First paperback edition October 2024

Book cover by Cherie Fox

Edited by April Kelly

(*Written & edited in Australian English*)

ISBN 978-0-6456561-8-3 (ebook)

ISBN 978-0-6456561-6-9 (paperback)

ISBN 978-0-6456561-7-6 (hardcover)

www.wesmhenshaw.com

Aubyn & Hattie

Thank you for being you,
Never change for anyone,
Always let those amazing souls shine . . . .

Again, all my love to you both

Love Always

Who am I? You may ask ...
Though, if you could, would I
*   even know.*
However, you cannot; you are
*   no longer here.*
You will return though ...
... one day.
Whoever, or whatever you may be
*   ...*

Herald for Eternity 1

Once Awake 3

Phil, the "Neverman" 17

Familiar Family 27

The Finest 34

Roads 43

Return 52

The Next Day 85

A Little More Action 105

Down Time, Downtown 134

Another Day 220

Ock 265

Farewell 276

Flourishment and Transition 288

A Supposed ... Afterword 298

Characters & Important Places (in order of appearance)

Getty – A boy, once crippled by the effulge of a unique mind.

Jesse – Getty's mentor in the ways of the world and maybe beyond such.

Phil/Phiolimmo – Member of the Neverman Tribe, cursed with a furry affliction.

Gretta – Getty's mother.

Jacara – Ethereal spirit of one of the protectors/guardians of Meritol. Appears in the form of a faerie.

Phor'tera – Phil's imbued spirit of the Boler'ata.

Ethel – Proprietor of the countryside tavern "The Finest".

Arigal – Once was one of the Shadow's finest recruits, now of the Higher, known as Semona before her initiation.

Dagda – One of the Higher, also known as *Dagda Eren'Gaturi*.

Kal – A non-descript guard in the Haze of Sorrow.

Mikki – The secretary to The Lonba in the Haze of Sorrow.

Hoanga – The Lonba of the Haze of Sorrow.

Higher Souls of Garoth – Known as the Higher. Party to Arigal, Dagda and numerous more alike.

Grapians – A race residing in the far north, a thick wool coat upon their skin keeps them able to tolerate the harsh climate.

Rendala – One of the Higher who frequents the Haze of Sorrow, sister to Londe.

Londe – One of the Higher who frequents the Haze of Sorrow, brother of Rendala.

Malinga – Maghari's personal assistant in the town of Dibrathella.

Velosko – Blind tenor in Vilenzia upon the world of Inarrel.

Ghareem – Main guard at the regional town of Dibrathella.

King Benjamin Jacob Aurelia – King of the province of Jacobs Well in Vilenzia, upon the world of Inarrel.

Balagor – Proprietor of the Blacksmith's Arms in Dibrathella.

Polett – Balagor's daughter.

Blacksmith's Arms – Tavern in Dibrathella.

Hop and Shovel – One of the prominent taverns at the centre of Dibrathella.

Mellor – A regular of all the taverns in Dibrathella.

Carla – Interim Proprietor of the Hop and Shovel.

Margus – Extravagant street performer in the town of Dibrathella. Easy on the eye.

Tillian – Margus' best friend. Also a performer.

Lawree – Proprietor of the extravagant tavern on the opposite side of the street as the Hop and Shovel.

Nagda – One of Dagda's home world, resident in the Hop and Shovel.

The Deliverers – An eclectic outfit of women who reside at the Spike of Meldori upon the continent Ungola.

Maghari – The Regional Marshal of the town of Dibrathella.

Lorel'eth – One of the Deliverers on commission to the town of Dibrathella.

Agda – One of Dagda's home world, resident in the Hop and Shovel.

Ren'egda – One of Dagda's home world, could even be his sister, but who would know.

Ock – One of the Higher, though of a race far from that of Dagda and Arigal.

THE LANDS

The Grampian Mountains

Grapton

Lake Baroona

T'YARIPOLE

o'Meldori

Angoliant

Elaclaxe

AuCLUDA

DANZY STRAIT

Newto

WEST DIVIDE

NEBR
BAY

N

DAYS BY CART

Ne

OF MERITOL

Haze of Sorrow

Hereherst

Hotspot

Dibrathellas

PLAINS OF DRACHT

Macam'bia

SHIMMERING SHOALS

UNGOLA

STRAIT

DRIFTERS DEMISE

Isle of Dreams

EAST DIVIDE

bras

Herald for Eternity

The night was the same as always. Him. Getty. Always slowly fading into that forever-away land beyond his dreams. Sometimes those dreams would take him from his bedroom and into the wooded land not too far from the large timber house in which he resided. It was an affliction only recently diagnosed but a madness – of sorts – all the same.

Events of the previous Vellum had subsided somewhat in his mind. So much so that he had begun to sleep peacefully wherever he lay his head, not succumbing to the overbearing unconscious – one that may well have been procured from far, far away. But still, he was where he was, with that fallible mind and body of his.

The events upon Inarrel would take their resolute place once Getty unravelled what secrets lay beyond. The scrolls he had been left only ever told of the point where Grehn and her unknown friends would discover some sort of requirement of services from the once-woman and now-faded Onberseeler, Morla. And these were always different over time; over the course of every reading, many had fallen in previous iterations, but this time all remained – for now.

The quests had been set upon the far away, time-unaligned world of Inarrel; though it was now time for Getty to become who he could be destined to be. He would one day learn of the fate of those fateful individuals and their close comrades, but for now, he had to discover himself.

I have left his diary – more his thoughts – here as a marker, something to help acquaint you with the next chapter. Before he is once again reacquainted with the world of Inarrel and, most notably, Vilenzia.

For that Darkness will not relent, and I have no recollection of how the whole scenario will play out, for I am yet to become, I only succumb to the way of things, whatever they may be. For I scribe only the way and let time do the rest. To one day, hopefully, be released from this forever-elongated burden.

I will leave you to Getty's thoughts. For now.

Know they are of his own. I am no party to what he may have said in the following, for that is not of my realm, nor do I know of what he spoke, for his tome is his, and his alone: as all of his kind would attest.

If, indeed, they were able.

Once Awake

There was always that thought that would occur to me, usually just before dawn, before a madness that – or so I was told – would take hold of my mind and throw me about our home. A frenzy of which I would know nothing about, save my mother washing down my legs, my arse ... or both. Bandaging me up from such traversal through my upper bedroom window and out into the woodland beyond. I always wondered why they persevered, keeping me up the steps; maybe they felt I would be safer from any intrusion.

I smirked, as I traversed a barren woodland far from my home, if only to myself, more to reflect on the image of my mother or father wiping my arse than anything else. Falling out of my bed was the usual offering, some sort of pretext to satisfy my own inexplicable reasoning for such injuries.

'To do with myself now?' I mumbled the thought to satisfy myself once more, for I was far beyond anyone else, by far further than a thunderclap's audible distance.

I had assumed.

And assumptions had been drilled, pushed firmly out of me ... *almost, but not entirely.*

There was no sound to alert me to what else was out there, but I immediately knew something else *was* out there. No inkling of how far away, nor how far they'd come with me, and not in which direction they, or whatever they may be, or where. But I knew; I always seemed to know. No alarm ran through me, though, not this time, for there was no aura about this place that added to any attribute of any cause for ill intention toward me. The immediate thought was to seek out the source of intrusion – that other than myself – of the sacred place, but I remained steady. Content to just be in that moment, even though not alone. No ... not ever alone, it would seem. But I continued as though I was such removed from the world beyond and all that dwelled within that world.

I would soon come to realise – though not soon enough – that the way of the world beyond the confines of the four so very familiar walls I was so used to for so, so long, would feel, for most of the time, to be held by the behest of the complacency as that my own. I would learn one day – not that day, as it turned out – as the scars marked across my chest would testify. As would my propensity for surveying one's surrounding environment, and then even beyond the traversal of such a sacred place that I had found myself.

I guess I was lucky that day. Got a bit lucky a few other times too on many a day before, and, no less, a many more thereafter.

*

The older, wiry-built gent looked at me from the other side of settled, glowing timber. I saw a frown slightly creasing his forehead; the shadows the crinkles cast told me so. He was the one who had sent me on that manic path toward the spire of stone stuck in the middle of a dense, forever vacant forest. The very same that was once home to the Epora – sacred beings who had once ... just vanished. Into the sky, they were said to have flown. To where? Or how? Who would've guessed?

Though who could have witnessed such, for the lifetime of

my ancestors would not stretch beyond that of a grain of sand washed up on the shores of Meritol.

Faded images had remained out on the precipice of the forest, splattered across huge monolithic stones that stood high out and above the ground, higher than most towns' and cities' central monuments – a warning, one to sway potential heroes from the horrors that lay deep within, or to come from such folly foray.

He was about to speak, for he was bursting to say something, though the look I gave him would settle his forever flapping tongue a short while longer. I smiled as he relaxed, dropping his back to the usual slumped arc he held whenever we broke for fire and feast. A touch of a smile now ran itself around his lips, for he knew the next part well and would take not so little delight in me retelling it once more.

The lady sat to my right, and the man whose lap on which she was perched had yet to hear this one, for they had only re-joined us that morning. They had been sent on a sabbatical, away from me, to allow me to grow the attributes I should so possess, not only to improve my confidence but to also boost strengths I thought only in my dreams.

The cold, end-of-autumn air had prompted the mixture of crushed apple, red wine, and a myriad of cheap spices to be brewed while the fire was starting to blaze, then given time to cool before ample and merry consumption. It seemed to me, the brew had brought a silent joy to those few who sat around the fire. It felt good to see my parents close once again, especially when my father grasped loving arms around my mother, just as they once would, long ago when I had arrived unexpectedly and thus before I broke them.

I watched as she swayed slightly, enjoying the moment. A twinkle of a smile also shone around her eyes. And I loved every second of it. Though that swaying would eventually subside, to be replaced with shock and horror as I told the story of how I almost had my innards spilt by something crazed and let loose upon this world.

The man opposite would lose his smirk, swiftly. For it was hard to smile when an angry mother was clawing at you, ready to rip your testicles off for sending her only son to an almost certain doom.

'And what else have you been up to, Getty?' she asked, once she had been subdued, to once again rest in the warm, loving arms of my father, though I assumed he was holding her a little tighter than moments earlier.

I thought to reply, then thought better of it, as my assigned master switched his eyes from side to side to advise me to "say no more".

Jesse had brought me a long way since we'd left the only home I had ever known, the one where I was pushed or dragged along whilst the passenger of a wheeled chair. And I suspected that he would take me much further yet. I complied. Like I always did.

The reason for such a task, to venture into the well-known void of death, that of the Eporan Forest, was to obtain what now occupied the majority of space within the large sack sitting on the grass between Jesse's feet and the smouldering coals; a large item that could only be described as an old, decrepit book. But, where it deviated from such was the extended flap on every page that could be unfolded, the flaps adorned with indistinguishable graphics — mostly of symbols or some elaborate scribble to annotate such images, I presumed.

The mysteria around the Epora reminded me of those wonderful, though every so often painful, times when my father would read to me, of the place near the south of Vilenzia, across the Divide, where all manner of magical and magnificent creatures alike resided. Though, I can assure you, what had stalked me through the trees would pale even the darkest evolen.

I had thought so …

I was disinterested in any distraction, for I could feel the pull of something strong. However strange the feeling, I wanted to move on toward the source of the pull.

For a short while, the shadowy being within the canopy's shade was happy to follow, stealthily, tagging along for whatever reason, one that would soon enough be revealed.

I eventually entered a large clearing, away from the shade of the foliage mopping away over the top of me. And the first step I took upon the nearest piece of unnatural paving I had graced within the forest, caused every tree in my vision to blur into pixelated stasis — not dissimilar to a frequent initiation to one of my once eventful dreams, where I would meet the Unknown, I assumed.

Then it struck. Not at me, as such, more at the block-of-stone effigy that was now ambling toward where I stood. It moved well for its size, no less its assumed weight.

I tried to move away, only to be repelled back into the fray by an unseen force. Though I could make out no features on the creature swinging at the boulder figure, I admired its tenacity and cause for my concern. The admiration was short-lived as it eventually subdued the bundle of rock, enough for it to return to where it had initially rested – back to the part of the wall it was set into, acting as a barrier to what lay beyond. As it blended back into the wall, I looked at its tormentor and saw two eyes peering out from underneath two bushy brows as the creature now set its sights on me. The face was almost comical, though its hands, full of blades, were far from such.

The thing raced at me.

And, as I flinched to form some kind of defence, another thought came to me instantly: move out of the way, you dumb shit. What else in that moment could I do but brace myself for the impact? Was it a thought of my own or one thrown from afar? I was unsure. But I reacted as told and moved sharply to my left.

'Uff,' a gasp escaped as the swiping fingers clawed through my new leather jacket and the next layer of my chain-linked vest, ripping three long dykes through skin and bone. To add further insult to the first injury, two large eyes appeared once more in the stone wall of the tower.

I may have cursed … more than once. I may also have nearly shit myself – and probably would have if I had consumed anything since my last deposit. But at least some luck was to be had that day.

I had no idea at the time why my pursuer would spend its energy fighting the stone monster. I didn't mind. It was a nice gesture, though I felt slightly aggrieved and slightly offended that I was not the most critical in overcoming at the time.

Was I less of a threat? Absolutely not, I thought, but I would hopefully get the chance to play that card later.

As the stomping stone of a mountain came back toward me, I noticed that its footsteps were wed to the pavers with a particular symbol engraved, none unique except the partial imprint atop each; that of a crescent moon. I made a move and ducked past the ambling wall as it swung a drooping arm of stone at me, hoping it would concentrate on the vicious creature now trailing me. I then realised that the arm of the rock was not meant for the other animal now following on the trail I left behind, but for me.

Then it all made sense.

Though the figure of stone pirouetted – akin to a well-versed winter skater – I was already on my way through the revealed opening and into the darkness it had left for me.

I stopped just before the precipice before being bundled over to fall down what seemed an endless number of steps by the one with the sharpest of fists and hairiest of bodies.

'Ah,' I thought as I tumbled down the winding cascade of stone steps, 'smarmy bastard played me well. Used me.' *But why attack me in the first place?*

Another stroke of luck was had on that day. My fall would ultimately be broken by the semi-naked fluff of a mattress of fur, that of the creature that had ripped my chest to near shreds. I didn't care as I rose off it, even as blood dripped all over a distorted, shocked – though natural enough – face.

It squinted and spluttered with some gargle that could resemble speech, a gurgle of something it was trying to communicate to me as it gesticulated its bladed fingers in some sort of obsequiousness.

A rumble caught our attention. Two blacked-out holes in its head trained themselves upon us, no doubt, as the rocky creature was locked back into its eternal jig of protection – whether from the outside world or within the confines of the space we now breathed. And we both looked up toward the top of the winding stairs; above each step, we had met solidly with our bodies. The doorway was now shut, closed, to deny any more daylight to enter what was now surely our tomb.

Maybe, it was just glad for some company and got a little excited, having spent so long alone, just as my mama was as boisterous and no less swingy with her arms, even when I had only been gone for no more than a few days.

Poor bastard thing, I thought, as I raised myself gingerly up off the haired mangle of striped fur, wrapped nonchalantly underneath strapped leather armour. And, as I stood, the thing beneath me started to convulse, not in pain, not in any final thro of taking that forever mortal breath. No. But a very distinct cackle that could only resemble a chuckle.

I had yet to see the humour. To add. I'd not yet seen any reason to smile for the previous four days either. Though the object I spied, one that glistened a way away up ahead, gave me some cause for optimism. But not humour. Until what happened soon after.

'Name's Phil.' I was stunned into a stupor, for my mind could not comprehend what had just come out of the man's mouth – if it could have been called such.

'I'm a Neverman; well, was once so …' Again, I could not muster the slightest response, for the "Neverman" spoke with such a commoner's accent.

'I … I … err—'

'Nay mind, lad. Sorry about all that c'motion earlier. Was all absolutely necessary though. I think.' And he shook his head to clear it.

I held out a hand, offering to pull this Phil fellow off his furry arse, then held it back to my chest as the razored fingers almost sliced mine clean off.

Phil was abashed by my reflective action before again he wheezed out the same sound earlier as he looked at his own hands. 'Ah, yes, I see.' With a shake of his wrists, the blades disappeared into its furry arms. He then held out two pink-padded paws toward my scraped and dusted palms.

I took it that time. 'Name's Getty.' The Neverman nodded at me. 'But how can—'

'—aye, of course. There's a story. Will fill you in on our way over.' He pulled off some of his leather breast straps and handed them to me. Then he ripped a few chunks of hair off his arms, squeezed them tight in his palm, and held them over each wound on my chest. 'Pull them in, tight, Getty, should be good enough to stem the flow. Don't want to leave you behind down here.'

Phil would tell me of how he was *once,* a Neverman, a gentle keep-themselves-to-their-self type of folk from far across the shores, beyond the east of my hometown. He explained how he once was not *too* dissimilar to me, how he was the victim of some unfortunate accident – or so he was told by some travelling benevolent kind of chap. He went on to tell me he had no recollection of how he had stumbled into the clearing, nor how he had indeed become that creature of nightmare – that told by the old folk in his village. But, he believed there was no accidental cause for his disfigurement, for he remembered, if vaguely, symbols etched into more than a few, though unable to recall how many, trunks around the edge of the clearing. So he just ran. Advised to run away by the robed holy man, for the villagers would soon discover what he had become. Telling me how he was lucky the stream of tears soaked into the fur upon his chest, for they would have undoubtedly led his parents on a never-ending search to wherever he had run to if they'd landed on the sacred soils. Wherever, anywhere, and over to nowhere, they'd search.

*

I had to ask, and I was a little surprised that he had not yet understood why he was following me. The answer was obvious, but to be sure. 'Phil …'

'Yes, Getty?'

'Why did you pursue me through the forest and then into here.'

'That I didn't. I've been waiting here for some time since I was told how to find a potential cure, if only a partial improvement to my newfound affliction. Was given the exact location of this here tower by some supposed wise old woman I happened upon in the province of Aucluda.'

'Any idea how long you have been waiting around here? And how were you able to survive in such a place with a scarce opportunity to feed yourself?' I rubbed my chin, even though it made me wince in pain.

'Well, it would be at least three summers, but not sure of how many days beyond that exactly. Once I finished my sack of dried backa nuts, I resorted to finding some edible bark. Don't taste too good, but mixed with some truffle, ain't too bad after a while, you just—'

'Three … summers …?' I asked, flummoxed.

'Yes, Getty. I was waiting for someone to get into this tower here. That same old woman told me that someone would eventually come along and shift that big lump of rock up there for me. It seemed never to notice my presence, no matter how often I threw stuff at it or pissed on its feet.'

'Well, did she at least tell you how to get out of this place?'

'Didn't think to ask, once she told me of some monster that guarded the entrance, wasn't too bothered by anything else … Come to think of it, I never knew that guard would be part of the tower itself, though once we were in, we would be able to waltz back out. Thought it would have been some dragon-type thing perched high up on top of the tower. But, no, I soon found out it was that cold bastard staring at us up there.'

'Guess that thing ain't going to let us walk right out of here with whatever be upon that dais.' We were getting closer now.

A mini revelation. There were three pedestals in this enclosed space, in a symmetrically spaced alignment, one behind the other. The largest sat upon the highest pedestal, first in line for plunder.

'Might tickle its nuts; see if that works.' I watched Phil's messed-up face twist again, readying himself for another bout of jacked laughter. He seemed to find humour in such a bad joke. And to think, only moments earlier, he had almost ripped me in half. I'm sure he found that funny too. But I was cautious not to hurt his feelings; for if he found such humour so quickly, he would indeed find shame and pain in spades.

I just went along with it. 'So, how long did those nuts last you?'

He looked sideways at me, two little beady eyes peering through the froth of fur hanging from his eyebrows. 'Have—um … had a big sack.' Then he just looked forward, offering nothing further, seemingly pulled by the object or prize he desired to procure.

'Huh,' I shrugged, not expecting the reaction or expecting something much more. 'Say, Phil … how long since you met that wise, old woman?'

'Far too long, Getty, far too long, bud.' Beady eyes shifted again before quickly settling back on the objects, or object, ahead. His pace quickened after he answered, as if not wanting me to see any emotion his eyes may reveal.

I watched on, through the haze of a heat drifting up off the scorched and smouldering timber, at Jesse as he reached forward and pulled the cloth sack closer to him. He loosened the tie and pulled out what was stored within. He struggled to get it free as it snagged the rim of string in every direction as he attempted to free it. But, after a few well-aimed kicks from the many that were not far from, it was out in the open. The little fire that was left between us threw what little light it held in the air to sparkle about the book's etched, metallic backing.

'Still smells like bastard backa nuts! Phoaw!'

I smiled as Jesse wrinkled his eyes and nose while assessing the condition of the leather cover up close. He handled it as would a mother coddling her babe fresh out of the womb, contrary to how he held my so-called fragile mind and body.

He then smiled at me. All his perfectly sized and aligned teeth on show, every tooth visible in the dim smouldering light offered by the fire.

'Ahh,' he sighed with some delight, obviously at my expense.

It was my mama that broke his smirk. 'Jesse ... please tell me you didn't send our *only* son into that retched place for another bloody book! I have had just about enough of all of them and their like!'

He looked sheepishly at the book, unable to offer the same armour to my mother. 'This isn't just any book, Gretta ... this tome holds so much from an age long passed!'

'Bah! All the same shit to me!' Again, I looked over to Mama, shocked at her sudden burst of sin, this time verbal. It took me aback more than the swinging of her arms. She settled back down quickly, resting her head into the large nook of my papa's armpit that he offered.

'Gretta, believe me, this was well worth the risk.'

'Why not go yourself, you bas— you wiry little sh—'

He smiled at her false cursing. 'You know very well why it had to be Getty. He has the lineage for such a task.'

I tried to remain removed from their arguing, but was sucked into the middle as my father nodded toward me, signalling me to attempt to calm my mother and save his arms from breaking with the strain she was asserting upon them.

'Mama,' I offered, if meekly. A part of me was enjoying the tables being turned on my past few years' saviour and tormentor. 'Easy, Mama. I agreed to go. I was enamoured by the fact that I would be gone from his constant abuse for even the smallest failure, if even only for the shortest time.'

'That I can believe!' She snorted with discontent, but settled back a little. She had grown, too, since she left to find Jesse, or the "Jester" as she had known him back then. Always had been stout, stoic, though with an internal will. That *will* now extended out to any who crossed her, or me. I suppose seeing your life almost cut from you would bring such a temperament.

Jesse fumbled with a few of the pages that spilt out of the book, trying to fold and then slot them back inside to where they belonged. After he had succeeded, he slowly slid out a page he had often tried to decipher, one full of images of another land. Of another race, he assumed to be the long-lost but probably not yet extinguished Epora.

She set her eyes on me. A look that always warmed my soul, for it was pure, meant; a promise. A promise to always have my back.

Just as it turned out, so too would Phil …

Phil, the "Neverman"

It would be hard to imagine again the shit we had gotten ourselves into. The whole time I thought of Peron and how Everos would chuckle at his expense when he found himself in similar precarious scenarios. However, this time, he imagined Jesse chuckling away in Everos's stead.

Phil tip-toed his way forward, almost reaching the first pedestal, when an almighty crash could be heard behind us. The hanging steps of stone had finally succumbed to the weight we exerted on them as we bounced our way down; the weathered connection that held them to the wall had cracked, thus bringing the whole lot down with a cascading crumble.

Phil chuckled, whether held with despair or humour; who would know? I wore a wry grin of my own, but mine was absolutely found from the former. The newfound knowledge of Phil searching for a way into this place … for years! had left my hope of a simple exit in tatters.

A pull of my own set my mind at ease for the briefest moment. I used that moment to settle myself almost entirely. There would be a way out; we just had to find it, fast. For I presumed I would be devoured much more palatably than I would find the alter – gagging on fur to remain alive – if it ever came to prolonging our, or one of our, survival.

The object was floating above the platform within touching distance of Phil. It rotated ever so slowly, so little so that I assumed it would take at least an hour to fulfil one revolution. A view garnered from since I had first spied it.

It had now rotated enough for me to see beyond to the next object. An object I assumed was what the hairy Neverman was seeking.

Roughly three large strides – or four small ones – beyond, a small jar, I presumed to be made of glass, rested upon its own perch. I squinted my eyes, almost closed, and rubbed them fervently to ensure I hadn't imagined what I had just witnessed.

'Did you see it just then too, Getty?' The smile he offered from underneath the cascading drop of fur needed no further clarification. It *was* what he sought.

'Yes, I did, Phil …' I had to focus hard, for that within the jar shifted in all directions too quickly to make out what it actually was. It appeared chaotic, though, on reflection, it was far from such: it was too soothing on the eye to be something other than a sequential rhythm floating about the innards of the jar.

Phil moved slowly past the first object and then on towards the second. 'What is *that?*' I asked, hoping he knew the answer. But Phil didn't answer initially, and I doubted he knew what it was.

He stood close to it. I moved to stand close behind him. Peering over his shoulder, he leaned his face closer to the jar to watch what was floating around inside.

I watched him. Soon as his nose touched the glass, what I thought I saw moments earlier reappeared, the effigy of some tiny, winged being assembled from the floating and rotating mist of crimson flecks. Its features clearly distinguishable, replicating that of a woman, though miniature, the size of a mouse—

It smiled, then went again on a merry dance, swirling about inside the jar.

'So, she is real, huh ...' He shrugged his shoulders and then looked at me. As he had mentioned earlier, I was lucky his chest was the way it was, for I would have been gasping for air as the flood of his tears would fill the void in this such small space. 'Never believed the old duck. Not in the slightest ... but what else could I have done?'

'What is it?'

'Not what, Getty. But who ...' A glisten remained in the corners of his eyes, though the glint of something more did not escape them, nor me.

'Who ... then, is she?' I peered at the jar again to see the misting of crimson form once again into a little girl with fluttering wings. She held a hand over her mouth and gestured a giggle. No need for any sound to distinguish that.

'She be the one thing in this world that may be able to save me; other than a swift blade, deep and quick to the throat, or a stomach full of poison, or tied to a stake atop a blazing pyre, one to send me on my way to that sweet, sweet, forever vista of nothingness.'

'Huh, you make death sound so ... so romantic.'

'I do, for that was once my only way out, though I was too much of a coward to actually send myself to sail that peaceful current the river of a forever darkness offers. It was. Til the day I met her. That day ... she gave me a hope I'd long lost.'

I looked at him as I held a hand to my chest wrapped in his ... soft fur, letting him know I still did not trust him, and he had hurt me. And, for whatever reason, it was far beyond unreasonable.

'So ... who is *she*?' I pointed to the figurine now solidifying itself more frequently. I was sure she could hear our words, for she reacted as such. She waved an arm at Phil to offer her thoughts on my question. Phil complied with her command, offering me only a shrug of both shoulders and raised palms as if I should understand.

I did. I knew all too well of how people would not wish to divulge too much, not so much to save their own skin but for the betterment of the other party and their unspoken wishes or opinions. So, I just remained still and silent.

I had no idea how she would or could help him. Unless she had contained within her tiny fictitious pockets a stick to beat the ugliness out of his face. Or, if that stick also held the world's largest razor blade, she was indeed … helpless. Just as much as he was.

'Getty,' he whispered as if he didn't want the floating figure in the jar to hear. 'I am of the Neverman tribe. I hold my word as bond. Maybe ask me some other questions. You know … ones that don't require a direct answer to—' he pointed a sly finger for my eyes only, from a hand clenched to his stomach, at the jar, hidden from the view of the little miss swirling inside.

'Okay …' I whispered back, which brought a scowl from the girl, who was now happy to show a constant, complete form inside the jar. She held both hands on her hips before I asked Phil. 'If I were somewhere else, and you were someone else, and that jar there held someone other than who it contains now, wha—'

The jar shook violently as the crimson cloud twisted around chaotically once more. It wobbled and set itself for a fall and would have hit the stone floor below if Phil had not put his large pink paws low, ready for such a potential outcome.

'Might not want to piss her off, Getty. She may be small, but my folk have written of and drawn images of her, which are much larger than this tower that keeps us imprisoned here.' He gently put the jar back upon the dais, shaking his head and smiling toward the figure contained within.

I shook my head too. As it was awash with all sorts of thoughts.

'You find what you sought yet?' Phil gestured questioningly behind, then forward, to beyond the second pillar.

Perched upon the final dais stood a shining blade – no bigger than my forearm, though much more conspicuous. It held a glow, even as the only light available to fill the space came from the low ember from the jar that had caught Phil's now undivided attention.

I was drawn to it. To *that* item, I was warned not to even attempt to look at, nay even touch, through stern warnings and horrible stories of all manner of ways I would draw my final breath should I ever draw *that* blade. I didn't care in that moment, I had only visions of glory and power, as that of the blade upon the *Spear of Starlight* from within my dreams, and I began my slow walk forward.

The whoosh in the room set my legs to ice. No less my body as I was confronted face-on by the apparition from the jar.

'Fool, boy. Shame on you!'

In response to the barrage of reprimands, I mumbled something, but nothing coherent.

'Do you know what power that blade holds?' I tried to muster a response but was cut short as my lips dried, bereft of all moisture. 'Of course, you don't. You seem only a fool for your actions, not for your sound knowledge of this once sacred place, that of the Epora.'

I stumbled a step forward, only enraging the hovering form before me. Giggling behind me could be heard, though I needed no further insight from where that chuckle emanated. I turned to see the Neverman holding the jar in one hand and its stopper in the other.

I turned back to the blade, though it was now partially invisible, only the glowing outline of the figure with hands to her hips left between. 'Only one blessed by the Epora, one of pure intentions and spirit, may wield such an item; one of a few scattered about their land here, their home. And, I do believe the Epora are no longer around to offer such esteem?'

More! I thought. Thoughts of the glories to be had with all the treasures crossed more than once absently across my mind.

Though, as my eyes lit up to follow my thoughts, the figure slapped me across my face, bringing me back to that level of calm Jesse had always instilled in me.

I rubbed my jaw; solid as a rock was her palm ... *who'd have thought.*

Phil came to stand beside me, humour subsided, and bowed deeply, almost to touch the floor. 'Blessed, Jacara. One of the remaining protectors of the realm once called home to the Epora, I apologise wholeheartedly for my newfound companion's actions here. May he still be naïve, but I believe him to be good of heart and intention ...'

'That I do not doubt, *Neverman*. I only offer defence for his apparent stupidity.' Her voice was angelic. Her eyes, though, shone cold enough to freeze any demon from the deepest of realms. Though not coherent, understandable just, were the words that wound their way through the air, wrapping around my head.

I finally dropped my eyes to the floor once my senses had returned from where they had departed, if not wholly, for I had indeed heard of such a being hovering gently in front of me, very animatedly, by Jesse.

She eventually turned her attention to Phil. I was happy to be relieved of it, though sad I had nothing to offer in the way of a reply; for I was in the graceful presence of one of the five legendary beings known as the Boler'ata – those who were hidden away from the world, to one day, if the legend was to be believed, break the world into five segments to enable all the armies sortied upon the surface to battle their way through demon hordes then on to the forsaken realms below, and to defeat the seven demon puppets of Bane.

'I assume you seek a remedy for your unfortunate affliction? And you believe I may hold such within me or my abilities?' She held hands on her hips once more and shook her head, slower this time. 'Another fool …'

Phil rubbed his hands together, no doubt his anxiety increasing exponentially as he reflected upon her words, and no doubt there was a dampening to matted fur around his padded palms too.

She went on, 'I do not offer such discouragement lightly, for I know of the folklore surrounding such an image as you portray to any of the Neverman tribe, for they are not such. Real. As you well know.'

'Blessed Jacara, the lady told me of you, of where to find you. I have been searching for a way to free you for many years—'

'Free? To free who? Me? Or yourself …?'

Phil stumbled with his response, only to let out a sigh, one of resignation. For she must have spoken true. And he knew it.

'I mean no disrespect to you, Phil of the Neverman tribe. Though, may I call you by your other name?'

Phil looked at her questioningly. 'I have only ever been known as Phil, blessed Jacara. Or Phiolimmo, if that would be your meaning?'

She shook her head even slower than moments earlier. 'No, Phiolimmo. Though you may feel cursed with the affliction affecting your body, more so … you have been blessed with a gift. You have been imbued with the soul fire of one of the *other*, as you would so name us, *Boler'ata*.'

This would have been the epitome, if a heap of a talking and walking pile of fur could ever look shocked. He coughed out a half-hearted laugh, though it had minimal humour. 'Surely not, blessed Jacara. I am fully the image of "Nightmare" to all my tribe, if not many beyond!'

'That may be so, and a well-meant myth be that. Though! One of the Neverman was always destined to wield itself as he.'

'Who?'

'Who else? Who other than Phor'tera himself.'

Though not entirely visible through drooping eyebrows, Phil's eyes shifted and drifted a crimson blankness across them. 'Good to see you once again, Jacara.' Phil's voice held the familiar accent, though the words tumbled out quite differently from the beast I had known for s short while.

He shook his head, regained his senses, and spoke. 'I feel it. I can feel it … him, within me.'

'Yes, that is the soul of Phor'tera. Well, not fully. What you felt was an echo of his former being. Your souls have intertwined and become one, as it had always been planned.' Phil looked incredulously at her. 'Fear not, Neverman. For he has sacrificed more than you could ever know.' She looked downcast for but a glimmer. 'All, but that he offered you. His body, power, and soul, of which now you are in control.'

'But I was offered nothing, not asked to carry anything. Not least such a burden you now proclaim so …'

Phil dropped his eyes as he raised his hands, drawing them closer to his face. Almost touching palms to eyes, he dropped to his knees and wept, looking at his hands again – forever to never be changed – and wept harder. For Phil, the Neverman would never be man again. Forever a beast. Forever to never return home, for none of his tribe would welcome such a beast of nightmare anyway.

My eyes almost glistened, too, held with a regret. A regret for tarnishing the beast with seemingly the same assumption, and as deadly as Peron thought of his first introduction to the dark evolen. Now I felt the same shame for such a thought – no matter the open flesh that still leaked through his fur and into my shirt.

I held out my hand.

The apparent Guardian nodded affirmation toward the heartfelt gesture.

Phil grasped it. 'Bet she knows a way out of 'ere, 'ey?'

He smiled as he rubbed his eyes with the backs of his hands.

'I sure do,' she confirmed, but not before laughing at where she pointed. Back at the stone figure stuck within its jig, high up the wall.

Familiar Family

My father patted my mother's hair gently while her head rested in the nook of his shoulder. The only movement on her part was how she moved in time with his chest as it grew, then shrank with every stroke of a breath.

The source of much-welcomed comfort, our fire, had lost all its blazing energy and settled into the forest to temporarily scorch the earth with its charred remains.

My father looked over at me, unable to shrug his shoulders, only able to throw a whisper, though that was lost somewhere in the distance between, so I had to make do with deciphering the movement of his lips, 'She be asleep … blanket.' He nodded to the enclosed cart behind Jesse.

I nodded back confidently. I knew precisely which blanket I was to fetch; the same one they had tucked me into every night I had lain stuck to my old bed.

Settling the blanket over her chest, letting it hang loosely over her shoulders, I hugged my papa gently as to not knock her, and kissed her head. As I backed away cautiously, her lips spread ever so slightly as she sensed my touch. She tried hard not to let that parting form a full smile.

My pace and poise remained as I backed further away, for I knew she was still awake, just soaking up the love and warmth of their companionship unhindered.

Jesse raised his head to shake it at me. Then he flicked scornful eyes that told me such emotional connection would eventually be the death of me. I shook my head back at him, smiling to show I did not care. He shrugged and settled himself back down. I would surely pay penance for such fluff of a response over the coming weeks. Again. I did not care, for it had been what felt like an age since I had seen both my parents, and to see them so happy and content, well … it just warmed my soul, filled my bucket, as such, with something other than adventure.

I gazed on wistfully as my father slowly lowered her to the ground before he gathered their pillows and his own blanket from the cart – wedged in with the mountain of horse feed they had carried.

They both would lay under the stars tonight.

Jesse was also content to lay beside the long-gone source of warmth, with no additional protection from the dropping cold as the night grew longer.

I wasn't tired. I was full of verve. A verve energised by the sight of my parents huddled together under both their blankets. There would be a couple of sore heads in the morning. Not mine, though, nor Jesse's. That thought prompted me to let out one last emotion for the night, a long outward breath of happiness, a sigh full of contentment.

In light of the content of the night, I decided to take a walk, away from the almost perfect circular clearing we'd found, though not too far away from where we set ourselves for the night, up to the precipice of the rock face stood high above the beginning of the lands that rolled on forever and beyond far below.

I wondered, whilst sitting there, straining to look at places I had yet to visit, those beyond the unseen horizon of almost total darkness. This world be finite. And beyond would be the same. I thought that of myself too, how insignificantly finite I once was, still am, and will be lesser so in the not-too-distant future …

I sucked in a sharp breath, a deep one, filling my lungs with the crisp air the night offered. I savoured the little peace I had to myself before the "tuition" would begin anew, either tomorrow or the day after. It would be brutal too. Though he was the fourth wheel, Jesse fit in well with us; completed the cart as such. He was much less firm while my parents were around, and he got on well with the both of them – most of the time, when I wasn't telling stories of how I nearly got my head split or my insides ripped out. That night aside, it was always primarily amicable.

I mistakenly told my mother what we had found, and how we had obtained such. My telling of the events was censored greatly, mainly to save Jesse's head, and, no less … that of my own.

I let the breath out slowly, and watched it disperse as it rose sharply away from my mouth, only to disappear just as quickly, reinforcing my previous thought of finiteness and the fallibility of my life, or any other, the same.

Though Jesse promised me he would teach me to cope with all this world had to offer, he thrust forth the fact that he would not be able to help me beyond this plane. So, instead, and until such time was required, he would vigorously offer me knowledge. Train and hone my newfound skills, all to survive *this* world until *that* time came. The time when I would be called upon to elevate. Whatever that meant, I did not know at the time. Though I was reluctant to leave my only family. I was

29

unwilling to be relieved of the few friends I had made in such a short time. Although, in the back of my mind, I assumed I wouldn't be done with either of them, even once I would be required to leave this wonderous place I had only recently discovered beyond the confines of my once forever bed.

The same could not be said about my mama and papa, that much I believed. Jesse was aware of that through my lack of progression under his tutelage. And that is why I thought he pushed me into situations and any precarious scenarios where I would have to be at my presumed best, not only to survive, but to develop further than I would un-assumedly allow myself.

Pulling my arms in about my chest to hold in the warmth of my overcoat, I felt a slight twinge in my ribs as I rubbed one of the three scabs that remained heavy on my chest. I smiled and rubbed harder. A painful reminder of a friend trying to find himself somewhere out there, beyond that sliver of a horizon, was now showing itself through the darkness.

How long had I been contemplating my future?

I'd best get back.

I must have been sat up there for hours, maybe, thinking of nothing much productive, just self-wallowing. I echoed that with another thought of a physical day ahead: training, most likely back up in the trees – with no sleep.

I lay down, rested my head on my hands, curled in tight near the edge of the high, sheer rockface, and closed my eyes.

Just a few minutes. It will only be a quick nap, at the very least, a short while before he finds me … he will … surely … underst—'

The intense pressure applied to my ribs was far from comforting as I began to drift away and think of my friend Phil. Not the reminiscent type of pain I felt earlier, but that of a big toe thrust swiftly into my sternum.

My immediate reflex was to grab at it as I was bolted wide awake; the shock felt like I had been dropped into the icy lake of Baroona from a great height. My hands floundered as they found no purchase before another toe cracked into the back of my ribs.

'Getty! Get up! You lazy, little—'

'Leave him be!' My mother came to my aid.

'We have work to do, boy. I find you sleeping up here again, or any other stupid place alike, especially with that tendency of yours to flee off somewhere once you're away with them fairies, and you will find yourself sleeping in a sturdy cage … hear me? Boy?'

My mother began to grumble, but my father shushed her gently. 'He be right, Gretta. No one wants to be scraping bits of our boy off the floor below to achieve some sort of proper burial before them scavengers pounce on his scattered bits. Least of all, you and me.'

'Sorry, Jesse.' I began while also rubbing at my chest. 'I just thought to have a minute. I had been awake all the night thinking of what's to come, and all that has been before.'

'Well, you will enjoy even more today, and a few days thereon, a whole lot less then, hey?'

I just mumbled something far from the sought affirmative. Jesse smiled, as too did my father. My mother, too, knew I had erred as the gaze she threw at me accosted my fear and pain more than the kicks to my still-tender ribs. And, including the day of

31

stretching the cartilage of the same as I grasped from branch to branch.

She shook her head and turned away. My father did the same, though he still held that genuine smile – whether that was because I was still here and not down there at the bottom of the cliff or for me just being that dumb youth he probably once was; I was unsure.

Family ... One day, I supposed, I would know how they felt.

Jesse walked gingerly over to me, head downcast, moving it each way slightly, the smallest smile still touching his lips. He sighed longer than the usual one he threw at me for such a significant misdemeanour. 'Getty, apologies for the kicks, and further apologies for my satisfaction with dealing them on you, but ... shit, boy!'

He walked to the edge, drew a large gurgle and let loose a spray out into the open air, the product to fall on some poor bastard trees below.

'What troubles you now?' He walked back to me and held a hand on my shoulder, squeezing it slightly as he continued on. 'For I fear we have healed your body somewhat, I still feel we could do some more with that fickle mind of yours. What say, you?'

I couldn't answer. I was still reeling from the lack of sleep, compounded by thoughts that prevented me from such welcome bliss. I closed my eyes. Squeezed my eyelids tight. Jesse took me in an uncharacteristic, seldom embrace with his languid arms.

'Pain from the past is a good thing, Getty,' he whispered. 'Let that pain guide you to where you *need* to go. Though, do not let it guide you where you had any inclination or indication of where you *want* to go. The past is the past. And in your case, that seems more prevalent than ever.'

I looked at him as a son would a father.

'Understood?'

A nod came was the only answer I needed to seek. Even though I knew not of what he spoke.

The Finest

I sat there stunned into silence, as a silence – that proceeded from the echoing final key being strung – eventuated, and that rapturous clang of a noise that would set itself free from the others by way of anything other than shouting and spittle would play itself out.

My silence was enough to settle for what I took to be true, as it was not negotiated by any, even as the laud of applause that was offered by all other than myself took the rafters on a merry sway – almost beyond their limit of the gravity being exerted now, testing its maximum limit. As, too, did the rafters below, undoubtedly rotted through by the spillage of a countless volume of draught – that of the same I held steady within the confines of the metal tankard in both hands.

One of the prerequisites for completing my study under Jesse – which turned out to be most of what I would study – had been how to interact with *general* folk – something I had not had the unpleasant pleasure of experiencing too often.

Unpleasant. Until I heard her voice sing a song I could not fail to reminisce again. Added with a surreal weight by that sweet string strumming to accentuate far beyond her untimely, soulful voice.

She was beautiful beyond compare, even more so than that distant mirage of Grehn's mother, Queen Jahnna as she would sway blissfully away under the dark blanket of the night sky on the longest of nights.

Did she just look at me? Or am I again dreaming of that

34

which may or may not be. Didn't matter. I took it as only that. No, now confirmed, as she once again looked my way. I was caught, stuck in a thick sludge of mud as her gaze locked onto and into my soul. I must say, though, I added a fair amount to aid the rotting of the timbers below and produced a slight timber of my own.

She smiled. A becoming smile. Before she moved her eyes onto the next patron, mirroring the same sequence of facial expressions she had adoringly thrown at me.

I felt nothing more than relief and a small amount of angst for the fellow to my immediate left. For he would be caught in that gaze and be forever weak should she ever betray the defence of the stage that held her away.

Many linga would be exchanged in this place for just the slightest verse conversed with her, or not so, in my case. I held but only two linga, the remaining coin left over from my menial allowance, stuck in the bottom of my tightly stitched pocket. I had no care for them anymore anyway; they were hers as soon as she approached the bar. Rather than a direct issuance, I was diverted by the bargirl's request to buy the woman a drink. Just so happened the woman asked for two of the same I offered, a *Sober Moment* – a drink of the silent herb "escleberry" concocted with vodka and ginger, and far from its name suggests – to warm the insides, not that mine needed such further coercion for aberration.

I smiled my best smile.

'Thank you.' She held her head back slightly, looking down her nose at me. 'How old are you, boy?'

Frozen, I could not return even the emptiest of answers.

She slid her head forward, down a touch, to look over her nose at me. 'Do you enjoy the company of *older* women …?' She formed a crinkle of a smile. 'I speak adversely; would you enjoy that of mine?'

I mean, she was probably not *that* old, but still, maybe twice my years.

Quickly I looked over her shoulder to see if Jesse had anything to offer. Anything to drag me from my dire attempt to woo such a woman. He offered a slap on the bar while he tried to stifle a giggle before it became something akin to a bark.

The woman who had accosted my vocals, and quite possibly my soul, turned to see what commotion was occurring behind her. Soon as she and Jesse locked eyes, he was instantly serious.

She blew him a kiss, and he caught it emphatically with his hand.

Walking this way, over-confidently, he smiled warmly at her as she turned to face him full-on. You wouldn't have thought he had it in him, not within that wiry frame. Or his gangly, elastic arms. But you would have been proven off as he held hands just below her hips and hoisted her high above his shoulders while twirling her around in the air.

Flopping forward over his shoulder, she giggled and hollered as he spun her around some more, her boots knocking all the drinks over that were close by on the bar. Also knocking a few punters' heads as she spun further on the pivot of Jesse. Startled, angry cries of grievance were dampened as they turned to see who their tormentor was. And the advertence of a wink from Jesse stumbled on such potential violence as he carried her back upon the stage. The *Sober Moment* still carried the full volume of its original content as it waded through the revived and roused, chanting crowd.

From behind the green-cushioned chaise he deposited her on – where she now lounged happily, supping on the cocktail I'd bought with my only coin – he pulled out a stringed instrument from behind where she lay. It resembled a guitar, though the deep globular body, and twice the number of strings suggested quite clearly it was not such.

Another set-up … The bastard.

The woman who had stolen my heart for the merest stroke of a beat – and maybe a couple more – looked up and over her shoulder at Jesse as he strummed a warmup melody. He looked down and back to her with a giddy smile as he sent his fingers on their merry dance across the many strings.

He seems to know everyone! And … that is not just a wistful gaze … He has bloody well been with her! The bloody bastard! She is probably half his age!

I contained a building rage by downing, almost drowning myself with the contents I held in my numbed hand; it was all muddled with crushed ice I knew from not where. The numbing of my mouth with the shock of cold held my mind as I sought to sit myself down, so as not to fall down. Who would come to save me then? Not she, not he! Not the way they are acting up together!

Jesse nodded toward me as he slowed his fingers, finishing his warmup. And might have whispered something, but that was lost as a trail of smoke belted up from one of the patrons seated at the table a step below where I stood a little closer to the elevated stage. My mind regained some cognition as the numbness around my eyes subsided.

A communal beat about the place had just been formed. It was echoed, if ever so out of time, with the tapping of feet throughout the tavern, though this only added to the vibe of belonging within. I watched the woman on the chaise stretch out and cross her legs, then bob the upper hanging foot in time with the beat, the glass in her hand bobbing too – when she wasn't gulping it.

Even I found the beat easy riding as my foot tapped— no, both of 'em, tapping unconsciously away on the brass footrest of the barstool I had found myself.

As the beat grew faster, so did her gulps, quickly reducing the volume within her glass to a void. Mine was already empty, and so was my mind at that stage. Eventually, I took the show for what it was.

The atmosphere grew and became dense in ease as all in the tavern tapped away. Two burly sailors, still dressed in their naval overalls, joined in with gusto and bravado, much to the delight of everyone, as they belted out their off chords. None cared as they were petitioned to join in with a large shout from the stage. And did they just. Not I. For my mind was cast back to when I was just a child, of when my papa would read to me, not only of the scrolls gifted, but also of other stories. I liked to believe they were more than just make-believe; stories made up by some dreamer such as myself, for they took me away from that bed, that room, that house and that desolate piece of wooded land we owned, to a place beyond my wildest dreams – and they could be pretty wild. I liked to think they would be real, as real as now. So, I soaked it all in. For I was living a life I had only ever heard or dreamt about.

The atmosphere was broken with a loud, repetitive banging that rattled the barricaded door. Much larger than any one man could produce with fists alone. A club eventually broke through, shattering one of the timber panels, and a face peered in the opening. I knew not who but was soon privy as one of the patrons shouted.

'Constable!'

All scattered like heated vermin in every direction trying to find an exit. I remained still, frozen. As did Jesse, who only smiled over at me and shrugged his shoulders. I had no idea as to why the commotion was caused. But would soon find out from Jesse that we were well past the standard trading hour. Seemed the volume of raucousness must have upset one of the few farmers who took residence nearby.

Escape was futile, and I assumed Jesse knew that as he strummed a little more, the fact he was joined by the woman who accentuated the solemn melody Jesse was spraying with accompanying vocals confirmed such.

The only other exit was opened hastily by a patron ready to make an escape, only to let in a stream of the town's finest, the few accountable for law enforcement. All in the room let their mood sink, and they settled back down as they found that any escape was off the table Jesse nodded to the Constable as he made his way over to the stage.

The Constable held a welcome hand to greet the woman. She took it softly as he helped her off the stage. 'Ethel, my dear. As owner of this establishment … seriously! How many times must I break down your door?' He swished his head from side to side in admonishment.

Her reply was swift and as soft as her melodies had been earlier. 'Darling, I always advise the locals when we have royalty appearing here, and they were all invited.'

'Even the children …' the constable said, abashed by the same hiding under the tables.

'Of course, my darling,' she responded, as though nothing was amiss having children up all night in a tavern, stuck in close quarters with some folk that could barely stand, let alone form two consecutive, coherent words together.

All names were taken, and a few papers were passed over. Including my own. Seems I would be another addition to their tiered warning system. Two more, and I would be eligible for a fine. Two more after that, and I would find myself in the watchhouse for a few nights.

What would my mother think of that?

All slowly departed the premises, but not before draining away their purchase, leaving the atmosphere deflated, bereft of even a slightly enthusiastic grumble.

But I wanted more! More of the … *this*. I had always found the magic of music so becoming, so soothful; even in my darkest hours, I would welcome the slightest harp of a melody.

I craved more. So much so that I was impatient to visit the next town, even if sparsely populated, as long as it contained a tavern, I would be overjoyed, even more so if it held more of the same as that night. And, now I knew that Jesse was an accomplished musician, I would always have the possibility of being entertained, as he never ever sang nor played whilst we were on the road.

We made our way back to the small camp, just inside a dense woodland that skirted the farm closest to the tavern. As we made it through the first of the thickets, we were greeted unceremoniously by my mother, hands on hips, not too impressed with our late arrival back to succour.

'Do you know?! Your father and I have not slept a wink! All night!'

Jesse raised an eyebrow, suggesting something unspoken as he looked behind her, to my father. 'Do not even think of going there, Jesse!' she bit at his bait.

'My apologies, Gretta,' he bowed just far enough to offer a meek heartfelt apology. 'Things just took their own course and sailed far beyond away from my control …'

She saw past his flatulence. 'Horse piss it did!' she dug both fists deeper into her hips – keeping them from Jesse's nose and the damage she'd like to do to it.

Once again, there it was … defiance in my mother's demeanour I seldom was privy to. I smiled, though I should have known better, for I was the next target. And on reflection, I really should have hidden the issued warning from the constable in my pocket rather than let the crumpled, yellow slip flap freely as if holding a prized catch in my grasp.

'Feel good, does it?! You getting yourself known with the local law enforcement?' She raised the questioning eyebrow, and I knew then that no local farmer had called into the constabulary's office to end the night's extended festivities; it had been her. No doubt to teach me a lesson. To make me feel a sense of guilt, and not to repeat such late-night shenanigans.

But I was buzzing. I couldn't wait to feel the way Ethel had left me reeling again. Nor could I wait for that burly sailor – whatever their name, or occupation would be – or whoever else, to belt out some loud rumble of a noise that should've resembled song, or if indeed, one day, it may. I looked forward to that day as my mother admonished me still as I daydreamed of all to come.

The swipe I received shocked me. Maybe it was more than just a lesson. Perhaps I had overstepped a mark.

Jesse took his well, a little too well for my liking, and accepted it for what it was. He did not smile, but the look in his eyes gave me an inkling into what he thought; *she let the night go on for quite a while, Getty. Don't be fooled by her apparent façade of care now, boy!*

I wasn't.

Maybe it had been my father who had suggested they let the night ride a while as he smiled gingerly, as though he knew I had indeed enjoyed myself. I nodded to him, carrying a wry smile of my own before my mama squeezed all the air from my lungs in a tight embrace.

'Silly boy … But I do love you so!'

It was Jesse who broke our tight embrace. 'I must go back. I said I'd help out with the clean-up once I got you back here safe.' And with that, he left us. Not to be seen until later on that next evening, just as we were set to depart under a cover of darkness, albeit on one of the brightest moons seen for some time.

Roads

A new wave of undue turbulence unsettled the bags we had piled onto the cart's side benches – once again – to try and keep them from sogging during any light rain. Jesse grumbled as he released the reins, sighing emphatically. 'Why must *we* take the additional cart when all that junk there is mostly *not* ours!' He then pointed to those pulling, 'Or theirs!' referring to the other hefty sacks containing all of their feed.

I kept my eyes forward, oblivious to all the shit in the back. Though then thought better as Jesse hopped off the seat to tend to the fallen baggage.

Making my way around to the opposite side of Jesse, I spoke loud enough for him to hear clearly. 'Why were you so long coming back the other day? Could have done with some help fending off, or at least deflecting some of the shit my mama was throwing at me.'

'You sound a little bitter, my young apprentice.'

'Maybe just a little. Do you know many such a whore all about the place?' I giggled and ducked out of the way of the expected rock to be thrown over the cart, aimed non-discreetly at my head.

'Tells me something when you can't bag yourself a guaranteed jaunt between the sheets … will have to get that out of you somehow!' Jesse jumped up onto the back of the cart and looked over the side at me. 'You should know … she was right into you. Said she'd not seen anyone so pure for some time.' He carried a laugh before he went on. 'Was keen to show you something you would never forget.'

I stumbled once more for an answer, even though I knew he was shitting with me.

'Though I would have very much liked to have fulfilled such a quest, there was no way I was going there once I knew you had been there.' My laugh replaced his. 'The very thought makes me shudder with revulsion.' If my earlier jest had not hit a nerve, the last certainly did.

Jesse slapped the top rail of the cart and turned away, taking my taunt with grace and returning to pile the baggage back up on the side benches.

I came around the back to join in the lugging, only for him to motion me to sit on the stepper at the back of the cart instead.

'Look 'ere Getty ... thing is, no matter your thinking of Ethel and me... we've never been like that.' He rubbed at the back of his head, eyeing me the whole time. 'See, I promised I'd help her clean up, and that was all it was. Can you imagine all that spillage when, once again, those officers made their way in? In addition to scattered chairs everywhere, cracked and shattered plates and tankards all over added to the mix too ...' He patted my knee as we both sat to face the well-trodden and sodden road we traversed our way over. 'Getty, me and Ethel go way back, back to a healing I could not offer, nor ever fulfil. The only thing I could guide was her soul. Well ... what was left of it after ...'

'After what, Jesse?' I pried, knowing there was something juicy to be divulged.

'Ah ... that is something I find too painful to tell, even to someone I could trust, even you. Some things are best left alone, for they are not my words to speak, for I could never do the girl justice.'

'What? Do you mean she—did she have once a daugh—'

'Enough! I said. Leave it!'

He hopped off the cart and ambled the short way to the road's edge to relieve himself. Not too far, just enough that if he turned, he would not sod the cartwheels.

'I guess the final offering the other night, as the lawmen made their way in, that was what all that solemn stuff was about?'

Jesse shuffled himself about a bit. And didn't say anything to me as he leapt back up into the cart – wiping a hand on my jumper as he made his way up off the intermediate step I sat on.

I will never forget to remember the smell of Jesse's piss for so long as I would take breath. Safe enough to say, it swore me off a myriad of condiments offered thereon that route!

Resigning myself to not ignite the subject, my legs hopped off the step, down to the ground, only to aid me in clambering back into the cart.

By the time I made my way up to help, Jesse had already restacked and strapped the baggage tight; with lightning speed.

I asked, 'Jesse, why such haste to begone from where we settled quite comfortably?'

'Nay, lad. Not that. It's where we're expected to be next. Hence why we travel alone for the time being. We are to divert off this road to follow a much narrower trail. We need to be at least a day ahead of your folks to get some good and ready training into you … from someone other than me, before your mother would be there to soften you up again.' As he finished, he squinted his face and puckered up dramatically to reflect that of my mother, aiming a peck targeted at my cheek.

To be fair to him, I was expecting it. And to my credit, I had promised to hold back a fist once he offered that churlish expression; for it was most likely his aim to procure such a reaction, thus becoming another lesson for me to absorb. So, I just smiled and made my way back to the saddle up front, hit the reins, and smiled as a loud, constant cursing cascaded away to silence as Jesse was bundled out the back and off the cart, into the dirt we left behind.

Jesse eventually jumbled back up to the front of the wagon, dusting himself off as if nothing had happened, giving no satisfaction for my part. He grabbed his own reins and shook the train forward.

A silence was held for a long time until we came to a fork with three routes leading in different directions. Three tattered timber signs held the names of the nearest two settlements and one other. We followed the one to "Unknown".

The road itself was not too worn, so we jostled our way through the overgrowth across the rocky and bumpy surface, timorously expecting to hit every divot – something we had a knack for.

We eventually arrived at another fork, this time splitting the road into only two directions.

'This is us, Getty.' His words were the first spoken since his piss. 'We will leave the cart here and take *only* our personal packs with us. Your parents can set up camp in that clearing over there when they arrive, as instructed, until we return from where we need to be. Here …' He threw my pack at me and hopped down. 'Help me with this tarp, will you. It should add some protection from any unforeseen weather. Also helps keep the animal shit off our things too. Should be no need to worry about anyone taking our stuff. Not up here anyway ...'

'Where is *here* anyway?'

'Somewhere we need to be is all I'll offer you ...'

We tied the tarp over the cart, unhooked the equine muscle, and led the pair slowly up a steep incline toward an ever-growing spire jutting high above the end of the trail and foliage we traversed.

Soon as we breasted the edging of the trail and reached the beginning of a clearing between the timber and stone, I knew full well why we were where we were; for Arigal greeted us with that stare, watching as we edged closer, glaring from a large window on the second floor. *Summoned? More than likely ordered to discuss my training – or lack thence.*

Our time there was short, much shorter than I had anticipated. Though, as we departed, I felt a sense of loss. I enjoyed Arigal's company. Not just for the angelic way she held herself but for that angelic kind of care. Truly, she would offer her life for mine, I so felt. Was that something more than was intended for herself? I would always wonder.

The three days seemed but a blip in time, for within the downtime – whilst I wasn't being tutored in many ways on how to avoid getting smacked in the head by their unseen magical projectiles – Arigal and Dagda were full of stories of their own, some I knew from my dreams, and far too many to fill the little time I had within their company.

I longed for more, and that longing left a hole that needed to be filled. "In time", they told me each and every time I begged for more, before my own dreams would take me away, dreams intertwined with images of battles and sagas told by the pair.

Firstly, they had given an account of why they had come, to resolve *why here*, almost in the middle of nowhere.

The funny thing was, we'd passed a few of their wards. They'd explained to us those same wards had the ability to dissemble distance and time for only a select few: only Jesse and myself included.

I had wondered why the horses shrieked and became bleary-eyed a couple times. We were told we were entirely somewhere else, still standing upon Meritol, far east of my homeland. And also, unbeknownst to me at the time – due to the dense foliage and the large, spired building – the sun had been switched to the opposite horizon.

Second, they had brought with them evil tidings of trouble brewing within the higher inner circles that Jesse and I were not privy to – at least, I assumed Jesse held no standing within. Apparently, time was growing thin to act. Once again, the commentary was sprung around the possibility of me being the *saviour* and enforced upon Jesse to act accordingly.

We were advised of an existential threat to all those poor bastards marked with afflation of such a title, and we were to proceed on our journey of knowledge and enhancement with caution … and alone. Meaning we had to cut my parents out of the loop for the time being – though I knew time could be a fickle thing, and it was more than likely a severance to last almost an eternity.

Jesse reacted to such a notion with a dismissive wave of his hand, advising that such a course of action would be detrimental to my health, but also his testicles.

An apparent reluctance ensued as the silence from the pair lasted a seeming age of its own.

The silence was only broken when Dagda departed to another room, rustled around for a moment or two, and then returned carrying something that resembled the same my father would read to me night after night when I was a child, right up to only a few years later. This one seemed to be scribed quite recently compared to the first time my father pulled out the worn old scroll.

Third, the scroll produced by Dagda was to be read by Jesse on every crossing of the old moon to me, and me alone. Though Jesse argued that I would benefit greatly if my father read to me on such occasions, as Jesse struggled to replicate the *verve* needed to stimulate me beyond sleep.

It all sounded like I was a pawn to some mad shit that was happening. And I had no interest in being a part of such *unsaid* shit. But who was I to belong in such company; the two seemingly immortal before me had ensured my mother still took a mortal breath. So there must be more than half-truth to all they spoke of. And to be honest, if only with myself once more, I was intrigued to see how far I could go. From being a stain on the world one day; to being able to deflect unseen blades flying toward my throat. Albeit most catching my bare chest before they dropped away, to fall through the terrain to their eventual rest on whatever plane that would be.

Trying my best to assess the situation I found myself in, as always, and never really having a say in what I wanted to do, the whole conversation about *my* life thereon went on. So much so that I found myself frustrated. So, I did something I didn't usually do; I offered my own opinion of things and how they should be.

Safe to say, it didn't go down too well with the party trio in the closed forum. The verbal lashing from all who thought best for me, more than probably, gave me reason to try me harder during the condensed sessions and aim for my throat rather than the legs as so often before.

I sensed an urgency.

Though they failed to divulge any further detail on the pending threat we faced, or from whom, or how they came to such information – I'm sure the threat was real, real as my newfound friend Phil, and that walking stomping rock of a thing that tried to squash me and my nuts – I felt they had only the best intention in keeping me alive long enough to fulfil my potential, be it only to find out I was not *he,* nor *the,* nor anything but a boy that once dared to dream.

I was finally asked as we were ready to leave, before we departed back to the cart we left on the other side of the world, 'What would I prefer?'

Would I prefer to put my parents in harm's way? To potentially watch them succumb to a darkness meant for me? To watch their soul fire be leached away forever – never to return. And for what? For whatever time was left anyway, was it really necessary?

'Yes, it isn't my decision to make,' I said decisively. 'I will ask them, and I am sure of the answer, but I will ask them anyway.' I shrugged my shoulders. So too, did everyone else. I was sure to see the pair once again, maybe not for a while, but I was sure, if I really needed them, they would be there for me – if not my parents.

I hoped, more than I knew.

Arigal left me with a parting embrace, and a whisper, for my ears alone. 'Whichever road you choose, I will follow. Whichever road *you* choose … understand?'

I nodded as her breath tickled my ear, then shuddered through my entire being. Forevermore, until the next time, I would crave her presence and the softest of words to be whispered only to me.

She was the road I would take, the one that would guide me beyond wherever I may, or could and would be. From then on, I'd always choose a path that *could* take me back to her, or her to me, wherever and whenever that may be … whatever road lay ahead, I'd take it.

Return

The road ahead turned out to be bleaker than any other I had ever known, though my knowledge of roads only extended just beyond a few years. The bumping flow of the cart seemed to enhance even the slightest flow of frosty air moving by. I itched to grumble something, just to let off a little steam that was building inside me, to bite out at the barren, frosty air that stabbed at our faces – more so our lips – even with the mildest of a passing breeze.

I couldn't keep the handkerchief over my face, no matter which way I tried, whilst also fumbling with the reins of the two compact packets of muscle. Any release of warranted strain I held would send them hurriedly on their own way, which was always away from where I needed them to go. And they knew it too: the stubborn shits. Controlling those two was now my only duty during our daily travels. Jesse had taken it upon himself to rest in the back for most of the riding, making it much easier for me to find that never-ending selection of divot.

I never could understand why Jesse sought out such a stubborn beast, never mind two of them! Or why we were heading out into the Plains of Drach't – a place of nothing, *not even bone,* Jesse had described what lay not out there. Even I, a boy stuck in my own room, in my own little world, had heard of them, and I had no intention of ever drifting across such a plain, especially now as I had my parents in tow not too far behind on their own mounted transport, albeit, evidently more manacled of mind.

The air stunk of nothing. Not the slightest scent of a faraway carcass nor that of any flora showcasing its ware to any potential folly of insect – even if putrid!

More worrying was the frequential cast of spraying shite that so often shot from the back-end orifices that wound not too far in front of me. And the way their tails would lift ever-not-so-subtly to make open space between me and *their* shit holes, then the way they seemed to squeeze their arse cheeks led me to believe there was some sense of humour shared by the pair as I strangled my wrists to keep them on course, unable to block my own orifice, be it my nose or mouth, depending on how I went with the handkerchief across my face.

Even the sky was devoid of anything that could resemble, well … anything. Yet another journey to learn more from. For him to teach me something more of that I already knew, but what he thought I could improve on, though with a little more *oomph* involved – be it ethereal, or maybe some other crazed beast.

He often told me, '*You may nay know who nor what you may have to deal with. And when words fail you, you must rely on that universal language, that of all of this world and beyond – may it be solid or no – it be that language of absolute violence!*'

He was not in earshot at that time. He had bolted on ahead, carried plumply upon a wide saddle; one he had taken before absconding from Dagda and Arigal's dwelling we crossed half the world to visit, headed onto some ancient ruin or whatever.

I had lost thought after a while and was thinking constantly of Arigal.

Of course, I was made to carry that hefty saddle back to

where we had travelled from, to where we would eventually rendezvous with my parents, back where the torment of my last few weeks nibbled away at the tufts of something – of what was now left.

They had set up a mini-camp, a small fire – now burned to ash – and a makeshift shelter. The camp also included provision for a toasty brew, potentially spiced cider, that bubbled away over a small patch next to the blackened patch of earth. The fading glow the coals emitted gave me the notion that the contents were well drained and fermented from where they stewed in the hanging pot.

Like most times, they seemed content for me to venture the short way over to them, though I was not met with the usual rib-breaking tackle my mama would throw at me. With a heavy sigh, she seemed content for me to bend down and cuddle her. I finished with a kiss on her forehead. My father was content to offer only a nod as he slumped against the stump of a once large tree, her using his padded thigh as a pillow. I was about to sit when my father nodded his head toward the opening in the woods we had made our way through.

'Pack up,' he said.

Though, my reply was swift. 'We have all our gear on the cart.'

He further advised *their* gear was his meaning, before he turned his head to the side and emptied his guts, a stream of burgundy coloured liquid – of that he'd drunk from the pot. It was, indeed, a spiced cider they had brewed, and not so little the amount I had assumed!

I averted the melancholy to regain focus. To gaze down that

future long, and winding road he had motioned his nod toward.

Oh, how it had added to my already low morale. It set my hands to ache, thinking of how they, and my patience, will be tested the whole way to wherever it was we were going.

The following day, Jesse had signalled I move on early. And to leave my parents to pack what little was left. They were to follow on when ready.

I was also advised to travel independently, keeping in front of my parents, and he would join once ready. 'Head down that long road,' he'd said, 'I will be sure to catch up with you before it offers a choice for any other direction. You'll know before you know I'll be there. You'll see.' He chuckled some and bound away with not even a sack of his own.

Though, during that morning, I enabled my folks to catch up quickly as I dropped the reins for the muscle to zigzag off the straight road as they searched for grub other than the dry stuff we had ridden with. To add more delay, I took frequent relief to stand near the stubborn pair while I emptied my bladder.

During that last dribble of piss, and as I sighed a fake relief while shaking it about – a sigh I had ensured for all my partaking of relief if Jesse was indeed present, I'd not be accosted as much.

Then came a slight rustle from behind a solitary, wide stump of a once large oak. I thought there was a whisper to accompany the rustle, so I tied my threads and peered around ... nothing.

Nothing there.

I shook my head, shaking off the tiredness I had been experiencing lately. A massive change from when I used to sleep like a babe, I had once assumed. The lack of sleep was the primary cause of why I found sleep hard to come by at night.

I had completely stopped the habit by that stage: the leaping out of the bed I was ridden to and then running some unbeknown gauntlet as soon as I closed my eyes. It seemed that the further I was away from that sunken obelisk, so too was the pull it had on my unburdened, unbridled dreams. That was quite apparent as soon as we had left my hometown. Though I had fountains of actual, meaningful sleep, a much deeper and calmer rest than ever before, my body ached from my eyes down to my toes from the weight of expectation now bound to me, and all I did or would do from there on.

As I approached the other carriage, my father, who undoubtedly still nursed a hangover from the night prior – evident from his gaunt expression as he swayed ever so slightly – jumped a little as if startled. I, too, heard it … again. And instantly looked back to see only nothing once more – a general theme for this stretch of land we traversed.

Nothing.

'You feeling 'right, Son?' he asked.

I nodded confidently and asked, 'You?'

A raised eyebrow told me all I needed to know. My mama was wrapped up in some large animal's hide and sat atop their carriage, snoozing away.

'Seriously, Papa? What did you two get up to last night? And … why?'

'Ah, was a long trek, boy, and it got a bit too cold, so thought to run us up something to warm the innards; you know what I mean?' He needn't have winked at me, so he didn't.

'Hmmm. Suppose I do, Papa.' I smiled at him. The pair of

'em seemed so relaxed those days, save the occasional swing from my mother toward Jesse – mostly warranted. And for myself, too – also more than warranted. It was as if the burden of looking after me had been lifted from them, and they were now free to breathe and enjoy what I had taken from them, a life once known. They would never admit to it – not ever – but I knew it be true. It made me happy, too … in a way. Happy for them, not so much for myself – as Jesse was finding a multitude of ways to break bone and spirit wherever we seemed to find ourselves: or more so, me.

'How far away you reckon Jesse be?' My father asked, hopefully. Only for me to crumble the hope left hanging upon his lips as he licked at them.

'No idea, Papa. He didn't say. Just told us we would get to where we needed to be … eventually. Even he paused as though he knew not when. I don't know. Do we rest up for a while here? Overnight preferably … Seems as though we could go on for another day and find not much better shelter.' He really meant that he was still struggling from the overindulgence, and I decided to put him out of misery. 'Mum could really do with the rest, hey …?'

'Aye, we'll tie these two little shits up over there.' He pointed to the tall stump I had just soiled.

'Aye, Papa. That'll be good.' I walked over to whisper in the ear of the nearest as they both nickered away, still trying to nibble at their reins after all this time, still failing. 'You enjoy yourselves over there, hey!' I patted its neck, a touch harder than that, a friendly tap. 'Night, night!'

When we settled down for the night, I was left to scratch around for anything that could be used for a small fire. Lucky we were on the precipice of such nothing, as nothing much could be found.

Sparse … barren … *they* would be the most appropriate words I could conjure, which would still be so far from the actuality of the place. My mind was playing tricks on me from lacking anything to comprehend. Exhaustion was also taking over, and I welcomed the rest too. Be it to lie in the cart once I unravelled the tarp, to attach once more over the highest rails.

A nag had pecked at me ever since I took that piss. Though I was exhausted, I knew that whisper resembled, to a point, what I thought was Phil's voice. And the nagging I sensed was maybe more a sense of loss of a good friend I had made.

I knew not of where he had gone to once we said our goodbyes that fateful morning, many weeks, maybe months after we had escaped the bowels of that Eporan tomb. Though I thought of him often.

The way he struck at me, he had explained, was of a desperate and manic madman, hell-bent on finding some solace within that single moment and a way back to being somewhat normal by gaining entrance behind the wall of rock. Just thinking of the flowing waves of fur, not the chaos he could inflict with his bare hands, made me feel warmth, that of a friend. I believed he was a good man, even if that stained image was portrayed as a legend of nightmare to his home folk.

Would I have acted in the same way? After eating all my backa nuts, hanging out in solitude for three and whatever long years in a woodland of legend, and that alone? Probably …

Especially if I saw the last and only light to a way back to a normal, former self.

After Phil and I exchanged goodbyes, I often thought about our discussion. Being so contained and unaware of much of the outside world here led me to embrace every paragraph of the scrolls – even if repeated a hundred times, that was my solace for the days I lay wasting away. My only joy, other than my mama southing my soul as she soothed my battered and bruised body with sponge and a loving, warm smile. That smile was a joy, too. For it was an affirmation of her love for me, one that must have been hard to wear every day. For I have seen that smile change since, all for the better, all for the better of both, to that of true love so often since we departed, for my father and me.

I settled under the tarp, wary of the empty sky and what such a sudden change could bring down upon you as you slept. I rubbed at my ribs gently. Though so long had passed, they were still tender to touch, so I brushed them often as a reminder of my first true friend and the only other than family, excluding Jesse.

One more look out the back to see if my parents had settled in too. No movement was a good sign as they lay in their sleep sacks underneath their cart. I drew the last flap to enclose the space from any draft that would make its way in – even though the air here seemed not to move a smidge. The nickering of the horses tied to that sodden stump caused me to chuckle; *they will make me pay for that tomorrow!*

That was my last thought before a mighty crash rumbled, shaking the cart almost to pieces.

A piercing scream set my senses instantly alert, fully awake, and caused my body to bound out of the cart. I raced out, the tarp wrapping around my head as I did, causing me to flounder as I fell out the back and scrambled to get it off as I wriggled in the dirt.

My first thought was of my Mama, though as I managed to clamber free of the tarp, I saw she was okay, other than slightly shaken. She pointed to the back of their cart and to a massive object that sat where their horses had been grazing, bridled no more to the cart but deep in the terra where they had stood not long before.

The large object before me was spherical: no imperfections, no dimples discernible, not even a scratch to be observed.

It was seemingly … perfect.

The only affliction to its perfection was the reflection of the moon, now warped upon and about its zenith, detracting from its pure red exterior.

The horses strapped to the fallen, sodden oak were now deathly silent and often cast a cautionary glance toward the clear sky, no doubt shitting themselves as if they were in for the same unfortunate fate. *Suppose it would be a way to go, and quick …*

My father ambled over, holding my mother's elbow as he helped her walk alongside.

'What in the world is that thing! Looks like a marble, but so close to it, you can feel it emits nothing but an icy aura.' He was not wrong; it did all that. Even from where I stood, I could feel a cold creeping around the place, an outward flow, though the sphere held no frost or any sign of an inherent chill.

Probably because there be nothing, no moisture to freeze about this place.

'We'd best go, hey? And quickly. Something here is far from

the norm …' I had not yet divulged any of the advice given while on our short trip across the globe, of their safety should they remain, though I thought this was not the best time to discuss.

'Bloody oath, that ain't right … look at it! Surely sent from up there!' As he pointed up to the dark sky, we heard a clattering coming from the direction we were heading.

Halting with a dramatic skid just before the massive orb, Jesse and his fine mount turned perpendicular to it. Jesse looked over his shoulder and drooped his bottom lip as he shrugged as if nothing was amiss. 'Close … hey?'

We all looked at him, knowing not what to make of his reaction. I could feel the heat of scorn appearing across my mother's face.

'What?! I had no idea this was to happen.' A slight guilt was evident by the squeakiness of his voice as he spoke.

'Then what is it?' I asked. From the corner of my eye, I could now see that rage brewing once more in my mother's. 'And why's it here?'

'Oh, yes, looks bad, hey!' he said, too calmly, as he looked at where the horses had once stood. 'Shit, are they under there? I only count two. Sure there wer—'

'—just get to it, you little shit!' My mother threw the verbal barb at him. My father held on tighter to her elbow.

He hopped off his mount and wrung his hands together, abashed as he approached. He eventually spoke. 'Well, see here … they wouldn't let me in.'

'In where?' my father asked.

'Where we need to be. Inside the walls of the place we're meant to be.'

'Inside where …?' my mother asked, the barbs now sharper.

'You know. Well, erm, no, you won't. But! We can still get in if we hurry …'

'But you just told us they wouldn't let you in! Why must we hurry if only to be turned back again.' I asked. 'How then, Jesse?'

'Look at me? Do I look like the type to seek refuge?' He ran both hands down his body as if to show he was a well-to-do type. 'No, I am not. Where we're heading is not far from here, only a few minutes' ride; if you ride as fast as I just did. I guess I should have waited for you all to show to add weight to the refugee persona …'

'And why *did* you ride so swiftly?' I asked, knowing the answer but letting him explain to those who did not.

'Oh. They asked who I was with and how far away they may be. Not so long after I had told them, I heard a "thwump" and then saw a big red ball sail over their unscalable wall, heading out in your direction. They confirmed my suspicion of them thinking you were bandits, or worse, ready to storm in as soon as they let me in … I may have given them too much information about where you had set up camp. Oops!' He wrung his hands tighter.

'Oops? Oopsy?! You bloody idiot! Look at that thing. What the hell is it!' It was now my father's turn to get mad at Jesse, something he had never done before, not to that verbal extent. I was also curious about what it was and how they had managed to throw it so far, not so much from Jesse; I wanted to know precisely what and how! From them!

Jesse looked at my father, abashed at the added admonishment thrown his way. 'It be a corkle …'

'A what?' I asked, tandemly with both my parents. 'A what?'

I asked again to reiterate.

'It's a solid piece of dense rock, cultured by some secret methodology; only ever heard about them. Though now they be true of word, I must also believe they have the stock of thousands, also talked about by the few that have ventured beyond. They didn't, however, say that the hosts were so inhospitable to just a short chat. Must be spooked by something, I reckon.'

'A what?' I looked at the thing. How could you culture stone so dense to form an object of such perfection and of that size?

'A corkle, did I not say?' he raised an eyebrow to ask no further. 'We must continue on, back to the gate I came forth. Apparently, they will know when to open their one and only gate, permitting entrance into the city, once the one permitted to enter is near! And now, it seems that ain't me …'

That may be the truth, but I pointed to the base of the sphere, to where Gertrude and Stephanie had once stood on weary all fours, probably sleeping, exhausted from their long day of carting my mother and father's cart and all their luggage, and they themselves over a shitty, broken road. The way Jesse casually raised one side of his mouth as he raised both hands, gesturing that it was not his problem, irked me. He was never the one to take blame for anything, "fate" was what he would always fall back on, the ultimate excuse unless the result was for benefit – then that would be on him.

He always seemed to, eventually, turn out to be right, though. For every time I found the worst in the world up against me, and for no reason, or any way out, the outcome was always worth more than what *fate* had in hand at the incept. Too many examples for elaboration. *Fate, hey. Fate could be as fickle as you wanted to make it.* And, for me, it was always the worst case. That way of my thinking had slowly changed with every eventual outcome, if ever so slight. Now, I would find myself revelling in the plaudits of fate and her mischievous, and eventual charm.

*

We trudged up to the gate with my parents' cart in tow, leaving my own cart behind – I was keen to get them inside, keep them safe and warm, with their own things, safe from any more falling objects, no matter how dramatically large, or perfect, or however intrinsically small they may well could be.

Jesse led the way, also the conversation with the innocent gatekeeper – no doubt the same who had initiated the eventual demise of the solemn, equine duo. *Feeling shame of a sorrow that they were not mine.* That very pair now obedient to every swish or sway of rein and vocal command – seeing your kind dumped below the ground they trod would do wonders for obedience *if only I had thought of that sooner! Bash an effigy of them with a rock! Save them trying to shit me off all day with theirs!*

The gatekeeper peered through the tiniest of openings and offered an apology on the city's behalf after seeing who Jesse now towed along; could be, indeed, potential refugees. The gatekeeper looked away and shut the slit in the wall adjacent to the iron gate. "Fire!" was the immediate, muffled sound from behind the opening; the cascade of the same caused us to look up as another ball of destruction was cast.

'Shit! look at that one!' I shouted as I looked up, before casting a cautionary glance at my mother. That *one* cast over us, and the wall, was much smaller and of a different colour, a solid blue, the same colour if you observed the azure coastal district of T'yaripole during the brightest days of winter – blue as blue. However, this was something created and not that natural wonder I had had the pleasure to explore.

The letter-box-sized window was opened slowly, and the girl behind offered her apologies as another ball of whatever material was again sent on over our heads. Slammed shut again was the opening.

Jesse pleaded for a parlay with a riddle of nonchalant tongue, and the opening was once again offered. This time though, the eyes were not that of the girl before, but of a man – aged far past middle years, hard as stone, almost as blue as the projectile that landed not too far away. The eyes shifted to each of us, holding a second or two longer than the last as they assessed each potential threat. Or target.

'Jesse? Was it?' the man behind the iron door asked gruffly. Jesse, though, nodded; to my relief, for I held a genuine fear of any close-range weapons mimicking those sent airborne.

'Jesse is but a name, one of many I be known by. Though your name for such as I may even be different from those I know of.' He finished with a slight flourish as if he were royalty.

'Nay, Jesse will be quite alright,' the man behind the tiny hole batted back.

Jesse angled to say more, slighted by the quick return to apparent normality. But the slot was once again swiped closed. 'Wait here, please,' a muffled voice came from behind the void struck through the massive wall, now filled with iron.

We heard nothing for a while, just an occasional sigh passed around while we waited. Though, when we did, it was much higher up the wall: a giant bird of a thing squawking down at us as if advising his kind in the area to leave us alone should we succumb before the walls, our demise being its stomach's gain.

I shuddered the thought away before my body did likewise as the temperature dropped dramatically.

Nonchalantly, I thought nothing of it. But my mother was the first to point out we could *actually* feel something for what seemed the whole journey. As if a switch had been struck. No sooner had she dropped her arms; another sound could be heard, an uncomfortable sound of grinding stone on stone. Then a hollowing appeared in the wall, not too far from the small peephole where we'd been communicating. *Another hidden hole in a wall; it seems this world be full of them!*

The rumbling continued for a short while. Though brief, the opening was not. Another sound, another block removing itself from the wall. At least that of an average man in height, in all three dimensions.

'I'll be damned,' Jesse said, awestruck. I, too, was impressed before I looked at the size of the cart versus the opening presented.

As if my mind was being read, a guard appeared from within the doorway. He took one look at the cart, stuck to the two remaining horses; *shame it was you not taken to the dirt,* I had thought, if a little too casually. And even obediently after seeing their kind disappear to the underworld – to a real sense!

Tapping his halberd on the wall, he shouted. 'Aye! Junpert! Need one more … on top of the others.'

A crinkling sound could be heard, and the opening grew

double its original size, thus permitting all well-travelled mass to venture through.

I could now spy through the large opening, and to the adulation of the place already formed in my mind, there was a row of four large battle stallions, fully kitted for their intended purpose. If those two lumps of horse meat needed any excuse to not nicker and carry on, they were the reason.

We were waved through by the one who had come out to greet us. Even if he did not acknowledge our presence, I was sure he tallied and assessed all immediately before him and then beyond.

Upon passing the four mammoth stallions and their armoured mounts, the obedience level of the two pulling the cart climbed to another level: eyes dead ahead, tails clamped tight enough to wipe where their balls used to be, waiting to be nicked and kicked, they were. I must admit, I, too, felt a little uneasy as we crouched underneath the overarching stares, even if through only the tiniest of visors.

The leather of their saddles and elaborate leather-studded boots creaked as we made our way by. All four mounts, though, betrayed their potential brutality as my mother passed them by; one by one, they removed their helms, bowed, and bid her "Good day, my lady". A slow nod by each toward my papa offered a silent warning; one to not disrespect the lady, ever, or there would be some consequence, *by what slept at the end of the hilt they gripped tight with leather gloves* – tight enough to add extra weight to the creaking of leather that caught the air.

We trundled on by, following the guard who led us through – assuming that was what we had been meant to be doing. Until he turned after at a point with a quick twist of his body and shouted – rather loudly – 'Stop!'

I looked about. First to the sky, awaiting our demise: to grace the forever unknown via a big ball of destruction, if perfection.

I suppose there are a million worse ways to go, I thought upon instant reflection of the pair now stuck in the mud underneath that reddish orb not too far from here.

Our horror, at least mine, was broken as a man appeared directly in front of us from a large wooden doorway. He approached, carrying a large shaft with a long sharp blade at the tip.

'Welcome! Chosen one! We have waited a while for your arrival.' I grimaced at the clichéd offering.

He approached the guard and whispered, but not low enough for me to mishear. 'You *are* sure they with him are true?' The guard nodded. 'Did you also seek out any others who may have been following?'

'Taken care of, sire,' the guard whispered back, then nodded slowly.

'Very good, Kal … very good to hear!' he whispered, a crooked smile accompanying.

My mother, probably feeling safe from the greeting, offered a few choice words. 'My husband and I were damned near killed by your projectile! Or whatever the shit it was!'

'Believe me, woman—'

'Woman? Was it? Damn you! Is that how the upper class here greet a lady? You should learn the manners of those back there!' she nodded toward the four, now helmed once more, alert as the gap in the wall was beginning to close through some magical method of which I was totally in awe at the unseen.

'But—' the man – seemingly in charge here – tried to jump in. But my mother was having none of it.

Again, there! That newfound, unbridled spirit. A gift of unbridled spirit, post almost being taken from this world, including any future other, now shining through.

'Ma'am, my apologies, for I misspoke … my haste with things got the better of me. I can utterly assure you; you are surely beyond equal here inside these walls.' The man handed the guard the spear and then walked over to us.

My father moved a shoulder to rest just in front of my mother's on the side he approached. A hand was offered to my father, the man's eyes pointed down at it, showing respect, for he understood my father's next move should he move any closer to her.

He took it and clasped it well, hard. Eyes finally met. 'Name? Before I let you go.'

'Ah, that's some grasp you have there, old fella.'

Finding some spirit of his own now, he replied, 'Aye, lucky it not be your throat—'

'Or your testicles, hey?' Jesse chimed in, trying to lighten the mood that was beginning to hang heavy all around us.

'Aye, be that, hey …' the man replied with a chuckle. 'Name's Mikki, assistant to the Lonba of the Twilight Clan: the mighty Hoanga!'

Still holding the big man's hand, my father asked sternly. 'And what in any hell was the need to almost crush—'

My mother stepped in between them, hoping to avoid any unnecessary confrontation on foreign ground. 'All good—thank you, Mikki, it seems you have bred some manners into your people here, and that I respect.' My mother nodded to Mikki and then to the four at the now fully closed opening as they made their way, synchronically toward a gate adjacent not too far from the one we had made our way through. 'I am sure you'll reveal all … in due course?' He nodded at her, and my father let go of his hand as the grip was relaxed.

Jesse came closer. 'Greetings, Mikki, I be the man known as Jesse, and I would—'

'We know of you, Jesse. We thank you for bringing the boy, unharmed, too, so would it seem …' I winced at the same time as Jesse squinted an eye, subtly enough not to draw concern from Mikki.

'Aye, not even a scratch on the boy …' he proffered before I could offer anything.

Mikki made his way over to me. My parents twitched slightly as he held strong hands on my shoulders – though, by now, I was sure they knew I was more than capable of defending myself from someone such as Mikki.

How wrong they could have been.

Not long after the unforgiving, firm touch did a large grin shine across Mikki's face – not one of malice or ill intent – as I found myself entirely in another place. This time, though – unlike many times before – I knew of the occurrence and shift to surroundings, for it reminded me of when Grehn was taken far away from those in the sitting room in the castle of Jacob's Well to a dream world be it of her own devices, or Holtonos', I could never decipher. It felt like the ground spun a full half circle upon its axis. That axis being me.

70

Mikki was still there, holding my shoulders, still holding that extended smile. The first thing I noticed was a sweaty smell – as though I had been labouring for days in the fields like so many I had passed in the taverns close by to their farms – as there were none around here, I sniffed at an armpit, and sure enough, the foul smell was my own.

'What you're experiencing now is a semi-transition back to the real world, that of your own. Unbeknown to you, or those you travelled with, you had crossed a divide into this world; onto the other side of the proverbial coin. Flipped into this dimension, the people of the Twilight Clan dwell exclusively in the place known as the Haze of Sorrow. Things can be warped here, to an extent that you can only imagine such!'

It kind of made sense, for the terrain looked eerily similar to the path we had travelled, less the massive city that stood where we ended up standing. The barrenness, absolutely. Though now different sensations touched my lips; that of a draft, a scent of dust, flower, or weed carried upon such breeze, if ever so subtle.

'So? Why are we here?' he asked *me*. And, to be honest, I had no shitting idea.

'Suppose another lesson? Always seems the way. I'm sure you have a valid reason, just like all those tuitions I have seen, or been through, before …?'

'Not quite.' He then let his hands off me. 'You see, there needs to be a place to escape to. When a madness descends upon this world like so many others. Others I'm sure you're fully aware of!'

'No, I'm not … seems to me that this one is more chaotic than that of Inarrel.'

'Oh … I see. So, is that the only world you have been party to?' He looked downcast as he looked about the barren landscape before sighing a sigh of defeat.

I nodded slowly, for I thought any quicker he may think I understood what the shit he was on about. I did not.

'I'm yet to get *your* name.'

'Just Getty,' I responded sullenly.

'Ah … Getty. You are herald of the fight to the dark. Whenever that darkness may descend on us here. Probably, it's already here … I guess, just there sowing itself into everyday life. Festering away, infecting our youth, just like those places destroyed from such initial subtle intrusion that set away over time.'

'You know of Arigal?' I asked, a bit too spritely, detracting from the seriousness Mikki spoke of.

A raise of his eyebrow to accompany the opposite side of his mouth told me all I needed to know. 'Hmm, you should know she hates that name?'

'Oh, I never thought … that was her name given though, hey? By them.'

'No idea, child, though she is known as she is now and was, as Semona.'

'Yes. Yes, you're right, I remember her whispering that name,' I blushed, thinking back at the pose, and the lips from which the whisper escaped.

Shuddering, the image disappeared through envy. Mama and Papa never talked about intimacy between a pair … or more there so. My father skipped over such *interactions* when he used to read the scrolls to me: though my dreams would eventually *fill those voids* once I became self-aware.

'You're yet to ask me, though I see it swirling within your mind …'

Stumped, I was. I had no idea where we were, or when, for my thought. 'How do we return to where we were moments ago, back to my family?'

'You count that mess of a man, family?'

'Jesse?' I answered and he nodded with affirmation to me. 'Well … yes, I do. For he has taught me much. Helped me even further. Further than I ever thought possible. And he would undoubtedly offer his body and soul to the dark Lady instead of my own. So … yes! I do.'

'Fair enough. You should know, though, you're not the first he has brought to us.' I twitched an eyebrow, admiring the whole charade he had played in bringing me inside the walls. 'Though I truly do hope you are the last … truly, I do.' The pause he left gave me some indication of the fate befallen upon *those* before me; the sad look on his face confirmed my suspicion.

'Here is a wondrous place,' he hoisted his arms and took a deep breath through his nostrils, 'full of so much potential. Harmony abounds here, for now, at least. So, when you end up doing your thing, can you look at doing it elsewhere, somewhere far from here, and quickly, so we can retain such a happy, quintessential existence upon Meritol?'

I looked at him with a wry grin of my own. 'I'll do my best, Mikki.' I, too, looked around and drew in the aroma seeping past, through the odour of my own. It was magnificent to sense; just as it was the time my mother had almost been swiped from this world when she had held me in the tightest embrace of my life,

I savoured every scent of her and my first feeling of a proper squeeze from her. 'I will do my best, Mikki, believe me. The past few years have taught me much. Before, I was content to hide under the covers of my bed, an easy life, being read to most evenings. Now I have gained a perspective of life, a life now immersed within so much of it. I want to protect all that exists, more than all that I love alone; for that enables existence of life to flourish unbound, of love, of pain, of all that we hold freely in our world.'

Mikki nodded his head as I spoke. He was a good man; I could tell that much. And I felt a pang of regret for my parents' admonishment of the man. I was sure he meant no disrespect to my mother, but only misspoke. I could always know how people were, empathically, if they were more than a supposed scoundrel. Always told myself to not judge on appearance, for I had seen, heard, and felt, so much as contrary to that image of people we would so often judge.

'How many dwell *on the other side?*' I asked, expecting him to tell me a rough number within the grounds contained within those massive walls.

His answer shocked me.

'There be many within our sanctuary, maybe just over a hundred. Many like ours, and many unlike ours; wholly dependent on the terrain they bound. Though, we know of many more sanctuaries spread about the plane beyond.'

'So … there are many more! Hidden away? Wow!' I was a little too enthused at the revelation. Until he broke such elation.

'Getty, they are also prepping for the end of this world. I know you feel a surge of adventure, but we see it far from!'

I knew I had erred. Suddenly taken back to that form lying on my bed, I thought of nothing only like back then! Now my knowledge of an entity demolishing civilisation as we know it, turning it to mulch, and feeding off the result of their pain and suffering, all was real. 'Any idea how many others?'

'No idea, Getty. We only know of another couple near this place, though we dare not venture too far. Who's to say? There could be a multitude of others, with such a setup as we …'

'That there could be. This world is a big place. So too, it seems, are the multiple layers upon each. Do you know what plane your *home* is on? Is it dimensional? Or is it another time or even place?'

'Who can say for certain, lad. Just gives us another out should the worst happen; that's all we need to know for now, hey?'

'How'd you get us here anyway? I saw no device, no words spoken, nothing of the sort to give weight on you doing anything other than smile at me.'

'Ah, we should be on our way back soon. Just hope my helper knows the correct sequence of code to set.' We waited a moment. He pointed to the air as a crackling fuzz surrounded us. 'You will find out soon enough. You will.'

With that said, we found ourselves in the same spot we stood before, between the walls of Mikki's courtyard, after the plane once again spun half-circle. I reckoned we had been gone moments, just as Grehn had been gone for the merest seconds when she disappeared with Holtonos upon Inarrel.

How wrong could I be!

There was no one left in the courtyard, just me and Mikki. Even the horses had gone, no doubt still grumbling as they pulled a cart now laden with contents that of two. *Surely compliant after seeing their brethren smashed into the dirt.* Who wouldn't?

'You look a little perplexed.' Mikki smiled, knowing I expected the complete opposite to occur, and he motioned me to follow with a finger pointed forward in front of him.

I complied.

'Lead on,' was all I could say. What else could be said? For more would surely be revealed, eventually.

I walked where he led.

First, through the doorway where he had appeared before we were warped away, then down some winding steps. *Undoubtedly those docile beasts had been led somewhere else?* Nope. The spiralling steps led down into a massive stable, an extensive array of other fine-looking horses.

The two had just been walked gingerly through the large double doors.

Behind them followed my party of three. No rushing to squeeze me *that time*. Just a pleasant "Hello" and "What took you so long?" was offered, my mother's grin amplifying the sarcasm. *So, not as long as I had assumed!* Maybe the whole scene had played out in real-time, which meant more than I could have imagined; this place *was* real! And not just a realm of fantasy contained within one's mind!

It may sound like such a small revelation, but this one opened more doors in my mind than ever before. I wondered how many more could be swung wide open in my messed-up space of a head. I was only interested in one, though; whatever it took, I wanted to fall free and into the arms of Vilenzia. Failing that, I wanted to preserve all that Inarrel was and will be.

My mind started to think of what Mikki had said, about the device operated by one of his assistants and how it worked with a random code set. *How many more could there be?* And, could one indeed take me to Vilenzia once again, wholly, in body, not just within a dream – as the more I developed, the less I transitioned into that dream of being there. Though, the face of that fuzzy figure who had greeted me in the in-between of that world and my world had been much more frequent, not saying much, just there, watching.

I had so many questions.

Of many, I was sure would go unanswered, as was the general custom and way of things. Some of those acknowledged as available to sortie through my quizzical mind would reveal the most wonderful things.

The world I knew, to the world I know, to the world I now viewed in front of me … was majestic, a grand scale presented. One to sway me forever. To offer me a path, the one I sought – the one most achievable. But I wanted more. I also wanted that second path, one to *her, to Arigal,* upon a whim: a whimsical and nonsensical notion … *for now.*

*

We had settled in a place beyond the stable; underneath the courtyard, I found myself being warped away, back to the real world.

Myself sunken into a button-punched leather lounger. The rest of the party mingling with a few other folk, unbeknown to me, stood around a small circular pop-up from which a few drinks were being dropped onto its solid surface, drinks that distorted the candlelight making its way through from the other side, *potent then* …

The room was dark, save the fire and candlelight, with a low soffit held up by a network of different sized beams and joists. There was nothing unusual about the initial appearance of the rooms we found our way through; other than they seemed to sparkle with absolute cleanliness, they were neatly laid out – symmetrical in design and size.

'So, how does that thing actually work,' I asked Mikki's helper, expecting nothing to come forthwith.

'Oh, this thing here?' he held it up and shook it a little. 'It be just a key. Useless without the door.' And with that, he let a slight wheeze out, amused with his own quip.

'You're right, I suppose,' I replied, not biting. 'The doorway though, what is that, and where was it before.'

'Not what, but who, Getty,' he tapped a finger to his head. 'Depends on the person creating that doorway as to what this thing here will do.' He shook it once more.

'A doorway is but a doorway between here and the next room. Can't see how that thing changes that.'

'Ah. Partly true. Though, how can you be so sure of what is beyond that door without knowing *for sure*?'

'Just makes sense. Doesn't it? Though the "door" is metaphorical, I get that, but the other side will al—ah yes, I see. And I think your metaphor is a poor one. It should more so be a … more a … Oh, I don't know, something like a travel carriage, and the stop on the route be the purpose of the "key". Not the door itself.'

The assistant smiled at me, placed the "key" down on the side table and leaned in toward me, elbows balanced on his knees, fingers touching their equal opposite, thumbs tapping at his lips while he thought. 'I like that, that makes much more sense; think of it as the fastest carriage there ever will be; almost faster than thought—no, not that, for some may never reach their intended destination,' again he chuckled, 'fast as …' he thought again a little longer. He could not come up with the required analogy in time before a ringing sound came from the woman at the centre of the popped-up timber servery.

I instinctively waved a hand over my glass of cider before placing a cloth to cover it, wafting away any tiny midges that would hover around or stick themselves to the rim.

Hmm, that's new. Unusual in itself, for there was always something hanging around such a sweet aroma, and you only sometimes ever knew once you spat the bastard thing, or things, out, most of the time over someone else! No touch during the swipe of said creepy graced my sensitive palm.

Thinking nothing more of it, I rose out of my comfy lounge and followed the assistant. I had not thought to ask his name, caught up in the madness of the past few hours, so I tapped him on the shoulder and asked.

He puffed out his cheeks and answered. 'You should know that by now, Getty, if not my real name. For whom I *actually* could well be.' He stopped, shook his head, and grinned at me before moving back on his way to the mass of bodies mingling around the prominent centroid of the room – the source of all the drinks being supplied.

It was not long before the bloke's true identity was revealed.

'All gathered here today,' the assistant belted out for all to hear as he held a hand atop each of my mother's and father's shoulders. 'If you could be called such! You are here for one purpose, and that purpose is supported by all those who reside here. Be known! That is our only purpose, to preserve the precious life offered to us, for us, to us all, by those we would call the Higher Souls of Garoth.'

I froze instantly, and so too, did my cockles and everything intimately related shrivelled. My father looked at me and twisted his head slightly enough to not cause any alarm. The Higher Souls of Garoth were of those who resided and settled at the highest rung of the Syltenerian ladder of ascension; they were the equal, I had presumed, of Arigal – or Semona – Lenjora, Everos, and Holtonos.

The assistant looked at me and smiled again, a broad smile, mimicked by all else in the room. I thought it some nightmare, that the whole world had gone crazy, converted to madness akin to that way of the Syltenerian order. And I was the only one yet to succumb!

The wink in Jesse's eye gave their silly little game away. I suppose he threw that wink my way to save me from slicing a few throats with but only one of the many hidden blades held hidden upon my once-bedridden body. I let them have their moment of joy, for it all seemed at my expense.

That kind of thought reminded me of when I was thence. For the whole time I lay, slept, and dreamt – mostly chaotically – I always remembered my parents tucking a small shift beneath my pillow after cleaning my cotton sheets: not much I could do with it, could barely lift my head, nay mind my arms. Sure, it was for them to sort out any incursion of my room – with what I know now – with a swift and covert swipe once they had been given leave of their final request to bid me a final goodbye.

I smiled too, eventually, and shook my head while I cast that sad smile. Though I was not the least enthralled to be the target of goading, I could not deny the fact if the hat was upon the other, I would have relished within such an atmosphere, one teeming full of camaraderie. They got me, and my papa, too, had sucked the extra essence of my pain away as he laughed out loudly, ripping that contained warmth from my existential being.

Another lesson! I correctly assumed, and I knew what all that meant instantaneously. *Never trust your gut, instinct, or family in situations like this!* I twigged it straight away; my family could well have been overcome mentally – like those docile creatures upon the plains or depths of Vilenzia, the bebockle and its land aboding like. I knew my parents not to be so docile. I believed they were mentally strong: for who wouldn't, looking after a waster like myself for many years and all the days those years entailed! I took the lesson well, took it even further, on how I could immediately distinguish malice or affection within those I knew, those I could know and those who I could never know! I had already had that kind of lesson – and not so long ago.

I was stunned at my reaction, stunned with my inaction as it were, as a figure came flying through the same timber door we had made our way through. I could not move; I was rooted to the polished oak floorboards. All I saw was a mess of fluff contained within its multitude of leather strapping. I leapt toward where I swayed mildly – the effects of my gloriously, languorously brewed cider.

I awaited the crash of his, its body, into mine as I stood stunned by the chaotic turn of events thrown at me by my closest and dearest. The impact came, though it was not what I had expected; that sensation of a fur upon my nostrils, a scent I had held once with much disdain, now only a longing.

Phil!

'Getty!' he shouted, and he embraced me, roughly. I was a little nervous he would claw right through me should he become even a little overexcited. Wincing slightly, too, I was. Phil backed off a little and saw me grimace. 'Heard you were in town. Raced here fast as I could.' His little teeth shone through a slit of a smile. 'How's them ribs, buddy? Hey? Healed yet?'

Seeing my mother's face twist slightly, I quickly knocked it on the head, for Phil's sake. 'Oh, no worries, they're fine, Phil, honestly. Healed soon after you tripped into me.' I swung my eyes from side to side to wade off any further talk of my once busted ribcage.

Changing the subject quickly, I asked. 'Tell you the truth, Phil,' putting a hand on his shoulder, I patted his matted padding, 'glad you're here. But tell me … *how* are you here?'

'Ah, yes, that!' He nodded to the assistant, who I now guessed was the leader of this place. A nod was returned. 'Well, remember that lass from the bottle?' I nodded; *indeed, how could I forget that.* 'See, she told me to seek out this place and more, in particular, him, Hoanga.' The man nodded, again, eyes downcast this time.

'Well met, Hoanga,' I offered, a little bow of my own.

My mother chimed in after an abrupt snort. 'Saw that a mile off!'

'My apologies to all of you. Much better to hide in plain sight, especially if any of you were here to do some serious harm. I am surely confident that none of you fall into that bracket. You are all welcome here for however long you wish to stay. But know this, some areas of this place are *off*-limits. Mikki will enlighten you about where you can and *cannot* go. You should also know that no harm will befall you here unless warranted through *your* own actions ...' He looked about the party, including Mikki, 'Understood?' He looked to us all once again, waiting for a nod of affirmation before he moved to the next set of eyes.

'Sounds fair,' my father spoke. 'There'll be no trouble from any of us.' He looked accusingly at Jesse, who reacted as if struck with a leather whip. 'We will abide your wishes strictly.' And nodded. 'I am, and I'm sure the others here have much to ask of you, many questions for you about this place and what you're all doing here!'

'That time will come, my good people. Plenty of time to discuss that. Now, who's up for another warm cider?'

Pleasant grumbles – to not sound too enthused – filled the air. I looked at Phil, and he the same back at me, *happy*. Happy to see my only other friend once again.

'Good to see you again, Phil ...'

'You too, Getty.' I smiled back at him. 'So, want to sit and talk again about how the hell we got out of that god-forbidden hole once again?'

'Aye, but maybe over there, out of earshot of my mama. That would be great. And! You must tell me of your travels since we last spoke, back in Elacluse. Say, where is Jacara?'

'Yes! And yes!' He leant in close and whispered, 'She ain't be allowed in this place, Getty; it's one of the defence mechanisms they have employed here, one she – or they, the Guardians, the Boler'ata – recommended should trouble befall the whole of Meritol. Come, let's sit.'

'How'd you get in then?'

'In time … But first, won't you introduce me to your folks and your man Jesse, your tormentor, so you had described him much too often?' He spoke the last loud enough for Jesse to hear. I smiled at the humour, though deep down I knew I would pay for such. One day, not today, so I let the time draw on – much longer than it should, drawing much more draught than I should have, knowing too well I would pay for it the following day. I didn't care. That was tomorrow Getty's problem.

The Next Day

I was woken with a thud to the front of my head – or donk, as Jesse would call it. My eyes opened to see nothing but darkness. The sudden jerk that ran through my body with instant fear revealed that I had only rolled off my slim bed and landed on my face. Sitting upright, I saw two furry feet hanging over the edge of the other single bed in the room, which confirmed we were still in the same place. Other than the pain throbbing in my nose from my short fall, my head felt surprisingly clear, with no dregs of the headache I had dreaded.

I wriggled his feet and received no response. I tickled the soft, pink pads he would call his soles instead. All given there was a quick swipe of his feet, swatting away my hands.

'*Phil*,' I whispered.

'Phil …!' I shouted. Nothing, again. I got to my feet and launched my body onto the bed he lay in, *take that you big bastard of a thing*.

Nothing.

I knew he was alive; dead people don't kick you, *or do the dead, possessed beings such as Phil?* His eyes were wide open too, and his tongue rolled about in his mouth – searching for the tiniest bit of moisture, no doubt – his fingers twitched as if dreaming of some sort of foray, probably slashing away at anything and everything.

I left him be. Standing between the two beds, I waited for that wave of nausea to hit me, to swirl around in my head after such a consumed amount of cider like so often it would. It never came!

I'll be damned!

I rattled my head around as if trying to wake from the dream and be deposited into that repetitive pounding madness that would make even the littlest sense.

The clear and coherent feeling did not.

We were perched high up in one of the West Towers, which looked back upon the way we came. From all sensical observation, I should have been able to see the city of Macam'bre, or at least its walls and many turrets, but I saw nothing beyond the wasteland we had traversed to get here. It put my mind at ease and that I had not dreamt of the happenings of the day prior. Nor the flipping of the world beneath me, for we had warped unknowingly into this realm. I had no idea when, where, or how, but it felt safe. I felt safe. What Phil had whispered echoed through my head much more than the cider; the reason *she* could not traverse such a divide made absolute sense. But that thought got me thinking more, why Phil, he too held the same essence of *she*, of the Boler'ata, or so she told us.

He, too, was to be part of the defence of the world we knew as Meritol. So why? *That* hurt my head; the answers would not be bought here, in the room I slept in. I would ask that kind of question later, whenever that would be.

I had no idea when or if we had arranged to assemble audience today. I could remember not much more than my papa playing a small flute, quite well – for I knew not he could play – and my mama dancing, swinging herself around Jesse as they locked elbows. Phil and I had settled ourselves away from the ruckus in the centre of the room, content to just chat, and drink,

86

and joke, all of which I could not recall. *Not the first time, mind.*

I thought to tidy myself and my bedding before I left Phil to his slumber – no matter how uncomfortable he seemed.

Not knowing what time of day it was, for the murky mist high above the terrain outside hid any clue to decipher such, I left the room and headed toward a large set of stairs that brought themselves up at the end of the hallway. So far up, I thought of the size of the tower I had found myself sleeping in. *So high! Yet so wide! A remarkable feat!*

My mind was cast to the massive orbs of perfection that had squashed my parents' ride. And I wondered how much of a stockpile they had created of such or how they managed to sail such a thing so far beyond the safety of the city's impermeable walls.

Intrigue set in. I was sorry to have wasted so much of the day, even if only the smallest of portions. I was eager to explore this place, for it brought a level akin to that of my dreams, years earlier. It brought those scrolls and books to life, in not just a dream – save if I was still, pending that almost fatal jolt of that next day sickness, the affliction of my own cause, that to pound my head into the sands of the Nebras over and over again.

As I twisted my way down those wide, winding stairs, I almost knocked over a couple of guards making their way up in the opposite direction. Their eyes focused on the step beneath each foot – for I imagined they would not relish the descent, bouncing back down so many steps in such heavy armour that belied their silent ascent. Two sets of eyes eventually found mine, the slight nod by each offered me a good day: and I was sure it would be – I had that kind of feeling.

The thing that struck at my mind once again – more tugged at it, as though something was amiss here – was everything was so … clean: free of any dust in any corner of the rooms I had found myself. Or the drop of a spider web vacant from every spot I would expect to find such. And, from what I could recall from the night before, the need was gone to waft away the cider-supping midges that had accompanied every mug of warm cider I had ever been served – say, if that *time* was only a brief portion of my existence. It all seemed *unrealistic*. What they had created here was almost perfection … almost – I still had to ask why they thought to sling those orbs at us and our docile cart muscle.

I wonder what those two little shits are up to down there in the stable? I would pay them a visit to ensure they had been looked after, but also to ensure their egos were not being inflated by way of constant pampering by the stable hands in this place or realm.

There! Another oddity yet to rear its head; there seemed to be only men who lived in this place. Though that answer would reveal itself and relieve me of my ignorance. An ignorance, one so prevalent wherever I had been – be it this, that, or any other realm. For one of the guards who made their way up the winding staircase earlier, their eyes, though stern and stoic, were softer around the edges compared to the other pair spying through the slightest of slits, a hint of colouring too.

I hated myself a little for such short-sightedness; maybe I had been exposed to too much of what I hated so that it had become an unconscious way of thinking! Though my mind drifted off to another question – why would they be wearing them indoors?

Maybe something wasn't amiss here. Maybe I just wasn't seeing it right.

I looked around at my surroundings much more the further I walked through the hallways and underneath their soffits. A constant sequence of majestic high-pitched arches repeated themselves. I found myself looking for any blemish other than the odd stonemason's deliberate touch of imperfection left here and there. Though I doubt even they were crafted and erected by hand, not from what I had heard or viewed thus far!

Eventually, a dizziness hit me from looking up and not where I was walking. A nausea caused by the spinning ensured I remained focused on where I was going. Forward. With no particular destination in mind. I was happy to just explore for a while longer. I would end up where needed eventually. And that might give enough time for Phil to wake and find me.

Once awake, he would have no problem following my trail, I could have been a bastard and walked the perimeter of the courtyard a few times just to confuse him, but I was keen to catch up with him when he did wake. For I had a few more questions for him, some no doubt answered during the night, though no burning recollection touched the surprisingly clear and functioning slab of meat between my ears. Another plus in this seemingly unreal place.

I like it! Could get used to this!

As I walked through the castle's many winding corridors, I could not help but take one more look up at the finely crafted stone arches. I stopped this time so as not to inebriate my mind with the nausea again.

A shout came from up ahead, 'Getty!' I continued inspecting the fine soffit; there were no faults, just smooth, polished stone.

'Getty!' again, a voice shouted. I shook my head – shaking

away any potential dizziness – before I looked ahead to see Mikki walking quickly toward me. He was dressed in a lather of robes which I presumed wore mightily uncomfortable – especially as he clawed at them with both hands to stop them from falling beneath his sandal-clad feet while awkwardly ambling toward me.

'Mikki! Good morning. You seem as though you're in a hurry for something?' I asked, showing him a warm, welcoming smile.

'Oh … no! I'm always like this. Much to do, Getty!' he proffered. I eyed him warily as he shuffled the drooping robes up a little more and then tied them a little tighter. 'There,' he said as if that would permanently fix the problem of too much cloth.

'I guess there is …' I had no idea what he was "to do" but imagined it was a monumental task.

'Now then, I was asked to find you: tell the truth, I was on my way up to your room to rouse you and your friend Phil. But, while I find you here, my master, Hoanga, requires your company. Yours, and your friend's alone … Should I go on and wake him?'

'I'm not so sure you can. I've tried. He will wake when he wakes. He will find me quickly when he does, I'm sure. As you may have observed last night.'

Mikki raised a questioning eyebrow. 'Aye, just like last night, eh?'

I had no idea what he was getting at, though something more than just chatting must have occurred, and what was he suggesting with that non-forgiving brow? *Surely not I!*

'Come on,' he said, quite forcefully, 'come with me then. Say … how's that head of yours? Should be more than a few fish swimming within, I suppose?' That knowing smile he gave me as he turned to face me, the way he came, told me all I needed to know.

The couch I found myself waiting on was not unlike the one I found myself sat the night before: of buttoned leather, not a blemish – no stretch marks, tears, or nicks – once again, other than the off-green colour as opposed to the deep red tanning.

Much more formal! I guessed the reasoning behind such a colour, not knowing that any colour held meaning other than red being dangerous, Or life-threatening.

I held my ribs once more.

It was mighty comfortable, though, and the longer I waited, the more it moulded itself around my bony arse! And my pointy elbows.

I waited for what seemed hours, but who knew in that place, before the main door was opened again to admit Mikki, who was followed in by Phil. He looked worse for wear, nothing like how I felt, and I wondered if that was because he held the soul of *one of them* that was not able to transcend into *here*! To a world meant to keep them out.

He looked absolutely admonished of mind. Eyes unable to focus on anything in particular as they darted this way, then that. Each pupil making its own way about the room.

Oh, I see! He is hating every moment of this, and I was loving every second of it. I let him know my mind as I smiled at him directly; my fingertips touched their opposite together knowingly. Yet to be admitted into the room beyond, I decided to prod at Phil some more while he wallowed away in a fragile state. Though, after a while, his dark blank eyes held unequivocal murderous intent toward me. Suppose I would have held the same stare had the shoe been on the other foot. But it was not. And I did not want to push my only close friend away once more.

I was about to offer my apologies for berating before he rubbed fists to each temple and smiled at me.

Feeling bad, I whispered over to him, 'Sorry, Phil. Just never seen you this uncomfortable before … without me feeling the same heavy load being thrown about inside my head!'

He looked at me through those two button-holed openings – one could maybe call eyes, perfectly round – piercing their way through the fur hanging all about his face. The fur slightly matted around his tiny mouth was another sign he was, indeed, affected by the inebriation of the night. As if I needed any further clues.

Well, and truly … *fucked*.

He tried to clear his throat to speak, though when he did open his mouth, he was interrupted by a clanging sound that came from the other side of the main door in the room, the one that opened inward, deeper beneath the keep, directly opposite the one that had admitted us into this holding room.

Mikki rose sanguinely out of his seat – a match of the same leather chair I was perched. 'Now … let's get to it. Much to discuss? I assume,' he nodded prominently to us both, but a little deeper toward me. Making me feel there was another lesson here I was about to partake – one of reception.

Phil did not miss my impending misery. He nodded with a smile as deepening his bow toward me; for I was now the one to be tormented, not for how I felt, nor for how I should feel. It was a secret smile for who he knew I was, and that trumped any hangover, it would seem. And that smile offered a return of the misfortune I guided before toward him.

Now, though, a separation was nigh, and that I was … completely … absolutely … well and truly … *fucked!*

So now, not the clearest clarity to their golden ale, nor too, their cider, could prevent that prevalent feeling of regret, no matter how pure the sample – however ample.

A sound resounded inside my head, of the world I had just left for granted, a "wild world" for sure. A wild world here seemed to be … *not*. And I liked that thought. Not entirely, for drama was what I was brought up by, to be read – more dictated to – as I lay there, wishing I was *there*, mingling with not just my mind in that faraway environment but my body and an accompanying soul fully engaged.

I could feel the gap between lessening.

Nodding to Mikki, I assumed the ringing sound was our summons, and that would be that. But no! Another ringing sound sang around the room, quicker in tempo than the one moments before.

Alarm echoed across his face as he looked about the room we were sitting in. He motioned with stooped palms for us to sit back down.

'Stay here,' he said before making a swift exit through the inward swinging door.

Phil shrugged at me as he crossed his legs; *lucky he wore those shorts today.*

'Seems like trouble afoot. Phil?'

'Meh, probably. Shit seems to follow you like—'

The doors swung open quicker than Phil or I had anticipated. 'Gentlemen, follow me,' Mikki looked much calmer and wore a slightly embarrassed smile as if he had erred in causing us undue alarm.

Phil proceeded to cough away, snorting, almost letting loose whatever he had left in his stomach from the night before.

If that sequence of a gargle was brought by any other person, I would have attributed the sound as a final breath; one escaping their mortal cage of un want.

Though I knew it was how he drew up after a good, long night on the ale, this one felt much more violent – I smiled to offer my heartfelt condolences as he choked on more of his bile, exasperating the whole process.

He held it in well to give him credit and did not drop one spittle from his quivering lips.

Mikki only dropped an eyebrow toward Phil, instructing him *not* to defecate with *any* of his innards on the fine leather, cloth, or the intricate rug he stood upon, no matter the pristine tiled floor. I assumed he was to be one who would be liable, as we were in his care at the time …

The whole interruption lasted for only a moment from my perspective. I imagined for Phil and Mikki; it would have felt much longer.

Looking at Phil, I wondered once more, as I often did while we travelled together, however briefly: how were people so becoming to such a beast, a beast who, by legend, would have stripped the flesh off of their newborn as if dropping skin, muscle, and bone of a spitted chicken leg down his throat then deboning the whole thing with the inside of his teeth.

The vastly different cultures upon Meritol aided our travels. Some places visited by us both had been challenging. Some are not so. It was easy to wrangle them to thought that he was from the far cold north, from a tribe most knew as harmless, the "Grapians" – if only through folk speak – most would never even know how they looked, so it was easy to sway their thinking, with the many differing looks from all over.

I only ever asked Phil to play along with that ruse and not slice through some idiot's neck with those ethereal blades hidden in his hands; for that would surely give him away, and the resulting cascade of town talk would ripple throughout the entire region, then beyond, to render us – more so, Phil – barred … indefinitely.

If not enough to only be rejected from every drinking hole: to be then hunted and then be removed from existence! Be it set alight atop a town square pyre, tied to some post, a swift swipe to the front or an even swifter cleave through the back of the neck.

He settled his throat, then looked to consider spitting out what he had gurgled up, but the big gulp and an accompanying wink told me we were good to go.

I followed Mikki, ignoring a couple of complaints coming from behind.

While I was at it, I thought of the few months I spent with Phil, remembering more than a few faces that had burned their way into my thinking more than just a few times, though none were so intimate to reflect upon in that way.

That burn would diminish in my mind over time. Though the

emblazoned outline of Arigal's face would not. If even a static frame of a face I could potentially love forever, for this life, the next, and any beyond.

Another thought became, depending on the circumstance of such burning, mangled thought, was … was she happy? For more than a few times, I sensed my only offering of empathy was the person or people within her company were absolute and complete shites!

I stopped daydreaming in just enough time to react. As I stepped over the threshold between the parlour and the room beyond, something had dramatically changed. As if I had been instantly dropped into the deepest, coldest ocean. The barrage of gravity pushing into me, then all around me, made it hard to breathe. My body wobbled from head to toe but eventually subsided as my senses grew to tolerate the new environment.

I risked another step forward.

'Feels strange, hey?' Mikki looked back at Phil and me. 'Lucky it passes so swiftly. Scared me half dead my first time, feeling that.'

Phil lurched and let loose the contents he had held in so stoically. Mikki shook his head at the mess. 'Sorry 'bout that, Mikki,' he said, wiping the dregs off his chin and matting the fur on his wrist too.

Was the whole charade of cleanliness now about to show for what it was? Nay, fate offered as we hurried forward to another threshold at the end of the short corridor that led into a cavernous space. I quickly calculated the height of the soffit and overlayed the assumed floor level above this place.

Impossible! was my conclusion.

Then I instantly remembered the fresh produce sitting on the stone slabs behind me and what had led to that. *Oh, goody! Another space between reality and make-believe, or somewhere far beyond,* it was tiresome, to say the least, that I was never prompted until post any transversal. That now irked me more than the bird shit.

'Say, Mikki, where are we now?'

'Getty … think not where, but when!' He rubbed his hands together like a greedy salesman who had just posted his pitch and was now waiting for the exchange of commerce to commence.

'Mikki!' I lost some level of calm, but not too much, just enough to gain some empathy. 'I'm sick of these games. My apologies for being so blunt, and in no way is it directed solely at you, but … for once, can someone tell me what will happen? For just once! Before it actually happens!' I let the volume increase the longer I waffled my bother, the last almost a shout … almost.

Phil laughed loudly. A full belly laugh. 'Getty! Look at you! You finally grew a little pair, my good friend. Mikki, you should know I, too, am getting irked by such revelations. Can you, in future, please let us know when we're to traverse plane … or time?'

Mikki was abashed, for this was another one of his surprises for me. It was not until that iciness was broken – as another resounding bout of laughter came from somewhere within that cavernous space – that my throat began to slacken a little. I meant not to offend Mikki; an apology later over a game of Fehlter would suffice … later, though.

A chair swivelled around to reveal Hoanga, clad in a funny

getup – one not custom to what I had seen thus far in the place we were temporary residents. Dressed in an all mossy-green, hooded robe that extended down to hide what he *may* have been wearing beneath his waist, or his chest, for that fact – if indeed, any *such* was hidden from our view. I shuddered at the thought.

'Greetings! I'm sure, without a doubt, that by now you have surmised you're no longer in—wait!' he held a hand up, reflecting his apology. 'Sorry. We are still here, just not when you'd know—'

'So seems the theme!' I butted in. 'Mikki already proposed the idea of not where but when.'

'Ah, yes, he did. And is that the reason for your outburst?'

'It wasn't an outburst!'

Phil began to cackle at me, which set off Hoanga to wheeze out an extended laugh as well, resigning me to drop my head for solemn reflection. I *had* fallen short in my reaction to the few present in this place. And that technique I had been taught would dissolve the anger building its way inside my already swollen head.

I wondered. *What's next from here? How many more invisible realms, how many more portals!* Be it time, place, or both!

The novelty was beginning to wane.

So too, were the many lessons I would undoubtedly endure after initiating such. I knew much was warranted, for I would need to react in real-time, in the real world, for when I was to be called for. But the benign crossing: to and fro, from and to, left me tired. A tiredness that drilled itself down, deep into my bones.

'Getty, do not worry about such trivialisation. We have met many like you, and even more far from. By the time they would

98

come here, they, too, had the same irk rattling their tiny mind. It seems this place here'—he stood and spread arms in the air and spun around— 'seems to give the … uhm … selected, reason and confidence to air their views.' He motioned all forward, pointed to a few scattered chairs, and then sat; his hefty frame dropping into a comfy-looking chair that scraped along the floor slightly as his arse hit the padded leather.

Phil was the least displeased as he leant back and lounged on an oversized oval-shaped chair – more a chaise – he was offered. Hands resting on the back of his head, he closed his eyes … purringly sighing.

I felt the seat was another stasis of my life, one yet to be told, of something more than I had known. Something to be told, maybe? So much repetition and yet not so much action.

For a fool I was. The revelation to be told would set me again asunder, again on that path, thirsty for more. To seek more knowledge that would fit inside my already heavy, overflowing "donk".

'Be warned, young man … for you *may* hold more than just fate upon those slender shoulders of yours,' he said. 'Of most importance to me and those who offer us this protection. Have your dreams subsided?' His head tilted down and forward a little to observe my answer through eyes spaced further away from their accustomed brow.

'I have not had any since'—too quickly I must have spoken, as his brows and eyes contracted as if he did not believe—'since I left Jesse and crossed the bounds that circled the Eporan lands.'

'You say, hey?' Now his lips and ears contracted, and not to offer a smile. Further guidance that he still held no faith in what

I was saying. I took it as he only thought it an oddity for what he must have heard from many before. That in itself made me a little nervous and a little excited, for I assumed all before me had offered, truthfully, that they had indeed carried on with whatever they brought that was thought to be special. I had no idea what, or if, they carried the same cursed afflictions as I ...

I was direct. 'Hoanga, *believe* me. I have had no such interaction with Inarrel since. Though I do feel torn by the whole thing, not being able to revisit, if only in my dreams.' My eyes glanced around the room, then to the floor. 'How many others?' I asked bluntly, even if not wanting to hear the response.

A long pause ensued, and then as Hoanga drew a breath, ready to answer, I jumped in. 'No ... best left unspoken.' I sighed as I raised myself out of the chair to inspect the spacious room. It did remind me of that gracious space packed to the brim with all manner of literature, high up in the City of the Columns.

The two of this place watched me as a short puffing sound escaped the lips and nose of Phil. I smiled at that; *rest up, friend* ...

Friend. Who'd have imagined me with a friend, and one so funny looking – but also so very lethal if he chose to be, be it with wit or slicing something or someone to pieces. Thinking of the almost fatal wound he inflicted upon me, I touched my ribs. Nothing. I felt neither the slightest fuzz of pain nor the tingling sensation of tenderness to touch. *It must be another attribute of this place.*

I made my way around the room's perimeter – if it could be called such. Brushing my fingers across the face of the row of books level with my elbow. Amazed at how they left no trail between the dust as I wiped across each spine. Something marvellous, though something that could also be cast as so unreal, this whole place could be labelled as the same.

Tarnished would be a perfect anonym, for such the place seemed perfect, if for the riddling questions and even further riddle of any answer. Though that was not confined to this place, but for all who would offer me some guidance or tribute.

A tome caught my attention, not for the fact it was sat proud of every other title, but for the symbol struck into the leather spine – no label, only a symbol – one I knew well, the very same outline scorched upon King Benjamin Aurelia Jacob's wrist, the very same as his daughter, Grehn's birthmark.

Immediately I looked to Hoanga. Who returned a stare above fingers that touched and hid his nose, not able to hide the knowing smile.

Another prop in this game in the attainment of knowledge. The look I gave Hoanga said as much, but he shook his head as if that was not the case. He stood gracefully, strode over to me, and held a hand on my shoulder.

'Take it. That's yours if I'm not mistaken.' He pulled it from where it rested on the shelf and handed it to me. The face on its cover held the same symbol, that of the three circles inside each other from each summit, forming a crescent beneath the top two; only … it was much larger than the one on the spine, so much so that it took up the majority of the cover. 'You *must* read this. You alone. Understand? None must know of the contents inside of this book, save for Jesse in the most extreme situation. For all of those who have ventured this far into this room, this place, they too have been presented their own volume, a look to their own future, just as you have here. Open it, feel the pages within, feel how your fingertips respond to their touch.'

I did.

The text within was etched, not inked. Scorched even, *but with what?* I pondered as the text would distort into nothing more than blank parch. It felt so … elegant, so well crafted, *but by whom?* I worried.

One thing left unnoticed until now, was for as my fingers made their way around the bookcases, there was the occasional skipping of leather as they touched the void of where there was once solidity; as singularity, I was sure – for whoever was destined to remove – for revelation of a destiny not beknown.

'This is an essential step. One of which all have taken before any ascension. What's that? You have a question?' My eyes had prompted his question as they scanned all the others that remained upon the multitude of shelves.

'The ones left in between or *those* left behind?' I tempted him to reveal more. Knowing full well I would only be gifted another cryptic answer. And I was pleased when a straight one was offered.

'None have been left behind. I assure you. All those who ventured this far have all been trained to afference such knowledge and of even further training. Though you're unique, so too was every being who has ventured into this place—'

'—being?' I threw a startled look at Hoanga, though he only nodded to Phil snoring away on the chaise to clarify his point.

I nodded, *of course!*

'Yes, we have all sorts coming through here … from all over.'

He swung his head slightly from side to side to stifle any question that would spout itself from off the edge of my tongue. So, I left it. 'They will all be taken one day, those that remain, to be taken to where they need to *be*.'

I was beginning to piece together much of what I had observed and heard. This was a central place, one connectable to a myriad of scenarios of time and place. Though place could be a fickle thought, and my own was anywhere from home to the edge of the cosmos, and that meant a multitude of the latter throughout each iteration of said time. 'So why so few taken?'

He knew I knew of the possibility and the infinite number of potential *beings* that *could* have graced this wonderous space. 'Ah,' he ruffled my thin crop of hair, 'smart boy …' He walked back to where he had sat before, not before telling me to scour further through the room. Telling me to not think too much of that thought. Finishing with one more sentence, loud enough so all could hear in the room, after kicking Phil's boots off his lounger. 'Who's to say that everyone else is but an extreme fraction of time behind you?'

My head felt even heavier at that thought. I assumed this place was not blessed with the properties on the other side of the door I had been summoned through.

My head spun wildly. I had many more questions now, though as I was about to throw them at Mikki and Hoanga, I was told to calm, for all would be revealed in time.

'For now,' said Hoanga, 'let us enjoy this wonderous place before we venture back to your family and Jesse.' He pulled out an aged bottle of wine – which looked like it had rested in some dark place for more than a few summers – and four crystalline glasses. He poured the fleshy, crimson contents into each glass before dropping the remnants down his throat direct from the bottle. Aged it was that: far beyond any other wine or spirit that had ever made its way past now tingling lips. I dared not attribute such a drop to that freshly crushed blackcurrant juice that I loved when I was young – for fear of ruffling the mood.

I sank back in my chair as a rushing mind-scene of images thrashed through the deepest, darkest forest. All its scents, truffle, bark, and myth – consumed my entire soul.

*

I had no idea how much time had passed from the initial tasting to the last drop or how many corks were squeezed from their respective stems. The final thought, though, was of my head spinning before I let loose a spray of my own to complement Phil's earlier. The last before a blackness encircled the periphery of my eyes and crept in … more profound, followed by a soft thud as I was dropped hastily to the chaise Phil had now vacated.

A Little More Action

The next day, the first thing I remembered I told myself to do, was immediately run to the window – just hoping some poor soul was not about their own business below. I needn't have; I was back in my room in the castle or whatever it was. Phil once more snoring away on his bed, me feeling as though I had bathed in a hot spring the day prior, feeling fresh as a spring morn; *this is an odd place, and though weird, it certainly is a wonder*. Once more, my head was bereft of any pumping or surging of blood through constricted veins around my temples and my eyes.

Phil snorted loudly and shot up to see me at the window. 'You had enough here that you thought you'd jump without me in tandem!' he chuckled. The only one of the quartet not to consume anything other than air the day prior, he was much brighter that day; his eyes showed as much too – much less than the previous day.

'How are you feeling, Phil?' I asked, knowing he was good, just breaking a little ice before he launched into song and dance at the state of my behaviour the evening prior.

He looked at me, little teeth piercing through the drooping of fur, always comical, ever since the first ever sighting of them, crunched together in rage as he swiped away at me as the colossal walking rock approached, ready to squash me deep into the ground. They hovered to say something, then he closed his mouth and grimaced as he looked towards the tome resting heavily at the foot of my bed. 'You read that thing yet, Getty?'

'No, I was instructed to read this alone in times of need or in despair of the mind. There was no further talk. No further instructions were issued …'

'Very well then, when do we leave?'

'I have not the slightest, Phil.' I had no idea. And why would he assume he would be leaving with us, having arrived there of his own volition and unknown reason. Was this just another game being played? Or a full-on coincidence. I doubted Phil would be that way. I had to ask. 'How'd you get here, Phil? And when?' Questions I had may have asked a few days earlier, though I could not recall asking or receiving a reason why.

'Been here a shortish while, Getty. I was told by a lady I met, deep within the Angoliant, that I was to come here and wait. So wait I did, once again, in such a short space of time at the latter end of my life thus far; I waited for something, a cure, a miracle: both the same, and then here you are! My saviour. Once again, here you came.' He chuckled some more.

'How long have you been here, Phil?'

'Not long … Well, to you, maybe longer, not sure of time these days being in so many switches and hitches of realms and the like, you know my meaning?'

'That I do, friend. That I do.'

Phil looked at me again, the bottom row of tiny teeth showing themselves before the upper lot. 'Say, just for demon's sake, and all *those* other beings, how long since we parted at the town of Elacluse.'

'As you said, Phil, we can only measure time—' I began to feel nauseous as I strode my answer out; I was becoming as cryptic as all those others. Maybe that was the doctrine inscribed over so long after the constant barrage of such machination. '—

well, it's good you're here now.'

'Say, Getty ... when are *you* thinking of departing? Honestly?'

'Like I said, Phil, I have no idea.' I pressed my lips together before he nodded acknowledgement.

'This place is pretty boring, to be fair, not much to do other than read, drink: which I may refrain from, for it seems I'm not immune like you or many of the others—'

'What ...?' I asked immediately, 'Others?' I spat out before he could respond.

'A few.' He shook his head slightly as if for me to ask no more.

I pursed my lips a little tighter to show I was not happy with any secrets he may hold, especially in such a foreign plane. Closing his eyes, he slumped more into the well-roughed bedding. 'Getty, you should know this is a place of an eventual last bastion or a last haven for those of this world. But! What you should also know, and I'm actually a little surprised at your question, is that this place is connected ...'

'Ah, to that room we were in yesterday. Yes ... I see. I assumed such before the wine was introduced.' I was instantly giddy about who or what else may have been confined between the innards of the pristine walls of this place. How many eyes ... how many hands ... what tongue would they speak ...

I was sorely disappointed when I eventually met these *few* foreign species, for they all seemed the same as everyone else, excluding Phil – of which I was hoping much more akin, or at the very least ... just as strange.

One, named Abal, was the sender of the orbs over to where

we rested for the night before gaining entrance.

Apparently – or so we were told – the docile things had been carrying an unknown rider within their flesh. Not just one, but many tiny parasites tucked deep inside the items, to be released here upon gaining entrance.

Abal appeared slightly older than me, though he had lived many times longer than my own. That revelation was a shock, though understanding why was a relief. I had asked what about the other two, and how he knew, and how they had such accuracy; he told me, in no particular order.

'Well, you have undoubtedly observed how barren the land be around the keep? We have gauged every possible coordinate for our range finder from each orb's departure from the *sender* – a catapult-like device. We roll them back into the keep, ready to be used again. We also have many ways of detecting such foulness: miniature bloodsuckers return here after their feast – which, in this case, was the trigger – and identify any anomaly once we squash them onto parchment to reveal, hopefully, a taint of colour in the standard range of the spectrum.

'Your friend there,' he pointed to Phil, 'returned a mighty vibrant colour, far from normal, though was lucky enough to be possessed with a boost of speed aided by an uncanny sense of something dangerous imminent that would quicken his doom!' His chuckle settled me a little; a similar slack of light humour would do that. 'It also seems that your rides were more … hmm, let's just say, resistant to being touched or fawned over.'

'You're not wrong there …' I left it at that. Abal was happy, too, as he chewed on one of the fig-looking things left out on a platter for the outlandish guests.

Excluding Phil and Abal, there were another two, just as similar and familiar with the general folk that dwelt on Meritol. Those other two had, as I was told, arrived together from when and where I was told not. I assumed they all held some lofty accord, similar to Arigal and Dagda's. They seemed the type, quiet and unassuming, though a cast across their eyes belied something not within, something powerful; hence their being here.

My mind began to wander, to follow the strings of ultimate possibilities to who, or what, was at the end of each. A sense of inconspicuousness piqued wherever my mind followed those imaginary routes; to worlds beyond. It made me nauseous again, and as I had learned, this place shouldn't do that. I began to work it away as I retraced each string back to this place. More so: the place I collected the book sat on my thigh yesterday. There! That was the focal point, the transection of time and space. And then there was me, a boy cripple with the whole world and more, weighted slightly on my shoulders – the weight gradually increasing the more able I became.

Is this a time for me to read the thing? I wondered.

Unsurprisingly, Rendala – one of the two otherworldly people – shifted her head as if reading my thought.

She came over to me. 'Not yet, child,' she placed a tender hand upon the top of the book and smiled, a full smile, full of warmth and a knowing. 'You will understand when you do, believe me.' She then pulled out a book of her own – smaller, but much more colourful, and holding a sparkle whenever the firelight cast its glance across its cover. Though the spine had faded, losing much of its texture, I did not mistake the symbol that flowed from top to bottom: two slender, winding animals the equal of the other: flipped. Immediately I muttered under my breath what I thought them to be, one animal that should have shrouded my dreams with nightmare, the same thing I found comfort in whenever I heard its name.

'*Dark Evelyn* ...'

She looked at me curiously, face scrunched as if I had no right to know what the etching should resemble.

'How ...?' she shook her head, a slight hint of confusion cast at me, nothing malicious in it. 'How do you know of such a creature? They are confined only to a world beyond your time and this place.' Again, she twitched. This time to better look at the symbol gleaming proud on my cover and then the spine.

'I know of them. Or, more so, the one that resides—um ... resided on Inarrel.' She shook her head as if I was talking from my rear-hole. 'A place I know well, offered through many scrolls while I lay still as a rock, crippled. Dreams, too, used to weigh, run heavy through my imagination each night; immediately after, my Papa would let me sleep.'

'What?! Your mother never read to you?' Now she was cross, angry almost. 'My mother would read to me assiduously every night I was lay.'

'Whoa! you too?!'

'Yes, Getty. I, too, was confined to observing the world from a bedhead's viewpoint. Though I did not have the dreams that followed. I would be fully aware as my body raced through fields with no volition of my own. As if I was in a dream, except for every knock and scrape I would feel.' She looked absently at her forearms. 'Tell me, though, tell me of your dreams?'

'Oh, I believe we have not the time for that ...'

'Oh, believe me, Getty, we have more time than you assume.' With that, she winked at me. 'I will see you again tomorrow. And then you can tell me of the creature emblazoned upon *my* book. And I will reciprocate. You will also tell me of your dreams, for I feel there is a connection there.' Another wink, more a twitch of a cheek. Then she turned on a heel sharply and was gone, striding through the double swinging door back to where she had come from. Still within the keep, I hoped.

It was then the other's turn to prod.

'Getty,' he shouted over to me. 'Come over here. Phil and I would like to speak with you.' Though Phil was different to the pair, he had settled himself in frequent company with them through a mutual bond of illness that followed a few nights of ... glugging and the resulting illness that followed on the morrow.

I made my way over, leaving my new book to rest on the button-pressed, tan-leather chair. I held no concern for its safety as we were the only remaining occupants of the taproom – other than the barman who concerned himself with polishing the crystalline goblets we hadn't even touched ... yet.

Phil was sitting, spark upright, not his usual style. His new companion, who had called me over, lounged a little easier into the dark green, lush fabric of the couch they both occupied.

'Does anyone find that *beast* sat beside you the slightest bit strange?' I asked comically.

Londe replied swiftly. 'No more than you, I would imagine. Many others, some not too unlike Phil, have made their way here to this place. I assume the spectacle would recede with each

111

occurrence. Now, you … You seem a bright lad, and that there book of yours looks mighty thick and freshly plucked! You care to read anything of it yet?'

'He's been told not to until when he needs to,' Phil chimed in.

'Well, how the shit is he to know if it would be useful to him?'

I shrugged my shoulders, not knowing an answer or what else to say to Londe on the matter. He was a genuine sort and was quick short with his words. No such mimicry of those cryptic and longwinded fluffy talks I was so used to. He was right, though; how was I to know what was inside. There could be nothing written there that could aid me in my darkest moments, of which I was sure there would be many. And, then what, when I finish said script? Do I begin again from the beginning, just as the scrolls read to me by my father … *Suppose that depends on how much I enjoy it.*

Our communique was interrupted by Phil's strange noise, a squeal that managed to squeeze out of his stumpy snout. His head started to twitch as if sniffing at something unseen. When he looked at me, I knew to run for the door before he could give vocal warning.

The two windows set into the façade of the room where we were mingling shattered inwards, throwing shards in the direction we all ran – more than a few catching bare flesh upon my hands, ears, and neck. Phil was unfazed; he had no exposed flesh, only matted fur. I imagined, as I ran, that he would be picking out small pieces of shrapnel for more than a while once we were clear.

Londe held a hand high in the air, dropping a shield of some sort all about his body, knocking away any glazed debris before it could inflict any damage upon him.

Carrying the splinters within my skin, we made it to the door before the entire room erupted with a blooming redness. Hesitant to turn my head back, I made quickly for the doorway. Being the first there, I held it open for the other two to pass through. All eyes still averted from where the façade had been shattered. Once through, I knew to slam the door shut and keep running.

Luckily, we did.

A blast erupted from the doorway, throwing shards of a different ilk – that of timber – down the narrow, enclosed corridor. Another stroke of luck, as I was first in the small chain-link of bodies, the barest of splinters – only the tiniest – managed to make their way through to anything of my exposed rear. A shout from Phil indicated that he received the brunt of the larger pieces once of the thick wooden door.

The searing heat came next.

We had only just swung around the first corner of the corridor as the heat blasted against the wall, singeing a good chunk of Phil's fur as he was the last to turn to safety. His bulk hit the wall hard at the end of the corridor. Panting heavily as he lay on his stomach, I stifled a laugh, for he now sported a bare arse, still smoking from the sudden blast.

There was no time to ponder as Londe dragged us both up to our feet and dragged us all the way to the entrance of the room from where I procured my book.

Throughout the whole time being dragged through whatever part of the keep, I surmised that the explosion had been concentrated to the window where we, or I, were settled. Other than the mild panic and constant stream of soldiers this and that way, there appeared to be no damage nor the slightest hint of an attack anywhere else.

Phil and I sat in silence while Londe paced up and down. The rustling noise as Phil shuffled, clearly uncomfortable with the cold leather touching his arse, was quite irritating. So too, was the waiting. Not knowing what had just transpired. Londe aired more through unspoken words. He had more than an inkling of what that may be.

Every time Phil or I would ask or gave the body language ready for such, we were shut down immediately with a stern "No!" accompanied by an even sterner stare.

Eventually, he would cease pacing to sit down beside us. His demeanour was now calm, and his face was full of candour as Abal ghosted into the room ever so smoothly.

'Still here, I see?' She raised an eyebrow to validate a valid question, not just candid chatter.

'Would seem so,' Londe answered directly. He, too, raised an eyebrow. For what, I was unsure. 'You took your sweet-arse time?'

'Sincerest apologies, Brother. I was busy neutralising the thing that launched those two projectiles. Seems timber and tort string are immune to the buffing effects of this place.'

'How'd you manage to subdue it so swiftly?' he asked.

'Lucky for you three, there had only been two projectiles loaded. There was no other ammunition around, unless they decided to begin throwing the sorry souls that pulled the contraption at you.'

'And?'

'All said shit have been neutralised. Efficiently so. Suppose you couldn't hear their screams or gurgles of dying pain stuck down here.' She wiped her hands together to clear off a dust I had yet to observe in this place.

'Any … more?'

'Yes, Londe. There was something else out there with them. Something we need to alert the council with.' She looked cautiously at Phil and me as if our ears should not hear of what that some*thing* could be. She raised her head and nodded to the door that led to the Library of Fate. That's what I would call it.

Before they both made it to the door, I asked, 'Who are *they* then?'

'You will know soon enough, Getty …'

And with that, they disappeared for only the time it took to shut the door, for it was immediately reopened – as if they had never left. Not enough time for me to stop shaking my head at Phil for the forever and never-ending stream of non-answers.

Before I stopped shaking my head, Londe spoke. 'I will tell you, Getty, who was out there, how they were neutralised, and how we must block off any further intrusion into the lands surrounding *this* place.'

'From where are they coming?' Phil asked.

'Questions I will answer once we are on our way to plug the gap in the barrier from which you entered. Seems our furry friend here might have separated it enough to allow those mounts of your parents through, and thus, the small but manic Army of Drach't able to penetrate it too!'

Phil raised his hands as if to defend himself but only let out another wheeze. 'Sorry … I didn't know, I was too busy avoiding those damn orbs you were throwing at me. And the smaller ones, well … I couldn't see them til they were about top o' my head!'

'As I have explained, my good man, a necessary enactment of this place's defences.'

'And, might I add, what an accurate projection you have. Lucky for me, I was able to use these little legs of mine to thwart such assumed coordinates.'

'In any case, we need to go beyond that barrier and snuff out any other potential threats while the barrier is being replenished. That also means … Phil, you're to remain on this side and deplete any that make it through. Understood? We can't have any more rips or tears.'

Phil raised a hand to his brow and offered a comical salute. One returned by Londe. I smiled at the connection between the two, no surprise to me; they had both, since the time I had known them, been so distinctly upfront with anything on their mind or when chattering about shit, no less any answers offered to my constant questions.

'Londe, you go do that; and be quick about it. I will go beyond once more, back to—' she held herself and looked directly at me. 'You know where.'

'Absolutely, you must, sister.'

'You go then!' she said as the door closed behind her, a chinking sound, locking or unlocking something. I had no clue. Though we wouldn't see her until our work was done, out there, beyond them barren plains. I had no idea where the precipice was or how we would keep whatever was out there at bay, and maybe that excited me a little more than it should have. I was

116

glad about it. What would my Mama and Papa offer as to their opinion, though?

Where were they anyway? I asked myself absentmindedly.

Time again. That was the all becoming, and often answer to things. Apparently, they had left half a day earlier, and with Jesse! And also with a large mission of mounted soldiers, keen to help stem any flow of unwanted guests toward this place. A mother and father with a profound sense of life was what it was. No longer hiding behind that role of nurturing the boy cripple, looking to save all in any way they could. *Fools,* I thought, and I felt foolish for such a thought. Who was I to belittle the people who had set me on a path to glory, who had looked after me for more than most of my life? And who was *I* to question? I didn't even know who *I* was.

Yet.

*

I had never worn a breastplate, or a helmet meant for battle. I would have expected them to be heavier, but knowing more about this place now, I did not question their feather-weighted composition – I hoped they would protect me far more than a thrust of the same.

It was not long, maybe a few hours, before I became satisfied the armour I was adorned with would withstand more than a brush of said feathers.

How many more strokes, though?

I had no interest in finding out as I swatted away their metallic swings of the same! Every clang received, though non-cutting, swept my mind away from the task at hand. The tremor flowing from such a strike left me open to another and always received. A swipe from behind, or from the side to clang again against my body. Never my head! For the little bastards only stood level to my waist. It was like swatting those pesky pests away from a tall bucket of bubbling cider: relentless but insolent of any style or guile. To be fair, I was happy I wore the armour. Still, I also wished for the same to cover my legs, for that was the prominent target for the short, nasty things we had clashed with on the other side of the barrier of the supposed unreachable sanctuary and last bastion of our kind upon Meritol.

Distinctly, the forest had reappeared in an instant from where we had left it days ago. Looking back was not something we had favoured, so when the forest and trail turned to wasteland, we assumed it was what it was. A break to another terrain. Not another plane completely.

Oh, I wished it so.

For me ... I was always of the assumption: I was who I was, where I was, and how each interacted together.

A nick to my leg caught me unaware. I had thought all the little shits had been dealt with. They had. Just not fully extinguished to be one with the dirt forever. A few still held their blades as they lay perpendicular to the brambled terrain, thrusting them skyward, even as their souls faded away upon the frozen terra.

Little fuckers, they were.

It was a scene un-beheld to me – observed from an obtuse reality. The blanket of small bodies littered all over caused me to lurch and almost heave, and I did well not to, once I realised who or what I was to let loose upon ... the dead – of some impressionable race.

Even as they raised what little weapons they had, failing to find any purchase, save a nick to the ankle or provide a puncture to the soles of our rubber boots, they went on relentlessly, rendered as useless as we trudged back to where we came; which included the crossing of a few streams and bogged ground between.

Didn't matter a bit to me. I would eventually find the time and place to let go and let loose my innards, away from all manner of past and present, to show my respect for the stigma of the hollow achievements of the fallen.

The thought alone would run through my body akilter, away from itself. To hide behind itself somewhat.

*

The place had been riddled earlier with a swarm of bobbing heads, blades held in the air, swamping across the brushland like a wave of wind gracing the tips of tall grass as the divots in the ground sank and the mounds that raised themselves higher. Now, only a slight shuffling could be heard – as a few struggled to raise arms once more – and the short sharp yelp of one of the soldiers taking a nick upon their legs. From all those that had ventured with me, back beyond the bounds of that ethereal world … all still remained. All intact, still mobile, and able to strike once more.

It seemed a waste, but I knew not of their beliefs nor their end goals. For if they were indeed instructed to swarm forth by the darkness mustered in their hearts, then a waste it could and should remain. *Would the ground take such foulness and turn it into flora for other fauna to feast?* I took a moment longer to consider, and that was all it was.

I spent a little time to source the whereabouts of the three who had trudged off so valiantly earlier. Even a quick glance at Phil set him on his way to seek and save my time looking for them. He should not have been here – there must have been some reconsideration of the severity of the situation beyond the bounds of sanctuary.

It became clear that this was not the first wave of the little bastards. They had attacked from a different angle. Noticeable by the divide and change of the colour dyed in their hair, from a heavy red to a light blue.

A familiar shout caught my ear, far away, from the direction Phil had bounded to, *Mama.* I could not see her yet, or my father for that, though I knew they were not far away. I just had to navigate through the sporadic thrust and minor irritation from the ground beneath me.

Eventually, I would spy something else familiar: the unmistakable fluff of my good friend. And then the spright, silly hat that Jesse would wear.

Where is he?

Not able to see the fourth figure I was expecting to see, I rushed on at a considerably increased pace, much to the little fellas' angst, as my boots caught them in all kinds of places, causing a grunt of a grumble from those souls not yet departed.

As I embraced my mother, she immediately whispered, 'All is alright, Getty …'

I looked for reassurance from Jesse. It was granted as he nodded that all was good.

'Where is Papa?' I asked for my own sake. 'Papa!' I shouted, this time.

'Over here, Getty!' my father shouted from somewhere I could not locate as I glanced around, the mist lost beneath my eyes now just an inconvenience of sight. I walked to follow the shout … nothing yet.

'Where are you?! Papa!'

'Up here, Getty!'

I twisted my head swiftly every which way before upwards.

'How the—' I held the curse well, knowing my mother was there, '—did you get up there?' He only smiled at me.

My mother was the one to answer the panging question rattling around my donk. 'Up there! Acting as our lookout, but these things just moved in so quick he got stuck up there. Tell a truth, probably best place for him.' She chuckled, and it did ring true. It was indeed. 'How'd you go?'

'Good, I suppose. We lost not one of our own,' I raised an eyebrow before asking her. 'You?'

'No idea, Getty. From what I could see, these *things* were no more effective than a stiff breeze trying to flock us!'

'Decoy? Maybe?' I asked.

'No, this is the only way into that place,' Jesse answered. 'Any other direction would just be the continuation of this plane. No … just seems to me that this was only fodder, mindless munchkins hell-bent on whatever prize in another afterlife they were offered. It seems they detest the hand they were given in this one.' He threw a big glob of spit at one of them, trying to raise a hand to grab one of the other soldiers, hitting it square in its lumpy face. Not caring to wipe the spittle from his chin, he

121

went on. 'We've tried to interrogate but are only met with the same response. All seems a bit dramatic, if comical.' Eventually, he did wipe his chin.

'How so?' I asked.

It was Phil's turn to answer. 'Seems they wanted to die ...' He turned his head away, as I assumed a connection was felt in their despair. I knew he would. And he should; that was what made Phil, Phil! He had never mentioned anything to me or even given any indication he was angry, upset, or mad enough to end the change the cards had thrown at him, thrown him away from his family, friends, and no doubt a love; for he was the most adorable being, with the most caring soul – save the slashing and crashing part he thrust and left upon me. Though now, as I had always suspected, there was a deeper touch than the few that predominantly shone through!

I walked to him, purposefully, for I didn't want my friend to feel alone in his moment of open grief. Nor in the moment of triumph either.

Putting a hand on his shoulder, I asked, 'Phil ... you 'right, friend?'

'Aye,' he squeaked, higher than he meant to, which brought back that enamel of the "fun guy" he always appeared, always was. I looked at him, his eyes bubbling as though about to break ...

'Come 'ere, big man!'

All the air contained within my lungs lingered no longer, no more breaths to be taken, for what seemed an eternity.

I didn't care as he squeezed me tight.

More, bring it on ... I wasn't panicked, especially when I felt

122

a droplet of moisture hit my earlobe and drop into the channel to tickle me more than anything ever before!

Ultimately, I had to let go, for the irritation of such an emotional tear offered was too much. This set Phil off on his cackling as I hastened to loosen a gloved hand and scratch the cause of the itching.

He wiped his eyes and nose.

I wiped my ear.

Nothing could wipe my smile.

Before we could embrace once more, a shattering noise rippled, and rumbled through the woodland, knocking all loose-hanging foliage to the ground, in addition to my father, who thankfully landed safely in a heap of unready and unsteady soldiers who were ready to catch him when he would have, eventually, leapt of his own volition.

'What in the world was that?' Jesse shouted, covering his ears as if expecting more disturbance to affect his overly sensitive hearing.

'I presume we will not have long to wait before we find out …' One of the soldiers answered, holding a hand to the hilt of her sword, pulling at it slightly to show she was ready, that we should also be!

None of this made any sense, especially to my mind. The whole premise of the place we had resided the past few days was that it was impenetrable by those not welcome. That was the entire premise of the place! To keep all said evil away from it! So how? How had the barrier been breached? I knew the cause was presumably Phil, but it hit me full-on in the face!

'Did you know, Phil?' I asked him angrily.

'Huh?' He shrugged, showing he had no idea what was happening here. The mighty army beneath me left asunder. Not a nick on anyone.

I turned to the next person closest to me in locale, and it turned, my heart, 'Did you know?'

My mother, unabashed by the question, only hooked hands on her hips and dropped a knee outward – almost catching my father in the nose as he still lay atop a couple of the soldiers he had displaced as he fell, them falling with him to the ground. 'What madness has you now, Getty?'

The question left me stumped. Left me questioning my own questioning. But I would not let it lie! *No, no!*

'Mama! Come now, for this be only another test or lesson for me, surely. And it seems you're all in on this one!' I swung an accusing finger around at all of them, all those I knew well and then those I knew not by name. Was it madness? Me throwing an accusing finger at all that I held dear. Probably ... but I was not to be outdone this time. I threw my madness at them all. Conjured up then served, in some kind: from the consistent offering of every lesson received, to be unleashed in an uncharacteristic rage at them all.

*

A thick crack to the skull brought me back to. Followed by a swift verbal barrage of her own. Dragging me forward, pulled by the shoulder, to where the ripple emanated, she shouted at me. 'Get over yourself, young man. This be no lesson. Believe me! I wish it was only that. Now, look! Down there ...' my mother pointed down a deep, wide ravine, to something moving through the trees, almost invisible – if it were not for the swashing of high branches and its leaves – as it made its way up, toward us, out of the fast-flowing water carried by the narrow dyke.

'Oh. Really? Not just another game then ...?' My eyes ached as they traced the path of the yet-to-be-revealed *thing*. Ached until it screeched once more, revealing exactly where its current location was. 'Oh ...' I said again.

The soldiers had already begun to make their way away from us, embarking on meeting the potential new foe in regimental style – forming three neat lines as they trudged over the now still and silent bodies of the initial onslaught.

We followed.

We knew not the size of the thing we would eventually encounter or if it was alone as it made its way toward us. Nor also of what may follow if this one failed to command its way into the other realm – that still bugged me. If, or even how, they could cross such a magical divide. Again, I looked to Phil.

Another wail was accompanied by the same brisk gust of wind that soared by us through the trees, brushing more foliage down into the space we tracked. Jesse looked over to me with a slight glint of fear held in his eyes. Phil carried the same. My mother and father, I could not tell, for they stepped further ahead and closed theirs as they turned from the gust, only to turn back forward, continuing on stoically once the draft had passed.

To say I was impressed by their conviction would be an understatement. I was absolutely enamoured with love, respect, and devotion. So much so, I clutched the small sack slung over my shoulder, wondering if I should soon read the text. If even the chance arose – post whatever trauma was to follow shortly.

Steeled by their determination, I pushed on ahead of them. Jesse and Phil carried in my wake: that wake would eventually carry the whole two legions headfirst into the path of the thing trudging its way, swiftly now, up the slope.

Turned out, it was not just *one* thing making its way toward us, but a trio of sharp beaks and equally menacing wings beginning to open up.

Orcindal! The very same creature that was bested by Gurengal upon Inarrel was my immediate thought of identification. But I had no further time to confirm such an assumption as they miraged their bodies away to once again be as one with their surrounding environment.

Though I had eventually led the charge, it seemed those behind me had been more prepared and much more game, for at least six empty metal drums appeared from nowhere, swiftly filled with arrows – which also came from somewhere and seemingly everywhere – with some fabric wrapped tight, abundantly around each tip.

It became abundantly clear what the wrapping was for. For each would lose their pale complexion, replaced with a dripping slime, one a shade of sin: dark and violent, the latter confirmed as each arrow held cocked was ignited by a source I knew not from where, other than a crackling sound before they were let loose simultaneously, as some unheard marshal's order had been given.

A minimum of twenty arrows shot forth toward the beasts. All found their mark with utmost precision, giving all assembled a good enough outline of a target. Though I was shocked, the three in front of us gave no grief of pain from the arrows shot forth – be it how tiny they were, I would have thought some cry would have sufficed. But then I looked back at those unfortunate souls lying beneath our footprints and how their whimsical jabs had only irritated us.

Poor – but irritable – bastards …

A crash of bodies was thrown full-on into the swinging sinew, and a new battle ensued as the three creatures eventually gave up their guise, turning to guile as their direct affront.

Not Orcindal at all! They appeared fiercer, much bulkier around every muscle, and held a heavier menace, less docility, in their eyes.

My arse began to twitch … just a little. Just enough of a parting to let out a little warm air. I clenched as I felt a rush of fur brush past me, *Phil!*

'Phil!' I shouted. If he had heard me, he didn't let it show as he raced headlong into the mad fray with a wrath of slashing to do some damage of his own as he outstretched both arms and roared with a rageful cry. His own natural weapons appeared simultaneously, ready to tear all asunder!

At least, this time, my mother and father realised that they were out of their depth, and so they went to aid the few healers within our troupe, helping the wounded as they dropped back from the front line – if they were able.

Soon they were overwhelmed with requests: more cries for help.

Not only I saw this evolving, but so too did Jesse, so he gave up his useless taunting toward the three beasts.

It seemed, lucky for Jesse, I assumed, that they were immune to a curse or two hurled at them, and the accompanying small rocks seemed along the same line, though I'm sure there was more to the madness on show from him.

'Getty,' he spoke, close to my ear so that I could not mishear. 'Now ... now is the time to release those shackles.' He looked deep into my eyes, each one in turn, and looked back at the chaos erupting behind him. Pointing to the *big* one, the one in the middle.

I held no weapon; I was barely holding in my guts. *How would Peron fare* – far worse, I knew, but that helped none. I shook my head at him to ensure he would not mistake my words.

'Are you *fucking* mad!' I already knew the answer, so I went on. 'No, I'll rephrase that, you're already so far past that ... Shit am I to do?!'

'Laddy, you do not need to strike at it, or they, not at least with a blade. Go there and deflect what it is striking with, and protect what it is striking at! Quickly, go ... go on!' He swung me around and pushed me forward with more than just a little shove.

'Be careful, Getty,' the soft voice of my mother penetrated through all the noise. I thought she at least would have been the first to stop this crazed man from sending me to – once more – a deathly peril.

It gave me no reassurance. More so when my father agreed with her somewhat. 'Just don't die on us. Will you, son?'

I turned and offered appreciation for their comforting words with a flat smile and a slow twist of my head, giving them all they needed.

When I turned back, the scene unfolding in front of me was

only full of maniacs, attacking without thought, thrusting away at the *just* as maniacal beasts' avaricious maws. The same collecting what their even hungrier, mighty wings or claws swept up. I let the comedy of it all calm the lunacy on show, let it dance around inside my head.

What I was about to do, or what I was about to *try* to do, would eventually counterbalance them each – their chaos and that chaos swirling inside, and outside far from my mind. It was like the weight of each party had been shuffled instantly to the middle of the scale, and I was walking along its centre, trying not to disturb one way or the other. As one … the twists, the fades, the slashing, they all slowed before my eyes. Not entirely, but slightly slower than what it was.

I concentrated now to further calm myself, thus that crashing in front of me.

Slower still.

Slower, I told myself.

To my dismay, when I took a moment to survey the entire field before me, the whole area to the front, then the back of me – for there was not much happening either side of me, other than a few soldiers that limped or were dragging themselves away from the carnage.

All now was *almost* still.

Now … this was comedy, indeed! To see such mammoth heads, splattered with teeth the size of my forearm and much sharper than Jesse's wit, in the midst of their chomp after a rageful roar took all the bite out of their ferociousness. It was akin to the bayer cub nipping away at a large piece of rope as its master supped away on some exotic herbal tea, holding the leash sat beside it.

I made a move.

Racing to the nearest defender, the next in line to take a swipe from the massive creatures' wings – for I held no hope for those already on their way south, inside any of the crashing maws of the three beasts.

I adjusted the soldier's immaculate-faced halberd into such an angle that would not only deflect the limb closing in on her but also cause unsurmountable pain as the slash would dig into the closest tendons. Its own momentum would do the rest to hopefully slice all the way through.

I did this for another two soldiers who had, unbeknown to them, found themselves in the same predicament. I also managed to carry back to some haven, four more soldiers to add to the pile tending to render aid.

It seemed my good deeds had not gone unnoticed either, not by the middle beast, the one that Jesse had pointed to – the largest of the three. For what must have been an instant for its eyes to process, I had been about my business for at least a few minutes. My legs quaked as it spoke, directly to and at me, the only thing other than myself that moved with any actual notice. The grinding, croaking gristle, deep. Also, the words clear, despite the echo of something within its throat.

'So … it's you I was sent here to sniff, then snuff out.' Its head moved as before, in time with mine. The poor soul spat from its mouth was suddenly caught in a semi-frozen state and hung languidly in the air.

The unlucky bastard had no chance, that much I knew; a drop from that height would shatter the smallest bone, nay mind the skull, which was to fall independent of its once host. *No hope for her!*

'You—'

'What? You piece of shit?'

'—you! Are what *they* seek …' it laughed, a smoky laugh, raised its chin skyward to accentuate its laughter and watched on as it chuckled away.

Fuck this! I grabbed the sword of the closest defender and then that of the next nearest and ran with seemingly unlimited speed to strike at the *thing*. It must have expected a mortal strike to its heart as it dropped its head to block and try to swat me away with its thorned chin.

But, I had been savvy. I knew how to deal with this type of foe – often – through the experience of being read the scrolls, and then, thus, the resulting dreams. A quick slash to the upper tendon, the large one connecting winged limb to chest, was met with a crashing sound as the other swooped in to swipe at me. Again, I was already moving, a high jump over the sweeping claw.

Slash. Downward this time, to connect a blade with the wrist of the webbed claw as it slashed underneath me.

A clean cut. Off it fell to the ground.

All around then played out to a mistuned chorus of utter madness. The larger of the three now limp, webbed arms wobbled all over, spewing a green pus from each fresh wound.

The almost stillness in the surroundings slowly dissipating into lightning-fast speed. Clanging and screeching returned abundant in the air. The larger of the three began to turn, knowing its time was almost nigh. It tried to flap its wings, but only one was able to unfurl – spraying ooze as it was raised in the air – the other was rendered to flopping. Off balance, the beast fell into the other, one to its left.

A hissing came from the other side as the third beast was sprayed with sizzling pus that covered its entire face, forcing it to cringe with a howl and close its eyes as the others fell beside it.

A swarm of soldiers used the temporary calm of slashing and dashing at them to quickly offer their own. Swiftly the three creatures were done. A hundred pokes would usually do you in, but the hundred or so stabbing away didn't seem to think that one thrust was enough.

All ignorant of the slightest drop of slushing of ooze that might burn them as they withdrew their weapon – be it spear, sword, or double-sided axe – they just wanted the job done. And I held no doubt they'd be alright once they left this place and returned to the sanctuary behind their *almost* impenetrable walls.

Either that, or they would have a few battle scars to show off as decoration from a rare sortie.

A snickering last remark was all that remained intelligible amongst the slurring last breaths of the trio. 'You will eventually be stopped … she, the Dark Lady, will not rest until you're gone …'

That was it. That was all for the day's play. So, it confirmed to me – not that I was unsure – *she* was prevalent in a multitude of realms and timelines, just as he who would rarely visit my pre-dream to talk shit to me just before the ever so vivid dreams would commence. I was sure many more would come before I was done.

I was not wrong.

For how could I be here, in texted script, and these memories of my time between this and that, there and where? And, where too next would I be found?

That! Is a question … for *where* is only part of the equation. Was I part of the cycle that resembled the readings taught to me of Inarrel? Would this etching become so distorted over time that the changes would not be inscribed by my hand? But of some other's swaying, brilliant mind.

There goes me, harping on, sounding akin to so many of my tutors and predecessors.

Who am I to question if this is indeed my own.

So, I let it go.

One: for how long now, I assume I would and couldn't have known.

Two: I love stories with a malleable ending, even if mine could be ever so.

Down Time, Downtown

We said our goodbyes to all the people who dwelled or were visiting within the walls, we had made our short, if eventful, stop before we continued on to the next bastion. It was much easier knowing that nothing would come and cause us the slightest bit of harm on our travel away. Until, at least, we would see any other sign of life; be it fauna or flora.

Jesse had advised us that our next stop *had* to be where we made our own way, just me and him. No Phil, no Mama, no Papa. Just us two, I assumed.

To be honest, there was a slight relief released when hearing that. Not so much for my family, for I would miss them dearly and not know when I would ever see them again … if ever. But my friend Phil, I would miss him immensely. And, he had his own course to follow, one that led to its own outcome for very different reasons. Though I was sure they all led to the same point. In their own right, even if I knew not of when.

It was a long while after we left the walls of the Haze of Sorrow that we found our ears ringing, alive with the chirping of birdsong and clacking of insects, hoping to perturb those singing from an easy meal for as long as they could.

The transition was transient, not as the time we left to battle with the little people and their beasts, but much like the way we had strayed into that void of *another realm*. Trees did not just appear, nor did the sounds; it was a gradual change, a cascading volume of all the new sounds, and also the growth we found ourselves rolling through.

Our cart's forever faithful and obedient draggers, the leading pair of our ambling charge did not blink an eyelid at Jesse or me since we left. I was unsure if the sounds of nature would bring roundabout their vocal snorts or, at least, their stubbornness. For now, they led themselves and their eyes forward. I shook a rein to remind them we were still there, and this only hastened the rumble onward.

So too, did that of my parent's supplied cartage. Those paid as retribution for the instant demise of their previous muscled pullers. That, and the small, weighty chest gifted as an offering for their despair from such an unfortunate occurrence in the middle of nowhere, in the middle of the night, before that ultimate pending thought of, *am I next!*

'What's in it?' asked Phil as he looked over to my father with a sidelong glance. He held the reins of his own gifted horse ever so softly, for he, too, had let loose a few stabbing jabs of his own as he reigned down upon the trio of beasts the days earlier. A rush of adrenalin, just as the soldiers, taking place of any inflicted pain. A few of his fingers still held bald patches from where the fur had been singed away, though he held them forward even though the mightily cold wind blustered as we crossed from *that* realm to the real – or what I assumed it to be, cutting at any exposed flesh to become near frozen.

'Nay you mind, young'un,' my father replied, with an even longer side glance of his own.

Phil pouted his lips and dropped back a few paces. 'Say, Gretta ... your man up front there can be ever so cumbersome, say ... what you get in that there box?'

'As *he* said, Phil ... never you mind, young man.' I watched as he shook his head to stifle a laugh and rattled a hand to shift his mount quicker forward to meet me – the driver of the lead cart.

'Hey, Getty—'

'—yes, Phil,' I smiled a little at him before he could speak.

'Your folks be just like you … did you know that!' He shook his head like a dog would shake off more than a few crawlers.

'Aye, that they are.' I left it at that, which irked him a little more. And he went to the only one not of my own kin.

'Hey! Hey, Jesse!' Jesse reared a weary head up from within the cart and peered sheepishly over its side rail.

'Phil! What?' he asked, woken from a slumber he had well deserved after the previous night's celebration. One I was not allowed to partake until we reached our mark: the large-ish town of Dibrathella.

'Oh …! Not you too!' And then he was gone, leaving us with only a trail of dust to follow. I assumed he knew where he was going.

My presumption was found well past unfounded as we caught up to him. He stood off his mount at yet another crossroad, both ways leading up a large hill, though with wide disparity.

'Phil …' I nodded.

'Getty …' he nodded back to me. 'Thought I would wait here for you all.'

'I'm sure you—'

'—yes, good that you did, Phil!' Jesse answered, interrupting my mother, 'I assume you have trialled each trail?'

Phil shook his head. I could tell he would have been

136

concerned to choose a path and then to follow, for he could well have lost us for a while and may not make up the lost time. He knew we had little time together, so he didn't want to waste any *potential* time on the grog or whatever else the town had to offer when we arrived at Dibrathella.

I must admit, I had my own curious thoughts about what may have been contained within that locked, ebony-encased chest. It was no bigger than my forearm, but the cost alone for the thing must have been up there with that offered in a King's ransom.

Was there some monetary donation contained within? Or something worth more than that and the chest combined?

Like what?

I'd never find out, all be told ... I didn't care *too* much either. For whatever it was, or could be, they never offered me an inkling as to the contents, which I can only assume was something they deserved and would put to good use once they were returned home – even if they would even travel back that way.

The prize that *I* received, the one I held tied to a rope slung around my waist in a tight, enclosed leather sack, was enough to recompense the singed hair spattered about Phil's hands and my time away from a reality I would've liked to enjoy, just for once, without the knowledge and foreign volition of being the so-called savoured saviour.

I had no idea what all this was for. What would all end up being? There was seemingly so much at stake, rested on such small shoulders. That all made me sick, as I knew many before had failed – to the best of my assumption. I doubt Jesse even knew, and he seemed to know more than all.

Jesse smiled as he pointed back toward the way we had come. It turned out a few hundred paces back. There was another fork. One overgrown – purposely, that much I could garner, as none of the obstructions were attached to anything other than those unattached to anything that eventually held solid to the ground. This one led down a trail, unlike the other two that led up. *I wonder where those two led to?* I'd never discover ...

I hoped, optimistically, Phil had scoured the terrain beyond each route to offer something beyond the benign. Surely he could not have missed such a planted route through the wasteland that was not dense enough to even call woodland.

But there it was, a trail wider than we had traversed. And much more forgiving for those that would feel the full brunt of any slight slump or bump in the surface. The road we now found ourselves on was immaculate.

A road that, if followed through to our intended destination, would see the smoothest of rides for those sat high in the driver's seat or resting up on the soft, padded benches crafted within the cart. Crafted anew, bettered, by those who did that kind of work back in the Haze of Sorrow, perfect craftsmanship.

That last made me laugh a little, for the stitchers were not of only men – if barely, but a fabulous team of all sorts – mostly elderly women and the majority of the rest, apprentice stitchers in the making.

We trundled smoothly down that winding road for a while before it levelled out as it took an almost straight path toward the centre of a widespread but not too towering skyline of a place. We didn't trundle long from there on before we were met with the initial town's en-guard.

The sorry-looking brigade of men and women, way past their middle years, set me to ease.

If slightly.

They were, undoubtedly, in cahoots with those cooped up behind those walls not too far from where we had ridden. Though I expected at least a more considerable resistance. *I suppose if we made it this far, there was not much else to do if, indeed, we were hostile!*

'Greetings, travellers!' shouted the only one mounted, sat at the front of the small brigade. He held up a hand, 'Hold on for the moment,' he looked behind to one of the men on foot, the man lounging on a planted spear, and twitched his head toward us.

'Ah, yes, right up!' Leaving the spear in the ground, the guard approached us and asked each for our name before writing them in a small ledger he pulled from around the back of his waist, wedged behind his belt.

I didn't honestly believe he was writing a thing down. For one, he held the scriber upside down. And two, I had never seen a scribe write so fast before he asked the next their name.

We all gave him an alias, of course. The mounted man seemed to know this as he shook his head. 'Now that pleasantries have been exchan—'

'—hang on a moment, there,' Jesse spoke, 'who of the elder blood are you lot?'

The man who had asked our name returned to lean on the spear again. The mounted man was about to speak but was thwarted by another, softer voice.

'We are here to welcome you to our town. Forgive us, we

139

don't get many coming this way, and I thought to give some of the men a little bit of a taster on how to approach those such as yourselves. A purpose of training and education only. Apologies, welcome once again, Jesse.' The woman dropped the hood down to droop against a roughly sewn, brown cloak.

'Pleasure's all mine, once more, Malinga.' They closed in on each other and embraced like a long-lost sibling – now found. An embrace held for a long time before he introduced us all. Upon mention of my name, there was a quick glance that held more than a little shock.

'Come! Come with me quickly, family of the saviour.' My mother and father were herded to the front, herded on by the mounted man. The woman, Malinga, leapt up into the back of the cart as it passed her by, and another embrace was offered, taken by my mama.

I was left with the rest of the contingent, who shrugged their shoulders and pointed toward my parents' cart with a spear as if to follow. So, we did. None seemed to blink at Phil. They just took him as he was, with no sceptical persecution. Which was a joy to witness once more. It made me feel more than a little guilty for how I had initially assumed his nature, but then that guilt subsided as I thought again of our first meeting; and upon our first contact: the fiery extension of a warm and gentle hand.

The vista before us was split in two.

The lower half, a wall adorned with many openings, all of equal proportion. Though intended for defenders to cast smiths' wares through, they each now held only a soft glow that flickered to give the appearance all innards of the large bastion were ablaze. That's what came to my mind: a sizeable walled stronghold. But where and why was it stuck here? Was there *more* beyond this place? I couldn't wait to see what. But that was for another time.

For now, I was beset on heading inside this place, as there were echoes of laughter and the thrum of some beating drum ... no, a multitude of drums, almost all beating as one.

The upper half of what presented itself before us was a darkening sky. Nightfall was fast approaching, and so too were the menacing, low-hanging clouds that drifted over our heads toward the town. Festivities of flame and music rang as a blessing to my weary ears. The flame now casting light beneath those dark clouds; they let loose not a thing to dampen anyone's spirits ...

Yet.

I was eager to cast an eye through the main gate when we could see what was occurring inside. *Whoa!* That was my only reaction. And I was sure the same response wasn't shared by my mother. Directly in the centre of the main road through the town, a large platform had been erected – and there lay the source and cause of my own, if all but one of my travel companions, blushing.

'Cover your eyes, Getty!' My mama shouted over to me. 'And you too!' she grumbled, pointing at my father.

Through all of the sloshing of grog that arced over onto the platform or the waving of arms that tried to capture the swaying beauties as they made their way up and then back down the elevated carriageway, all was lost in my mind as I fixated on her. She was hanging, more dangling, from a bar high above all else in the street, holding it tight with the back of her knee while the other kicked and flicked in time with the thrum. Though I knew her to be not naked, I wondered profusely how she could fit into such a tight-fitted garment that accentuated *every* crease, *every* mound, and *everything* else that would make one tick that way.

My heart jumped, almost fell out of my mouth, only to be caught in my throat as she dropped from the bar and caught herself in a ribbon that joined the two, swiftly transitioning to a slow rotation all the way down to the platform where she would join the train of sultry swaying – as a water droplet would join its destined crystal-clear trickle down some magical crystalline ravine – heading in my direction as I drove the cart through the wide gate. Quickly, my hand was rushing through the loping mess atop my head, trying to fix straight the months of growth. All in vain as she turned to march back the way she came, not even casting a curious glance at the newcomers to her town.

As she disappeared, hidden by the swaying of all who held carriage of such a spectacle, the rest appeared fully, as did their revealing outfits, men and women flaunting themselves provocatively at the baying crowd – a mix, equally split. Each provocation met with that forever unendearing slap of rejection as they made their way on to the next punter in the crowd.

I had no idea what was happening here; was it a dream? It all seemed a bit much to be real.

But, hey! What was real during those days …!

And I couldn't wait to get in line for my first rejection. I cast a glance away, no matter how hard it was to, to the town itself: its side streets and what may lie down where they led, then up and down each side of the main road to be greeted with a multitude of signboards hanging from gilded hangings bearing

142

all manner of creature, which spoke to me of each as a potential tavern!

I was not wrong …

Abruptly, all was to be lost after the dark clouds were rent of their contents and decided to dump the lot on the entire street, extinguishing all flame – be it for light or show. All spirit had been dampened, too, as all rushed to congregate under awnings deftly offered by each that held an animal of some, all kind high above their glowing entrance. Their doors barged open as the eager landlord proffered them to move inside swiftly.

I would end up in one of them … eventually.

Not that night.

We would make our way through the main street, past the goggling throng of punters who took refuge underneath large flapping awnings while we were drenched, and then on, up the same street as it took a wide right turn. The turn followed the terrain on a mild incline toward a grand, gated complex stuffed full of greenery and a few turreted buildings that popped above.

Surrounding the wide street we trundled along was more of a residential offering, with only a few small taverns poked between the tightly packed houses and small retail or commercial tenancies. And, instead of the lurid platform running up its guts, a finely manicured, raised garden bed split our two carts as we moved closer to the gate.

My mother was a little more impressed with this street. This was more to her taste. I watched her reach over the cart's upper rail to brush the now moist, blooming flowers. Malinga watched on, too, smiling at my mother as she caressed each that hadn't been trimmed back while my father was trying his best to keep the cart's wheels close to the marbled upstand wall that lined each side of the last stretch of the road leading to large gates – giving her close proximity to brush with her fingers – each he tried to avoid, ducking and weaving out of the way, except for the ones the horses took a nibble on, flicking what was left into his face, unable to move out of the way of the slash quick enough.

Where did they all go? was a thought that rattled inside my head – and no doubt a couple of the others as they looked about auspiciously for any sign of those lining the streets moments ago in awe.

'Nay mind, Phil,' Jesse poked. 'We're sure to bump into them sometime over the coming days before we all go our separate way.'

Phil looked downcast for but a moment. 'Aye, you be true,' licking his lips, then his little teeth, he went on, 'could use a good brushing and a good cuddle at that.' They both laughed, Jesse slapping the big, furry beast on the back before pulling him close, shoulder to shoulder, as they both sat on the back of the cart.

Jesse whistled a little tune; one I had never heard. I liked the sound of it. It cast a happy melody into my ears. Though, a hideous attempt by Phil to sing along caused all but he to laugh.

'Ah, Phil. Can you never do that again?' Phil pursed his lips together and flapped his lips as he pushed the air from his lungs through.

When he finished his composition – reminiscent of an ass's arse letting loose – Jesse began whistling again: the same tune, only louder.

'Oh … *why do we sway, whilst our boys and other loves are so far away* …' the sweetest singing voices came from the cart ahead.

'… *And, oh, why do we women have to stay here for another day* …' my mother joined in with Malinga. The words were now more pertinent than ever to her.

Jesse stopped the whistling to join them lyrically. All three sang in tune while my father hummed the chorus. Thankfully, he didn't attempt to participate with song, for he would indeed have made the big fur ball sound as talented as Velosko – the blind tenor from my dreams upon Inarrel.

The song continued until Malinga hopped off the cart as we stopped at the large iron gate. She approached the three men who stood behind, spread equal distance apart, and passed through the rails a small parchment to the one in the middle, the only one of the three with no helm, only a tight wrap of cloth pulled over his head. He read it. Not once, thrice, before he passed it back to Malinga.

He then went over to the man on his right and whispered something. Again, not once, but three times to avoid any miscommunication.

The tallest nodded back, then trotted the whole way up the grand driveway splattered with tiles of extravagant mosaics. Then the message bearer walked a short way back, turned to face us with hands resting behind his back, and signalled to the remaining guard to open the gate.

Once the gate was opened, the man standing facing us shouted a grandioso welcome to everyone, introducing himself as Ghareem. Welcoming us to the humble abode of the Regional Marshal of Dibrathella. I looked about and saw nothing modest about the place except the shoes the soldier who opened the gate for us wore. *There'd be no running in them! That's a given!*

Up ahead, far behind the man belting out all kinds of things related to the town and all its glory, a plump man waddled towards us. Flanked on either side by two others, taller and seemingly much nimbler, carrying a seductive sway rather than the off-putting wobble of overindulgence — a swaying that was so … so becoming, much as when we made our way up through the guts of Dibrathella.

I decided immediately that I would enjoy the few days I would have here.

'Greetings! Greetings, my good people,' the plump man offered whilst struggling to bow his head lower than his breast, so he slipped a knee behind the other to drop a pompous curtsy, if slightly. The two women did likewise, much more graciously and far more profoundly. 'I do *believe* that we have a most special guest with us … and you too, Jesse!' he laughed and slapped a knee, chops flopping as he sucked on his tongue whilst chuckling away.

Jesse mimicked the plump man. The two women on either side of him giggled, drawing, in turn, a stern look from Jesse's target. In the end, all was in jest as Jesse hugged the man. 'And greetings to you too, old General of nothing but a shitty wasteland! How've you been, Maghari?'

'Oh, you know … busy.' Jesse looked over his shoulder, causing the man's plump round cheeks to flood a crimson tide. 'Not much else to do here, you see …'

'… That I do. That I do …'

'So … this is he?'

'In the flesh!'

146

'Its name?'

'Begging for your pardon, you rude man!' My mother pushed forward before accosting him some more. 'And what kind of seedy place do you be running here? Hey?' She stood, hands firm into hips. She would surely knee him in the chin if he dared to bow again. And to be fair, I wouldn't have blamed her.

Its name! Seriously?

This place seemed to be positioned here for a reason not many of its populace would know why. It was too far from the region's capital to form any defence from the sporadic nomads or the elusive territorial outlanders. There was nothing between here and the Capital, Hotsper, other than a few other minor towns. Jesse had told me that most of the riches flowing west from the Capital came here. And it seemed they were being put to good use!

He also told me this place was one of a number of the same, scattered around the perimeter of that void and the battlement we had visited; to act as a bog and slow down any attack that may be forthcoming. *Like that worked on the opposite side, where we battled those beasts and those pesty little shites!*

It seemed that this place was in for a full-on rollicking once those who made the call to set these proxy defence towns up, found how much of their funds had been squandered. With little else than a wall defended by only a few, that few too who partook in such debauchery.

Not that I cared, not a mite. Though I thought I would if I were on the other end of that proverbial stick, holding that sack of coin over the town, seeing it drain away down the many grated sewer inlets placed in front of each tavern – and there were more than a few here! *Surely there would be some audit of their spending.* Or maybe not; it all depended on who provided the funds to these satellite towns. I doubted the occupants, be they resident or holding some office in the major Capital corresponding, would venture too much, too far, behind their own walls of safety, if elegant comfort.

Walls! What was it with walls! They were only useful or solid if someone tended them – if at all.

But who was I to judge? For all I could think of was what the town could bring to soothe my own itching. An itching felt all about me, one that could not be scratched as a remedy. I was now sure what could satisfy such an itch, and it wasn't the ale alone.

I caught my eye drifting past the wide man – for all his girth, it was not a hard thing to do – to look at the two standing on either side behind him.

My mama turned and walked away, with some pace, far from the sultry look of those that thought the Marshal some sultan ruling over some exotic foreign land. Where, in truth, she knew, he was just a slobber of a mess. And! When whoever decided to check on *this* place – for I had no inkling of what life was like elsewhere – there would be a reckoning, and at least one head was guaranteed to metaphorically roll from rotund stem! If not all those that cascaded away from those towns closest to the precious bubble, set up for any future defence to offset any attack beyond this plane.

After our introduction was made and countered with aplomb – once more – we were led toward the right as we approached the main building of the precinct. A wide, covered awning above us kept the darkness of the night away. The sound of hoof hitting marble far from detracted my opinion of this place, nor the man ambling with some difficulty in front of us down along the same road that led toward a small, detached residence, no doubt our temporary accommodation!

My sureness wasn't well rewarded as we ventured through, underneath the large canopy, to be led into one of the most exquisitely laid out courtyard I'd ever laid eyes on. A residence fit for royalty.

We were motioned to dismount our ride and follow the two women that had swaggered as we followed.

One of the pair led my mama and papa to their guesthouse. The other led the rest: the rest being the ethereal fur ball, the Jester and young me, to our own place. Malinga followed the latter, or more led us, to our individual dorm and explained, more told, we were to remain there until the morning. Until we were sought, *summoned.*

'Refreshments will be brought to you,' she added. 'Clean linen and towels have also been provided. Trust me, they are crafted with the most exotic material, nurtured and only found to the east of this place. You should be more than rested by the time you wake in the morning.' *No doubting your words there!*

My stomach grumbled, not with the thought of offered refreshment – for I was sure they would be absolutely delicious, if bountiful. No, a thought that had been spinning around in my head since my eyes graced upon this town, one to venture out, to mix with the masses hoarding inside the nearest tavern from where they were drenched.

A thought now dashed. Tired as my weary eyes were, I could

surely revel for at least a short while.

From the way we came, two youngsters approached, a boy and girl, there to take our rides to where they would be stabled, preened, and then groomed as if they were the finest racehorses in all the lands.

Phil yawned. Jesse too. I also reached a fist to my mouth to stifle my own.

Malinga waved away the women that had led us there, pulled a small key tied to a piece of string out of her pocket, and opened the two doors we had been presented.

'Jesse, you're in here. The very same dorm as last time. How long ago was it? Since you were last this way? With anoth—'

Jesse jumped in as she glanced at me. 'Say, Malinga, it be at least five summers? Six? Maybe …'

'That long, hey …' I was sure I saw something else in her eye, the way she drew them around all of Jesse's face as if to take in every tiny detail.

'Much happened here since?'

'No, not really. Not much to do … It's good that we do get a few visitors now and then. You'll be the second crew to make your way through in the past seven days. A large crew, too, the others were. We don't usually get a new group, or traveller, in such quick succession.'

Jesse raised an eyebrow. 'Really? Where they headed?'

'East, to the Capital, Hotsper.'

'Really?' Jesse raised the other brow.

'Is that not what I said?' She raised one of her own.

Jesse rubbed the back of his head, then walked over to Malinga and hugged her gently. 'Good to see you again, Mal.' He opened the door and offered us all a good night of rest.

'That was weird,' Phil yawned again. 'Well. I'm stuffed. Can you hold those refreshments 'til morning?' My stomach grumbled again, *maybe I am a bit peckish*, for I was to bunk another time with Phil, and that meant I, too, would not receive anything to settle my grumbling.

'Of course, Phil.' I was immune now to the fact that everyone, since I was reunited with Phil, took him for normal. Even those in the crowd earlier who watched us trundle through the rain from their relative safety of standing under an awning.

He still freaked me out a little, though I supposed none of those others had ever been mangled, almost to death, by him: that would maybe sway their view just more to the offside.

Turning to me again, she asked. 'Something on your mind, Getty?'

'Oh! Nothing. Would I be able to take a little walk?'

'Of course. I will escort Getty around the grounds for a short while. Phil, off you go inside and get yourself settled.'

'Well, I hoped to be alone for a moment or maybe two. Not had a break from everyone for a while.'

'Of course, Getty.' She bowed to me deeply, giving her acknowledgement. 'Don't stray too far. And, if you're feeling peckish, I will have one of the girls find you with a tray or two.'

I nodded my acknowledgement. 'Oh, no bother … I'm sure to be fine.'

She turned immediately with her own offering of "Have a good night". My stomach turned too, more than likely upset with my politeness in declining a free snack or two, and from one of those two with the hips no less.

Phil helped me unload the cart, taking only what we required over the next few days. We knew the tarp to be soaked. Unbeknown was the small tear that had trickled water through onto my clothes sack. I still threw it into my room with haste anyway: I would deal with that the following day.

One thing I did take, something I had yet to get into, was my Book of Fate, or so I called it. I clutched it tight underneath my jacket to hide it from the diminishing drizzle that had followed from earlier downpour. The book I held was a personal thing. Though I was yet to read it, I wanted no other to see it before I had the chance. I didn't want anyone to read it following my own perusal. What was within? Finely crafted and scripted pages? I was nervous to find out.

'Hey, Phil. I won't be long, mate, but don't wait up. I will sneak in as not to disturb you. Alright?' The answer: a short snort and licking of lips as he rolled over, already away dreaming of what I would never know – I reckoned I'd be too frightened to know of what.

Malinga hadn't left us the key she used to open the door. There was only a snib on the inside that could lock the door, but I didn't trust it to operate as intended, thus locking me out, Quickly I pulled one of Phil's travel shondals – a pair of footwear, a cross between a sandal and a shoe – off and stuck it between the door and its frame, leaving it slightly ajar. *He shouldn't be sleeping in footwear anyhow! And certainly not those filthy things.*

The path I followed was made up of all sorts of shapes, all made from some fine marbled material – if indeed marble itself. It was a narrow track that led through some winding, immaculately curated growth on either side. I felt my hand beginning to rise, trying to feel the soft, dark-green foliage. But I held it back to avoid further saturation of the jacket I had slipped on before departing.

The path would eventually lead to a small courtyard with ample seating, created by the many upstand walls that held back some murky water and the flicker of orange darts that occasionally made their way across its surface. One portion of the wall that caught my eye was bone dry, sheltered from the rain by an overhang constructed of metal and stone, also draped with some fabric on either side.

Setting my way toward it, I spied a figure approaching the square from one of the other three entrances, carrying Malinga's offered tray. I knew such to be surveillance much more than tending to my digestive need.

I grumbled slightly to myself for the intrusion as I sat down in the offering of the petite nook, dropping my weary arse onto the surface with a cushioned fabric whilst I awaited the offering as the figure approached through the gloom.

To my dismay and that of my stomach, the tray bearer was none other than Malinga herself. And, what she proffered was not for the consumption kind; not an oral consumption in sense, but a hefty looking scroll that looked so atypical to this perfect place with its crisped, cracked edges and tattered skin. Something else to be consumed by the ever-expanding mind of mine. One that had exponentially grown from being splattered with such since I was *gifted* to my parents.

'I believe you to be the recipient of this *thing* ...'

The binding and seal were still intact, pristine, even after so long curled up – I assumed it was a long time from my observation of its condition.

I waited for the follow-on comment, some instruction, some direction on how and when to use the thing … All I received was a smile.

She handed it to me, then left with nothing more to say. The sinking feeling in my stomach would not weigh me down before I read the contents. My mind was racing as to who could have left such a thing for me. I hoped for the sender to be *her*. But how? As it must have been sent some time ago.

I still hoped …

For Getty's eyes alone. A scribe of elegant ink read along the side of the scroll, passing underneath a ribbon holding it furled.

I sat lower. Lowered myself to the backing of the nooked bench to rest my weary arse against such a delightful pose. I sighed. Holding both book and scroll in each hand. *So much for a casual walk.* I shook my head and eagerly picked the waxed bind to the scroll with my fingernails. *Suppose no time like the present.*

My eyes drifted over the text to scan the final few lines of the vellum. Only to find a disappointment once more …

Regards,

    Dagda.

It read as a spike through my heart. For the signature I was hoping to find had not struck to mark the parchment … not *Arigal's.*

Those feelings I left to the mist and returned my eyes to read from the top, knowing of its potential importance, written by the prescribed scriber.

Dear Getty,

There will come a time to pass when your whole world may shake. And that shaking may take more than just your held breath or the merest of beats from your most precious asset.

When that time comes, it will signify a shift, not only to your balance and the path you have taken, but a divergence for everyone who has, is, and ever will dwell around the stars for more than a moment.

Getty, I need you ready. We need your total commitment to what we see as true and righteous for the betterment of all after we eventually leave this or whatever place we call our own.

In this moment, you must remain steadfast and let your training take control of your senses. For in that moment, all of creation will depend on the actions you do or do not take; your reaction will be pivotal to determine a final demise or a new dawn – a future free of the filth that has plagued my life and that of many others for such a while.

It is not yet time for your fate to reveal itself. Though, when it does, please use this as inspiration rather than falling into despair and the wallowing of desperation you may feel. It is only fate, your fate, until you change it. That it may be, but that does not define you.

You! You are someone thought of that would look at fate and cinder it to forge into blocks as something we are to build from.

He was apparently running out of room to write as he was only halfway down the scroll, and the space between the lines became shorter, and the text began to dwindle in size to allow more words on each line. The man, or whatever he would or could be called, added words to the rest of the scroll.

Important as they were, they seemed hastily written, as if under some duress of time, not in such a way of volume, more the slight rambling in parts.

Entirely, I do trust you have not yet been able to read any text or symbol coherently within the tome you now undoubtedly hold tightly about your body whilst reading this, my rambling.

Would he have been mad at me if I didn't? Luckily I did hold such.

For even so, if you have, the pages would be left unintelligible until they become relevant. They will react to you, and you to them, thus untangling the script etched within — much like the scrolls your father read to you, if much more complex.

That is the point of such, the whole key to the resolution we seek. You must not! Must not reveal the contents of this message, one sent long ago, or any of the content contained within your other arm — if you do indeed hold such — to anyone. And that includes Arigal or any close to you. For the ways of those trying to break us are extreme, even with the lightest of touch, and they will not hesitate to consume all you hold dear to get to you.

So, my point is, my advice is also something to be considered herein and then on. The bearer of this message was, and is still, dear to me. She is one of the few who have turned away from what 'we' do so they can do what 'they' do to help the likes of yourself get through what needs to be done.

Now to the point ...!

You must forget every being you have met since we first met. That is key! You must go back to your reading of the scrolls. Once you do, you will understand.

Hopefully, you may even read of me, drafting this such missive, and to cease knowing all you know!

That is key also! For since the time we first met, the scrolls have taken a different path, one not of our liking. The burning of the scripture has never been observed in such intensity ... so we went back there, and it was all

156

wrong. Another force at play is swaying the balance; this and that way to the limit that each may withstand!

The reason to forget all you have met since that meeting, since we came to you and stopped that mad manic army of shadow is that they are already seeking you out. They will throw a myriad of creature! Armies! Devilishly seductive demons at you: those you must resist their words, their sway, their charm! They look to control, not us. No! They seek those of your world, those few that hold a spirituality, a connection with the natural essence of the world you reside. That, and so much more! More being, they seek to influence all such on every other world! Here, on Inarrel, that is of the four demigods — the creators! — on your world, it is the spirits that cause life, cause death ... cause so much to bloom, inadvertently sending love or pain of an emotion to where it needs to go. To fill the proverbial bucket of the Holy Unknown and offset all that darkness that is creeping up around more than just my peripheral.

In essence! You must relinquish any friendship, any acquaintance, any lover. Anyone who could be used to track your next whereabouts.

Lover, I laughed at that. Who would, or could even love someone like me, once a cripple, other than those he now called *friend*. There was that slightest spark in the village where we resided in a barn, but no more than so.

I read on, waiting for the punchline, or the gut punch, which seemed the most likely. But as I read on, my heart fluttered, my head swayed, and my crotch slightly tingled.

Go into the town, enjoy your last few nights of freedom! But be warned, you must not disclose to anyone who or what you may be! This is your last chance for a rodeo before you are thrust into the next level of ultimate commitment.

The next level of training, to be taught and mentored by he known as the Jester, and she known once as Arigal!

And ...! For if we are to ever meet once more! I will be shouting the rounds for us all!

Us all? Does he mean to send the same to all who come by, pass this way, then beyond even this plane? I cared not! I would enjoy the next few nights and the many beyond under the now confirmed tutelage of Arigal, Semona, or whatever her real name may be. *Who knew the truth anyway ... of anything?*

Please make swift demise of this scroll so no other may lay an eye upon what is written, thus taken, to soak within one's malleable mind.

For a better future, for us all and everyone else!

And I could just make out the scribble of hand to signify the writer's signature, which was out of key with the text above. A well-practised sign-off to signify it was not a first. *Hopefully not his last!*

Dagda Eren'Gaturi

As I rolled the ancient light-weight scroll tight, ready to rip it apart and throw it to those fish bobbing in the pond – in the hope the parch be edible once dissolved of its crisp state – around me and to finally dispose of as Dagda instructed, another piece of parch revealed itself; much more agile and lightweight than the scroll parchment. So thin it was almost transparent. I gently unfurled the scroll and placed it to my side, less gently

158

than I took the paper. At first glance, it seemed nothing more than a protective layer, just blank, maybe to protect the scroll from ageing. When I ran my finger across it, then felt the slightest grate upon my fingertip. I held it up to the artificial light coming from the stumped, low-burning candles around the courtyard, as there was none offered from the cloud-covered sky to confirm with one other of my primary senses.

A trickling of a symbol shone through the paper. Not so much that the thing was marked, more a sliver of silver revealing itself upon the surface, clear as a merchant tracked a trail through the winter snow. It was one I was always well accustomed to.

Almost, always ...

For I was well aware of the symbol. As per my vivid semblance of a dream, once again, the scorched mark upon King Benjamin Jacob Aurelia's wrist and the very same above the hip of his only daughter Grehn. And then the alignment to signify the holdings of that same prophecy!

Oh, how much could one's head hurt! Then I thought of those little bastards whose heads had recently been smashed by nothing more than a sharp tread of a boot.

Before I looked anymore, I ensured the scroll was well torn and thrown to float away forever: to never be recovered.

Something was off, though, with the iteration of this same symbol. I was sure that it was supposed to resemble what I knew and had observed many times in my dream – or whatever that could have been construed to be, resemble, or even be factual!

So, I was happy to see out my final few days in this town. For I could see no other town offering the same. This one, beneath all the pomp, grandeur, and flagrance for clothing, and disregard of one's innards, was indeed my kind of place.

Ultimately, who can say that I, Getty, was a pomp or bore? At least they, or someone at the very least, would see me as someone they'd like to know!

So, I thought nothing more of the symbol on that thin covering; I would deal with that later. For what could affect the next few days beyond the new beginning of only more shit for my mind and body to consume?

I held that thin parch as I made a decision. Folded it twice so it could slot inside my book, then focused a thought on the words left for me on the scattered pieces, now bobbed at upon the surface of the water that rippled in all manner of directions as the prey cascaded and thus multiplied opportunistically from the disturbance created by their brethren.

Hmmm, I thought Dagda had no time for me …? Maybe written long before he met me … the latter I doubted, for he knew where I'd be and what I'd be up to! He also referenced the onslaught he and Arigal gave the shadow demons – or whatever they'd be called. I held his visage again, the frosty look he always gave, a firm, plastered pose that frightened my mind and shook my knees! And those eyes … resemblance of a deep freeze, would still all, save my mother! For whom he happened a not-so-small soft spot; either that, or he had once tasted her pork and potato stew - a stew crusted with the most deliciously crumbled pastry, which made the dish ever so!

And … why? Why would he tell me to do the opposite of what I would have expected him to say or sway me from? Was he expecting me to be that cliché of a child and do the exact opposite? Just as that expectant way of all those spoilt brats I

160

had read of …? Not likely. Not him. That was not his way of things; he was always so direct, and that! was something I admired more within someone than those who would seek to direct my path with riddle and/or false rhythm of truths!

So, I guessed it to be a valid instruction. One I would relish and be glad to oblige. That was for the next day. Instead, I found myself searching through the winding hedges to where I could find the tasting plates. My hunger was now causing me to feel more than a little nauseous. The added weight I felt in my stomach helped a little, but that would subside once I was resting, and I hastened to think of my stomach being unsettled before our venture out into the town.

*

I woke up excitedly early. Long before the dawn could fully usurp itself through the crack Phil had left in the door. He, too, must have been eager to venture out, or his appetite had exceeded its limit for lack of substance.

Stretching out, relieving a few joints off each other, I wondered how the sensation made me feel. More than just a relief of the niggling ache, it set my mind back to when all my waking days were meddled in with the large bed back home. It had only been a couple years since I had really begun to see that. Maybe it was my mind holding back my body. Jesse had held true to his, *those* words, though initially they may have been more suited to a dockland tavern.

He had almost helped me fulfil my forever want … to one day look after my parents through their own trials and tribulations – be it age or some other foe. I had yet to repay that favour … fully, many a favour so offered without thought for any retribution on my part. Now it seemed my time was running low to offer such hearted promise. They would go one way: back home or venture on to wherever they so fancied – now that I was out of their care – and I would go my own way, taking all that memory with me, hoping I was allowed to retain such: for my own volition of compliance may well lead me back to where it all began, if they would even let me … *just as those that left the fold within the City of Columns! When they were cut from the tutelage, forever to never remember who or what they once were.* Would they throw the same penance my way, one to follow my own nose to nowhere in particular for the rest of my sorry, sorrowful days!

Phil barged back in through the wedged-open door, two hands full of fruit. A vast array of colours on show. Of all he carried, he had taken a bite of each, as if selecting the most edible for his over-particular palate, and no doubt tossing the rest that didn't make the cut away unceremoniously. Thrown so far, they could never roll their way back to him.

'You want some, Getty?'

Luckily, I had found that offered tray the night before and had devoured every last bite laid out upon the large stone platter. I was sure I would have been half tempted, even as I looked at every already bitten fruit.

'No, I'm not too hungry. Thanks, though, Phil,' I smiled at him, and he smiled back at me before he munched at a piece, almost taking the whole thing down – core and all. He would always do the same with anything he had, always offering me before he would send all to digest in his ironclad stomach. It was his thoughtful way, *would he ever catch on, or was that his way of humour?* I found it comical, at least, every time we engaged when he had food on board. I thought again of the fur balls that must be garnered by the swiftness, and non-heed, of what he was biting away at, tearing out the matted fur surrounding the two soft-padded oars one could call hands.

'Your loss,' he mumbled whilst munching. 'Say, I bumped into your father out there. He mentioned that your mama had been absconded to attend Malinga. Sure she will be pampered no end …' Phil looked absently at his nails, clogged with fruit, before he went on. 'Your father's spirits were heightened at that revelation. I'm sure, I'm sure so!'

A wink from Phil gave me the same thought, though I doubted it would eventually end up being the same notion. I was sure he would be happy for a day away under the guise of making my mama happy and actually being himself in front of me! And not … for the flavour the town offered the night previous! I have certainly been wrong before; would the man I loved the most prove me wrong once more …?

I truly hoped so.

The place we were now was so far from home that the duration of the night held was far beyond any time during our bleakest winter night, and it began to mess with my head a little. There was no annual Festival of the Night here, on my world, unlike that three-day-long night that occurred across Vilenzia and other parts of Inarrel. Still, I expected this was going to be the closest, in similarity, I would attend, and last night's stage show was surely a taste of what was to come, or I was advised by none other … than Jesse.

Jesse and my father were waiting inside the well-appointed foyer that led into the complex's main building. The stained windows were throwing a myriad of colours across the floor and walls as the sun finally crept its way up, still sitting tight to the horizon. The few scattered clouds that drifted across the sky would occasionally stifle the rays of light, rendering the room back to its original extravagance of opal flooring and intricate stone cladding that filled every piece of available wall.

It truly was over-the-top indulgence. The funds provided by the Capital indeed were being spent with the best interests of Meritol in mind.

Another burst of sunlight flittered the colours around once more. An ample pane covered Jesse's face, colouring it a bright purple and my father's a shade of pink. *No doubt a comical omen. One, once we have indulged enough today and certainly even more through the night.* I was apprehensive of the day ahead, more so for the sporting accompaniment that would cause me to be written off on the morrow. Phil saw it too and looked at me, his bottom teeth forming some kind of a hidden smile at the shared humour. Jesse shielded his eyes and, in doing so, saw us both smiling.

'You, both … really do need to grow up,' he turned, then sauntered through the large opening into another, more prominent, antechamber. A high domed ceiling took your eyes away from the floor, and four similar openings to the one we graced led in different directions. We followed, assuming he knew where he was going, or at least where we were supposed to go …

We milled about for more than a few moments, waiting for someone to arrive. Who was supposed to greet us? I was unsure.

So, we just inspected all the offerings of this room.

I was primarily enamoured by the intricacy of the paintings on the ceiling. They seemed so life-like, yet so warped, they made my head spin. I had to take my eyes back to the tranquil floor, only to be greeted with another quandary to my vision. The random mix of unmatched pavers set each eye to wander its own path.

The uncomfortableness my head felt soon broke as my eyes spied an actual target to focus on. The main man of this place was followed by Malinga and the two maids who flanked the two, just as they had the night before.

'Where is my mama, Malinga?'

'Oh, she will surely be enjoying an extended soaking within the deep, hot baths in this complex's North Wing.' She looked at the four of us, wearing our best clobber, shoes buffed to within a smidge of remaining leather. My jacket and trousers were still slightly damp from the weather, but I cared not. I thought I looked quite smart, and would fit the part as we ventured through the town's central district.

She looked at each of us again before going on. 'And, I'm sure you all will welcome the warm waters, fresh from the piped springs in the morning or whenever your empty heads arouse from wherever you'll end up!'

Lucky my mother was not there, for my blush bloomed a crimson tide at her quip, my father, too, blushed for more than my own share. The sound of a hot bath would have suited me just fine, for I had not yet washed deeply, other than the spattering of water contained within the ceiling space in a side area to our dorm. The time would come when I would bathe within the North Wing, just not when my mother is undoubtedly wallowing, wearing nothing more than her *complexion*. My body shuddered a little at the thought. Then we were off on our merry way. Jesse held back briefly, speaking with Malinga, who never took her eyes off me. Then he hurried, four, long bounces, and was with us. A clasped hand grabbed my and Phil's shoulders.

'Boys … boys, boys, boys! Are you in for a time. Believe me, when I say this town is a constant for revelry; the riches flowed through to here, supplied by someone far away, and seem to be used far from what they should be. But I reckon there is only so much you can do to prep for a doomsday – that final reckoning. I dare say they have some defence lined up, and I am glad I will not be the one to receive such a buff.

'A good wager to be had here; if you had the right equipment, hey, Getty …' He squeezed our shoulders tighter. My body shuddered, from an expectance, for the expectance, to finally … once, to be in tandem with that anticipation.

I felt good. My body tingled, and my mind was at a saunter. My soul … *burning!*

My father grumbled as he walked a few paces ahead. 'Jesse, you're a good man; don't you let me change that opinion of you …'

Phil and I laughed. Then began to tease my old man. To give him credit, his wit was as sharp as ever. Commenting on how Phil wore nothing more than a leather napkin around his crotch: *to hide what?* he had said.

How he had caught me, fully stiff, in my room on more than one occasion – me unable to hide the cause of embarrassment, as my constricting mind would not let my constricted body hide the protrusion, usually at his eye level when I was stood stark on my bed.

We carried the banter with us until Jesse called for a halt. We waited for a while outside a non-descript hole in the wall. I tried to ask what we were doing, but all I received in return was a shush, followed by a hand to his ear – advising me to shut up and listen.

I eventually did. The eeriness of the quiet settled itself in and all about me. There weren't many people, not the kind of people I had hoped for anyway. Just a few families were making their way, flittering between a few of the windows of stores on either side of the broad street, buying fresh, earthy, or freshly butchered produce.

A dinging sound caught my attention, something other than small chatter. The sound came from the other side of the door we stood near. The double door opened to reveal a man with a hammer in hand. For what, I was about to find out. He fully swung them open and knocked the bolts down into two holes made for such an operation. The small towel he held over his shoulder fell off as he swung the last knock.

Jesse bent down and placed it back from where it fell.

'Wahey! What are you doing, man?' Jesse was a wiry thing, lucky for him, as he instantly bent back, saving himself from losing a nose or worse, as the hammer swung around at him.

An instant later, the burly man's face twisted up with recognition. 'Well! If it ain't, the Jester!'

'Just Jesse now, Balagor,' Jesse held out a hand which was grasped tightly, if a touch roughly, then was pulled into a wide embrace, squeezing the air from the *Jester's* lungs. A pat on the back was the last of the greeting. 'Gentlemen, this here be the worst pourer of ale in all of the world!'

'Aye, that's why I employ the best.' Balagor turned and shouted back through the wide door. 'Polett! Polett …'

'What now! You old codger!' A screech accented the reply.

'Come 'ere! You'll never believe who be 'ere!' He turned back to us, waiting, and began to wipe down the hammer in his hand; I hesitated to think what was to be wiped off.

A young lady came to stand half in the door, a hand resting on the frame as she peered through. Quick as a drip, she was onto Jesse, all arms and legs wrapped around his gangly body. 'Jester! You came back! Oh, how I have missed your tall tales and witty skits! Please! Tell me you're here for longer than last time …'

'Now, Polett, steady on. We're only passing through; we have some important business to attend to.'

Her eyes dropped heavily as she slid herself off him and looked at us all. 'Oh, I see. But you promis—'

'Ah, ah, ah,' Jesse wiggled a finger had her, 'I promised to come back one day with even more tales of the world. And that is what I'm to do, though only over the next few days before we must depart.'

She was evidently still unimpressed, with how she crossed her arms and swung a heel around in the dirt. 'Ain't you going to introduce me to your … *friends?* She stopped squeezing her arms to her chest as she spread them wide to encompass the three unbeknown to her.

'Yes, yes … of course, my dear,' he nodded to her. 'Come, come closer.' She did. Her first port of call was to stand before

Phil. Phil stood awkwardly in front of her, not knowing how to greet her, so he just assumed hugging was the way from her earlier rendition of greeting.

She snuggled into him, enamoured by the warmth the soft silky coat gave. 'This be Phil, he is of the Neverman, though now cursed with saving this whole place once it all goes to shit!'

'Such a beautiful being ...' she squished herself in, closer, arms wrapped around as much as she could reach, eyes closed – so too her mouth, thus avoiding any straying clump of fur. Phil could only pat her head and back as he looked toward me for any assistance.

My smile offered was the least favourable answer, at least to him.

When she finally let go, she cast him a long gaze, a deep look into his eyes. It made him shuffle that little bit more in those ridiculous shondals he always wore.

She turned to me. Oh, did my heart miss a beat as her glacial orbs assessed what felt like my entire being!

'Is he another one?' she asked Jesse.

My heart sank at what she must think me of. *Another one ...* how many had Jesse sauntered through here with? All those *saviours ...*

The terror I was experiencing was calmed when Jesse gave her my name. 'And here we have Getty and his father.'

It was my papa who approached her first. I was still frozen, solid, lost in those glacial orbs.

'Excuse my poor boy there. He rarely gets out, especially that rarity does not extend beyond his, our own holdings. Even further beyond that rarity of what you truly are. He will be right soon enough.' She giggled as my father bowed and held out a hand for her to hold as his eyes ascended to meet hers.

'Oh, we get them, even here; though we're a distant and somewhat isolated town, some of the boys here avoid even eye contact, nay mind the speaking part. You will be fine, Getty. Just be yourself, and you will be fine.' Her smile forced my eyes away, and they all laughed, even her … *oh my life!*

Balagor eventually came to my rescue, ushering Polett back inside whilst saying something to her. 'See the men a table, somewhere t'other side from where those last few stragglers are still lying from last night's debacle.' He turned once she was inside and ushered us to follow him in.

We made our way inside the Blacksmith's Arms, to a well-furnished small opening, set underneath a bulkhead covered with all manner of items: from small round emblems to a multitude of knitted scarfs emblazoned with even more colourful, larger emblems, many the same as the circular carvings of timber. A couple of the emblems I knew of, or at least I thought. I wondered on while we were seated on the polished timber bench wrapped around a half-circle timber-topped table, inlaid with a tanned leather topping, leaving a gap filled with timber to rest our elbows as we waited for our first drop.

Delightfully, to everyone's surprise, Polett brought over a freshly baked loaf, accompanied by some liquified butter and a couple of other dips – some of the colours could surely not be found in nature. When we had finished that one, she brought over another and then another until we could stomach no more. *We* meant Phil, as I was done after the second helping, and so were my papa and Jesse. All this before we even had a chance to sup on anything other than the dripping butter that now plastered the tabletop … and our chins.

It was a huge relief when the drinks did start to arrive, though my stomach was well settled from the thick loaves.

'Trust me, gents, you will thank me later!' offered Polett with a smile. A not-so-subtle wink was thrown Phil's way. If a brush could blush, Phil's face would be the epitome of such an event. Not for the colour his fur-covered skin would undoubtedly be changing too, for his eyes now darted aimlessly, not knowing where to look. *Lucky her old man isn't here to see that little interaction, for his face would surely be soaking crimson by now … with a swift blow from the man's hammer,* now resting in a metal hoop attached to his thick belt.

Now it was my turn to smile. The embodied spirit of *the world spirits* would not be able to miss this smile.

Jesse had a little chuckle, then offered the explanation to the perplexed company that sat with me, including myself. 'Believe me, you will be thanking that girl for giving your stomach something to absorb the shit you lot will hopefully be drinking today. And, as a suggestion, one I think you should be taking quite seriously, you will do well to keep up the intake of grub throughout the day if you wish to, at least, have the tiniest amount of sense left to observe a night filled with much revelry.' He raised an eyebrow. 'Or … just don't write yourselves off. Okay?' He slinked backward, 'Just consume moderately …'

We all laughed at that, including Jesse. Though I thought he held a genuine laugh back as if he had to force it out. Something was bothering him, for him not to be in the mood, and from what I had seen this far, this place meant something to him as he looked back toward Polett with pride in his eyes, almost like a father would.

I knew there was nothing romantically kinetic between them other than that type of fatherly bond; she was too eager for his stories than anything else. Whereas she seemed already smitten by Phil – in what aspect I was unsure, cuddly, or amorously – and she also seemed intent on teasing me, in front of my papa no less, and her meathead of a father.

Though my palate was well tarnished by the butter, I was eager to taste what this small tavern had to offer; for if Jesse had a thing for this place, then my tongue would surely welcome the washing away of such a *delicious*, if slimy, coating my tongue held.

And that it did!

The full stomach allowed me to slowly enjoy every sip, every gulp until it was almost gone. At which point, the bread began to reappear. I was hesitant to take any more, but thinking about what Jesse had said before, and he being such an intelligent bloke, I took heed and nibbled away. But this time, using the ale as a substitute for added moisture to swill down the crumbs that left themselves trapped underneath my tongue and wedged in between my teeth.

Another round appeared, of a different complexion to the last, but even more so … delicious. I hesitated to think of the cost of the brew, and, for that, who was footing the bill!

Jesses saw me thinking on something; he always seemed to know, or thereabouts at least, of what. He shook his head at me.

'Drink, do not worry of your pittance stuck at the bottom of your coin sack; this is all on the house, or more … the town. Whatever we spend in the next few days will be covered by the treasury coffers controlled by Maghari as it always is, for all visitors, save a few ...'

'So why do they get so few visitors then? This place seems almost too good to be true,' I supped after I bit a little more of a new loaf.

'Almost, you say, well ... maybe you're right. Tell the truth...' He leant in close to me and whispered in my ear, out of range of the others so consumed with the fresh bread making its way through again impatient lips. 'You remember Malinga said there were others here not so long ago?' I nodded. I did remember. 'Well, it has me a little on edge. Who were they, why were they here? And where the fuck were they going!' he shouted the last, which caused both Phil and my father to pause mid-chew. He remained silent for a moment longer, looking over at the few remaining revellers from the previous night as if he could be after some information they held that he did not, no matter how loud they were still snoring.

He twitched nervously, fumbling to grab the glass before him, none of the contents yet consumed. Such a precious commodity for such a small holding. I was yet to check if it was even glass; for a town full of such frivolity, it could have been carved from a diamond, though I assumed such a luxury was even a stretch for this place.

As the pause continued, Phil and my father began to pull at the warm loaf again, keeping an eye on Jesse, expecting him to say more. The only sound was a large sigh from Jesse after he downed his ale.

A sigh of despair?

'Don't you think you're overreacting a little?' I took a swig, keeping an eye on him for any reaction. 'I mean, like … they could have been anyone?'

'My point exactly, Getty … could be no one! Could have been someone else. I must find out more about these people.' He pushed the glass away. 'Apologies, Getty, I must relieve myself of any more today. I must investigate and find out more about them to be sure. You enjoy yourself, all of you, for I feel our days of freedom will be short-lived from here on in. At least ours that may be …' He said the last as he looked at me. I felt like crawling into my glass and hiding; he was bringing the whole mood down somewhere far deeper than I was hoping for.

'Can you at least do that on your own? I think we will soon be sick of your fidgeting manner. You're hard to be around at the best of times …' I smirked at him to reinforce that it was meant only in jest. He lifted an eyebrow, *received*.

Then he shot one back, just as he always would. 'Well, who will be there to wipe your arse and carry you home, even before you can pass halfway through the afternoon! Like so many times before …'

My father and Phil cackled at us both for being so petty. At least some of my company still held some humour and seemed to be in the right frame of mind. So, I gulped down my ale, not plucking anymore at the warm loaves that made their way to our table from whoever knew where.

*

Jesse failed with his pursuit for information and continued to sulk as he nursed the same ale that had followed the first.

My thirst had increased the longer the late morning burned.

174

Bells rang all around the town as daytime passed its zenith. It also seemed to signify the beginning of proceedings as the tavern began to fill up, the people of the town starting to drip in.

Chattering clatter began to fill the tavern until it became just a blur of noise. I spied Jesse straining his ears to take in anything that may rend further digging. He seemed to perk up once the tavern shuffled to a new beat from the one we were introduced to. He partook in the occasional bit of banter between his concentration when eavesdropping – only enough to show everyone he was not snooping.

'Why don't you just ask some people?' I asked him. The look returned said I knew nothing about intelligence gathering … nothing at all.

I got up, and my head swayed slightly as I did. Pushing past Phil and my father, I mingled with the closest cluster of shifty-looking folk.

'Say, any of you men know anything about a few other men that passed through here recently?'

'Say we did?!' the meanest-looking one answered, 'What's it to you anyway!' I shrugged my shoulders and dropped my lip. It meant nothing to me, of course. Not yet.

'Was only asking …'

'Well, ask somewhere else, *boy*, and take your cuddly bear over there with ya!'

Phil heard the retort and stood immediately. He meandered his way slowly over to where I stood, fists clenched.

'No, Phil!' I shouted before he would take the head off every one of the small gang leering in his direction – to forever frame the smug smirk on each one of them. I could see it in his eyes;

that was his intention. Seen it before, many, many times when someone had only, in the slightest, *slighted* me.

Polett jumped between him and them, turning angrily toward each and all more than once. 'Do you know who these people are? You knuckleheads!'

'Friends of yours, I assume …?' the red-faced lump of a man jested, expecting more than the little whimper of laughter he got from his buddies.

He looked over my shoulder, and his face turned to mud. I did the same and saw Jesse waving a finger at him. Then when his eyes locked onto mine, he shook his head.

I will be punished for this, no doubt! Seriously, though, why couldn't he just speak to the folk? I would be schooled on such reasons when my head cleared, and we had cleared out of this town, from where he could discipline me without the vengeful eyes of my mama watching on!

The man backed away, offering his apologies. But Jesse motioned him over to where he sat. The man obliged, wringing his hands together as if waiting for a paddling to his arse from a no-nonsense grandmother.

It never came. They took turns whispering into each other's ears, a lot of the lump swinging his head from side to side and a lot of Jesse nodding with affirmation. In the end, the man returned my way, bowed his head slightly, and offered myself and Phil an apology.

That … apology was followed by an offer. 'Say, why don't you men come on with us? We be heading just a short walk up to the *Hop and Shovel*.' I instantly thought it was another drinking hole, which certainly sounded like one. I turned again to Jesse, who nodded at me as if he heard the offer as he listened in, intently – though acting as though he was not.

'What you reckon, Phil?'

He still blazed his small round eyes intently at the plum-faced man. Though the murderous intent had subsided, he still remained alert, hands clenched – though not as tense – ready to strike out at any moment. I calmed him with a questioning look and a shrug, one he returned.

'Let's go then,' my father confirmed. 'Your shout, though ...'

'Mellor, Mellor be my name, and ...'

'I'm Getty's father, and this here is Phil. And I'm pretty sure you all already know the man sulking over there in the corner?' Jesse made a sign with his hand toward my father.

'Aye, too well, it seems. And my apologies once more, Getty. And to you, Phil. Your man over there, the Jester, told me all about how you could've ripped me open like a bear tearing away at some stranded fish. And you, Getty, how you could melt my innards with just a few moves of your hands in the air.'

I let it be. For that was far from the truth. 'You'd do well not to forget that too, Mellor.' I looked around at his drinking crew, 'All you men, too.' With my attention diverted, I hadn't noticed the prominent space that had now appeared between us and them all around us, nor the distinct quietness of the tap room. 'Let us finish here, and we will join you. You'd better make it worth our while, though! Hear me?!'

'Oh, laddy, I will be sure to pass on to the landlady who be gracing the tap room at the *Hop*. Believe me, when I say you will be well looked after ...' I was unsure how to take the wink he left with me before he and his vacated. *Sarcasm?* Probably.

Subversion or subduction? Less so. Either way, he had caught my intrigue.

Polett shook her head, 'Mellor be a big soft one. He has some issues with controlling himself, always wanting to be the big man and the centre of attention. Though he knows his place in the world, this town, and – especially – he should in this place ... my home.' She looked over to her father, pulling draught like a man possessed, contents spilling all over, arms bulging with every pull, hammer still at his waist – I understood now why. 'I will be finishing my shift, hopefully before nightfall. Will you still be out and about?'

I was frozen once again. My mind now included! For if I was to see her again that day, or even frightfully ... that night, I would have to refrain from gulping so much, and so fast.

Phil answered, for I could not, 'Yes, of course we will, my lovely Polett ...' Thus shattering my frozen tongue, now thirsting to loosen the chains held around my mind every time she spoke. I had never known Phil to be such a *smooth* one with the women. Confident, witty, ferocious, and wild. But also soft, caring, loyal, and frightening. When combined, I supposed those traits *could* be quite attractive; once you saw beyond the shondals, fur, and knuckle extensions. Not to mention the intrusion of some spirit of nature imbued within his own.

'Great!' She ran at him and squeezed him tight, softening even further the tension he held within his matted frame.

Great! I thought as my mind melded back into the alter-rhythm of my consumption thus far. *Seems she must like the hairy type.* And, apart from my frothing fringe, I was far from such!

Phil was now finding it hard to contain himself, now almost skipping down the street, every stride accentuated. My father ambled close behind. Jesse skirted around wherever we walked – still on a ledge of despair as his eyes darted all over the place, looking for something that was keeping itself hidden for any purpose other than to blend in.

'Jesse, have you spied anything out of the ordinary yet …?' I asked, for his constant scanning was annoying … at its best.

'Getty, believe me, when I see or hear of something, you will be the last to know,' he looked to Phil, 'don't want you two charging over and chasing … whoever, or whatever, away before I would have chance to talk with them – if indeed, that was all it needed to scrape such required information from their lips.'

'Hmm, you can be damn irritating sometimes … especially lately. I remember when you used to be so much more … fun.'

'Aye, Getty, and much more inclined to work your skinny little arse into shape!'

'True. And … I did enjoy our sessions back then, for it was all new to me; being able to actually walk, unaided, if eventually.' I grimaced, as I should've been a little more respectful to the man, something that had flittered away the more competent I became in my abilities. Without Jesse, I would have still been stuck within the confines of my bedroom, *I supposed*.

Sometimes, I did reminisce of the time I spent wallowing away there. Though there were many times I wanted nothing more than to hear that inconsistent crackling of firewood beneath the warped hearth in my old forever haunt of a bedroom. Nor nothing more than to close my eyes and wonder, as my papa took such delight in letting my mind wander as he read all kinds of stories. It was not always the scrolls he would dictate more than often. He loved to read through his own favourite childhood readings. Those I was enthralled by how he would embellish dramatically, throwing his hands, arms, and voice around. But none of those stories compared to when he read the ancient scrolls to me. I felt a connection, and though I was immobilised, I sensed the slightest tingle sparking about my body, if only the slightest touch through my muscle and bones. It was enough to ignite a world that seemed to connect when I slept – as if my bodily motions, whilst I dreamt, were in sync with the notions spoken and articulated so passionately by my father. But now I knew that was not always the case as the words took on their own volition.

Oh, take me back to those days. I laughed a little inside. *When the world was ever so small and even more so simple.* I often wondered about the happenings upon Inarrel and, most notably, Vilenzia. Even more notable, the missions – or quests, adventures, I liked to think them – set by Morla, one of the original Onber I knew of from the ancient scrolls. A world I had once believed and now knew to be true. Though from which timeline, or even where in which forever foreign alien plane …

I knew not. My best guess was it was far, long, gone. Though still touched, touchable if not reachable, somehow, given the malleability of the text and constant tweaking of the storyline, my father would read to me every time we went through the motions of dusting off each of the scrolls back from the top of the bookshelves – deposited in the only place they would all fit, and the least likeliest place to burn if our crooked and charred timber hearth should finally give way; save any fire sent from the heavens.

I wonder who, if anyone, would be tending to that old hearth and the larger, more angled, and crooked bookcase made of the same spread of oak — probably sawn from the same massive log, judging the similarity in its fissures and rings.

A nudge from Phil brought me out of my reverie, back to the street we had been walking, back to approaching the *Hop and Shovel*.

We all stood next to each other, waiting. For what I could only assume would be some introduction to the place.

None came. Luckily, the large swinging double doors would accommodate us all if we did proceed to walk in side-by-side.

Luckily, Jesse led us in.

The place opened up into an ample, cavernous space of a proportion akin to a well-off royal's ballroom: even furnished with a candled chandelier with an elegant array of what – I could only assume, given the breadth and frivolity of this place – was more than just glass beads suspending from each other to create a circulation of a cascading sparkle of refracted candlelight, throwing off every available colour across the now stunned, and silent face of every well-dressed punter in the tavern: if it could be called such. Tell the truth, it reminded me of the *Grousing Potter*, the famous *Grouse*, located centrally in one of the oldest cities in Vilenzia … Jacob's Well.

I couldn't smell the general scent of the patrons that would frequent this place; or more so, I couldn't smell anything at all, anything other than the hops, which did twinge the nostrils in the right kind of way – the freshness of the smell alluded me to the fact that they brewed on site, but from where was a mystery to me.

Turning to Jesse, I ignored all the stares from the upper echelon of Dibrathella. 'You smell that?' A glorious, charred smell had twinged my sensitive nostrils.

'Time … my young friend. We will eventu—'

He failed to finish what he was saying. He noticed Mellor thrusting through a throng congregated before us, barging through a few of the well-dressed punters that stood condensed together, and slapped a hand against a shoulder each of myself and Jesse before he could finish.

He appeared … a new man, now not shabbily dressed like before, or, at least, he hid the dirty from view with an elegant jacket woven from some fine, weighty thread.

I had no clue how he had shifted himself out of his not-so-elegant and baggy trousers and into some tight-fitting thread, entirely akin to his jacket's patterned dressage, and in such little time between conversing.

'Boys!' He patted our shoulders as if to dust off anything foreign to this clean place or what we may have left stuck there from our first stop. 'What took you!'

A bell rang. A vigorous repertoire of different chaotic dings killed off every preceding note before it produced the one and only fullest chime to vibrate away without disruption. After the last, one remaining, victorious note fulfilled its one and only duty for the world, had stilled the air for a while, did the place resume its – I could only presume – previous state of normality before our benign interruption.

Affecting a myriad of proceedings taking place, most notably, business dealings and talk of commerce, which became now top rank.

'Well, as you know, we carry some important cargo. I wanted to be sure that the present be delivered to its recipient … abridged, somewhat,' Jesse winked at me, then at Mellor. 'The young man would like to know the source of the fine scent wafting over all this … crust.'

'Of course, *Jester*.' The very whispering of the name caused a ripple of disquiet within the ample space. Stares toward us all of a sudden from each small group. All looking at Jesse as though there was a higher station to be held through any commercial agreement made with him.

Jesse only smiled back to them all, then offered a communal shake of his head to quiet each and every one, quelling their evident ambition for further wealth by way of his behest; and of further ascension up the hierarchal pyramid and its ledges of respect. Rather than being one of those on each lower level looking up. They knew straight away to steer clear unless prompted. I could see it in their eyes; not so disappointment, more a relief they would not need to compete with the other factions scattered about the expansive, dark-timbered floor.

I cared less for them or anything other than finding a comfy seat – which seemed unlikely now we had ticked well past midday's fulcrum.

Mellor, though, led us undisturbed through the throngs of every man and very few, if any, women …

Yes! Every man! It was abundantly clear that nearly the only people in this place were middle to well-aged men. The few *others* were darting between, trying to avoid not only the sickly leer of many an eye but the eviler caress with a privileged pad of a palm – if that was all.

He led us to an isolated corner of the large room, the only such that pointed out into a nook and the only space, it seemed.

We had to duck underneath its bulkhead to sit within a horseshoe-shaped bench.

Behold! I found myself sat, or more so wedged, at the return of the cushioned bench, squeezing my legs together as I was crowded on either side by my party and that of Mellor's, coming in to squeeze on the other way in.

My attention was eventually caught unaware, thrown away from the assembly seated through the middle and across the long table that now wedged me between a familiar and an unfamiliar friendly line of bodies. Caught by a swish of hair, so out of place in this market drinking hall of debauchery.

It made sense, that tingle resounding inside of me. Whether that was because I had yet to see one female in this place other than those with hair tied back, carrying a plate or tankard, I was unsure. What followed, as she laughed heartily every time she leant in, whispering something to the woman opposite her, was a sense of glee for me. Sure, they were talking about the men of this place, passing over opinions of each and all. And the way her eyes moved … I was enamoured to learn more about her.

'Careful, young'un,' Jesse said, seeing my glazed eyes fixed on where the woman stood. 'That there be the proprietor of this place, in the stead of her old fella, who be still to return from … well, best you know not!'

A shawl she held loosely over her shoulders covered the slightest bit of skin exposed to the air. Her tight-fitted dress was of the same fabric Mellor held stitched together: much the same pattern and thread – not so much its weight.

'You don't say …'

'I meant what I said, boy. *Steady*. Hear me?'

I nodded back. The look had become deathly serious. A seriousness he very rarely held at the worst of times. He twitched his head in annoyance at the obvious thought I weighed.

She *surely* could not be this place's sole heir, if only temporarily. She seemed … far too young for someone to be running such a marvellous establishment. I wondered who, or what else, was helping. Where was the playing hand in the shadow to be found.

She turned, locking a gaze directly into mine, just as I was about to shake my head to knock off the thoughts racing along a long, winding ledge. I shook it anyway and looked elsewhere from her gaze.

Still feeling the burning stare on the side of my face, it was torture not to look back at her, though in my mind's eye, I knew she was smiling, enjoying my excruciatingly bad attempt of offering no interest in her … *None at all!* Mentally I repetitively reminded myself.

I didn't notice where, who, or what I was looking at. Until I eventually realised, it was all being played before me.

Obviously, Jesse's broken mood was *it* as he stared at me with the broadest grin I had ever seen. Then he stood up, smiling at something else. I knew before I could hear, or see, who he was about to greet. I knew by the scent that had wafted so seductively into my burning nostrils.

She had made the short way over to us.

'Greetings, Jester …' I dared not turn to face her just yet, for my mind was awash with thoughts best left … as just that. But now the scent had drifted, made its way all through my body and back to my mouth. I let out a little sigh, a little too audibly, judged by the humorous stare both Phil and my father gave. Even in the most insincere of circumstances, it was enjoyable to see my father enjoying himself.

'Ah, greetings, my dearest Carla,' he would have bowed, I was sure, if not for the small crook we found ourselves wedged into, bowing was our natural sitting position. 'Though, I am a man of many names, and that is one I have forsaken forever more.'

She eyed him curiously, 'Really …?'

'My dear, I shall be known now and—' he realised he was being overly extravagant once again, 'Only Jesse, my dear.'

'Again. Really?' before Jesse could reply, she asked about another. 'And who is this?' I knew for sake she nodded her curls toward me, for she ran few fingers through my own. I would have thought that strange, though it seemed a common theme throughout my days.

Once more, my tongue was tied to the back of my throat. I began to turn, to look up at her, but was grappled tightly by the fingers caressing my scalp. 'Did I ask you? Young man.' She seemed angry. At least she thought of me a *man* and not some over-pepped boy.

A good start, I supposed.

'This here be Getty.' I could see him cringing for me as his lips twisted slightly, as my eyes twitched upward in some pain. I winced as to not release or show any pain through a leak of moisture; for that would set me back some in her eyes. And I doubted she would entertain even slightly the soft type.

She turned the clenched hand, my hair still wrapped between her fingers, forcing me to look up at her. 'Well, Getty ... you are by no means the worst-looking lad who has chanced an eye at me today, and I dare not say you would be the last. At least you had the grace to relieve me of offering you the offending shake of my head, one to reflect rejection. Unlike the majority in here, who are just arrogant snobs who think the sun shines out of their arses, and I would be forever their property if only I gave them half a chance for them to show me how well off they were. And for that, I thank you for not wasting my time.' Her face was hard, though her eyes gleamed otherwise.

'I suppose you're welcome ...' my words eked out.

Her face softened somewhat, and she looked at Jesse. 'You have far to go with this one ...' she said, as though she had been in this scenario before. 'Your other candidates were far more brash and forthcoming ...' she warily eyed me, then Jesse, 'or is this just another tact? Another ruse?' She pulled my head tighter, closer to hers. Looking me deep in each eye, I flinched as she angled *my* head rather than her own. Eventually, she seemed content with my true, innocent boyish ways and released me with a little shove back to my seat. 'As you know, everything will be on the house. Everything ... except our best batch, of course. As you already know, Jesse. Have your man there, Mellor, keep tabs, and be sure he'll be honest in his marking.'

She winked at Mellor, who offered that bow Jesse could not manage, no matter how much his chin squashed into the timber top. I rubbed my head, more to feel if she hadn't yanked off any of my thick mane.

I was beginning to like this day less and less the more it went on. The butt of the joke I was, every time.

Phil cramped himself tighter to my father, probably trying to hide himself, if impossible, from some of the barrage of barbs being shot at us. I was taken aback when she did eventually speak with him.

'Welcome, ancient spirit of the world before that of our own.' She offered a sincere bow of her own, 'Welcome!'

Phil was suddenly abashed with her direct nature, his little teeth coming quickly close together then drifting apart a few times, showing me he, too, was nervous under that thunderously beautiful gaze.

'Ah, Carla—' he tried to stand but bumped his head – luckily for him, it was well protected with layers of matted fur atop his noggin.

'Sit. All of you, sit,' she offered politely. We had no choice; we already were. 'Mellor, you're to follow me.'

'Aye, miss.' Mellor nodded. He had lost all previously held bravado and now obeyed her upon a whim, be it Jesse, Carla, or anyone else in the town that held some clout, I assumed.

He had to scramble over a few of his friends, who too had changed, may I add, into more elegant attire, to make his way out of the hook-shaped nook.

Mellor returned with another two. A boy and a girl, both most likely not far into their adolescent years, though they had an air of confidence about them that belied their seemingly immature age – but who would know the fact of such from what I have been party to. Their faces strong and perfect, they gracefully, as if gliding, drifted over with two platters each. The girl held a myriad of assortments, all delicately arranged. Some even steaming.

To his credit, the boy held his higher, perched one side of each platter on his shoulder, not swishing a drop of the bubbling, amber liquid over the rim of the too-many-to-count tall glasses he carried. The gleeful, shifting eyes of all but one of those within the nook were almost audible.

Mellor helped divide each serving into equal portions for us all onto the white plates he had carried over. Carla relieved the boy of the weight resting on his shoulders, carefully lifting each drink off so the tray wouldn't topple over.

Though all within the nook were eager, none were brave enough to dabble before Carla gave us the go-ahead.

She smiled knowingly. 'Enjoy! All of you.' She opened her arms wide, a gesture of goodwill. 'Jesse, would you mind?' She raised a brow and flicked it toward the end of the bar.

'Of course, my dear.'

I was the only one to notice them make their way to sit on the only available high leather-clad chairs at the long bar. The others were a little too content with the provisions provided. I watched on as Jesse smiled warmly with her; speaking only a few words set her to giggling, inaudible from where we sat, but a smile could transcend more than just the space between.

A pang of jealousy crept in, though I knew Jesse wouldn't be flirting with her – I knew more than hoped – I only wished, once more, that I had the balls to carry such suave as he. *One day,* I told myself.

When Jesse motioned for the barman to approach, she

glanced in my direction, moving the spiralling hair that had fallen to her cheek back behind her ear. She finished with a smile and turned back to Jesse as he handed her a steaming goblet – most likely mulled cider- with some exotic spices added to the concoction.

Not for the first time in this town, my heart was a flutter; in the space of only a day. It gave me much cause for optimism that I would hook onto someone eventually; *maybe I do heed Jesse's advice … and pace myself, for the day is, indeed, still young.*

I snacked a little more than supped. Jesse acting as the produce bearer, was discreetly complimentary to my new method of navigating through the day, more so for following his advice, I assumed.

It would not take long for us to become acquainted with the hand residing in the shadow – Carla's right hand. A man, both tall and full of a solid bulk. He approached Jesse from the opposite side Carla was seated.

It wouldn't be long before her other hand appeared, this time from the side she sat. A woman in a full-length body suit wrapped almost too tight around her body, adorned with a few strapped sacks all about her body.

Carla nodded to them both, and even though Jesse squirmed in his seat slightly, he still greeted both with a confident, knowing smile. A pat on the back from the big man, and a kiss on the cheek from the other, was given in return, soothing what little concern I held for the briefest moment.

No sooner than a hello or a how are you could have been exchanged did they drift off again, to rest upon their respective perches, back in the darkness.

Jesse sat a little easier once more, an arm over the back of his chair, a leg folded over the other.

I continued sipping and nibbling while my father and Phil became a little more acquainted. Phil was telling my father stories that made him giggle; the ones he told of me in the most uncomfortable or unfortunate situations forced the biggest smile and laughter from him.

I didn't care; I had a few of my own to tell – at the right time.

The chatter expanded somewhat to encompass the whole table. Men greeted us and offered their names, something I was never able to remember, but faces ... That! Was how I would remember anybody and everybody. A good deal of time was spent exchanging stories. A few were quite cumbersome, but the majority were wildly fascinating, vastly contrasting in style, poise, and result. I could have sat there all day but for the constant uncomfortable glances from Carla.

Someone who hadn't remained seated was Jesse. After Carla had left him to resume her role as patron at the other end of the bar, he was up and down, in and out, mixing in with the pockets of what I assumed were wealthy cliques scattered around the floor, keeping themselves always more than an arm's length away than the next bubble of a crowd.

I had kept my glances fleeting, at best, never to stare for too long to not draw much. I constantly half expected a dagger to be touched to my throat for my leering gazes to be viewed as a threat. Relief set in when she had removed herself from my direct line of sight. I found my breathing more concise, easier, and my concentration on the conversations around me fuller once more. And, by the end of our time there, my mind would be … satiated.

Jesse eventually came back to advise we should move on.

Or, as in his words, he had "ruffled enough feathers".
So, we bid all farewell, and they us. Though no doubt was left, we would be seeing each other further on our merry way around the town, if not in the streets later on, once the sun left the horizon with one long, final caress.

We squeezed in a couple more taverns, or better described as hardly-reputable drinking holes, before we left the twilight. I stayed true to my thinking, a sip and then a nibble. Or two. Pretty much the same were all the taverns. A firm mixture between the first two we had sampled; a minority of both at least, and the rest that spread the breadth in-between.

As we flittered between those taverns, a mild commotion grew to organised chaos the later we wandered the main street. The sun had set early, a lot earlier than I was used to, though the cold it brought didn't bite too hard for apparent reason. Phil was probably sweating, even though he held no cloth to cover his body other than where it needed to be covered – to provide a social interactional benefit to the viewing recipient who'd be viewing such a mess – and that leather strap of his.

I sensed Jesse becoming more agitated, and he sensed me looking at him shuffling about, too, no doubt a little cold himself.

A shake of his head told me he had heard something on his hunt, his search for that littlest breadcrumb of information about the troupe that had passed through recently.

A hand he used to give visual measurement from the ground to measure roughly the height of a child.

The look of, *Oh!* Flashed across my eyes.

Jesse nodded that he knew I knew. And I would need to speak with him urgently, for ill tidings would surely abound.

Unwelcome at the worst of times.

Wondering set me asunder how in the world no one else had been able to give him something before now. The crazy little people would surely have brought attention to at least a few, if not many or all, in this tiny town, no matter how inebriated they always seemed to be. There was more to this story, for sure. I would find out soon enough …

We were hustled through the bustle, trying to gain admission into a large building set dead centre along the main street. Another similar building towered just as high, on the opposite side, and it was just as hectic down and around the identically constructed entrance. *This must be the best spot to view the town's frivolously endowed antics later!*

I could understand the reasoning for such the crowd, pushing, to only get squished in, for if this was indeed the spot to be, I wanted the optimum position; or, at the very least, the closest spot for the evening's proceedings.

Hoping it was more of the same as the night before, as the sky was as clear as it could ever be, with no rain clouds anywhere on the horizon. That gave me optimism for an extended rendition of soul.

'This is serious business, Getty!' Jesse said.

'No doubt!' I replied.

He looked about shiftily. 'What concerns me the most, other than confirmation of them … *little fuckers*, is that no one knows of their passing through this town, other than that minority I know well.'

'Yes, I thought that immediately when you exhibited such.'

'Pay no mind tonight. There isn't any point in us moving while you're so … unfit for travelling. Though tomorrow, we must go before midday! Meet me, as the sun meets its zenith, in the main hall of our host, where we gathered before we departed this morn.'

I knew what that meant; this night would be my last with my father. Another thought choked me. I would only, if even, have the morning with my mama. *Was it ever easy?*

Phil sensed my angst. Communicated so with a large pad on my shoulder.

Jesse shuffled again, ever so slightly, as the drooped fur from Phil's arm brushed his neck as he reached over to comfort me.

'Where will you go …? Spirit from a time before?' Jesse asked, half turning to Phil, humour not abounding in his voice.

A pat to Jesse's shoulder told him all he needed to know – he had no clue.

I looked at Jesse and could tell there was some strain within him still. Of what he was wrestling with inside, I knew not. 'Phil, say should you become more than just as you are—' Phil's furry brows raised themselves rather high, 'No, Phil. I mean this most sincerely, more of an open-ended question.' Jesse thought a little while, two fingers to his chin, before asking again. 'Well, let me rephrase. *Where* would you like to end up?'

Phil looked at me.

A slight shake of my head shattered everything within me. I was cutting off the only true friend I had ever known ... The pain in his eyes I would never forget. Not anger; a complete understanding of what I was saying without really saying anything. That hurt the most, that he would not beg me to stay by his side or for him to tag along – though I was sure he would be the most welcome ally of physical aid should we need some extra muscle or any scything to be done.

It must have reason, I told myself.

And I hope it's a good one, a very good one, my heart screamed.

The night passed on by. Though the atmosphere had been somewhat subdued after that discussion, or lack thereof, as it were. My father was content to just sit and listen to the banter, a quick glance at me here and there to show he was slightly concerned about me.

Jesse still wore that same frown, the one implying a held impatience. I constantly looked at Phil, and he always met me with that warm, small smile of his; he was a master of charade, if unintendedly so.

Wondering began to take the place of the lump hanging heavy at the bottom of my throat as to when the entertainment out in the street would begin. I had seen nothing of the sort so far; we were well past the time we had journeyed through town the previous night. And ... there were plenty scattered in each tavern to imply a potential for it to rival that of last night: even a familiar face here and there? Maybe ...

Indeed, they *were* familiar, potentially those that *did* strut along the stage last night. That was confirmed as a few extravagantly dressed dancers swanned through the large entrance with over-the-top aplomb. Eyes to the nine, legs to the eleven, hair to the full ends. And heading my way.

My immediate reaction was to stand, a show of greeting, only to be pushed back down, bringing much delight to all those around me.

A deep gruff voice came from the one who had roughly sat me back down, 'Prepare thyself, big boy ...' The man squeezed through and over Jesse to straddle me. Vigorously grinding and rubbing a haired chest in my face, the laughter grew with every alternate interaction the dancer threw my way.

My father laughed so hard I could not help but do the same – when the man's chest permitted. His laughter was soon snuffed by the dancer's comrade, as he, too, mimicked all kinds of poses while bouncing all over my father's lap.

It was Carla who eventually came to our aid, 'Margus, Tillian, leave those poor gentlemen alone will you ...' She raised her eyes toward me as though she thought I was enjoying the man thrusting all over me. I quickly shook my head to ward off such a notion. A wink from her told me I had taken the bait, prey caught with slight banter of her own.

Margus, I assumed was the burly dancer holding his full weight atop my trembling thighs, whispered gruffly in my ear. 'I feel that there, that little bump,' he threw his head back and boomed a burst of laughter, then came in close to whisper again into my ear, now tingling with fear of what he would say next. 'She seems to like you ...' my tongue froze, and my slight bump too.

'Ooh!' Margus giggled as he relieved my legs of any further

discomfort. He sauntered past Carla, talking loud enough for all to hear whilst flourishing a hand about the air. 'He's all yours, that horny little sprite …' Carla tapped the half-exposed arse hard, bringing a little yelp and another satisfied giggle from the man.

Tillian wrangled himself off my papa, and a few blokes sat between him and freedom. He, too, brushed past Carla, wearing an expectant smile as he prodded his bare cheek for her to pat. She did, but not as hard, bringing a disdainful frown from the big man.

I wondered once again.

What! In all, that was not insane …! Is going on!

Jesse smirked at me, knowing full well what I was thinking. Then, when he shook his head in tandem with Carla as they caught each other's eyes, that told me all I needed to know. Forever the pessimist, during *plentiful* bedridden years, before my optimism had set itself to the forefront of my world, soon as I could move even the tiniest of muscle, even the slightest, whilst I wasn't dreaming. Now a balance between the two had set the baseline for realism and all that came to follow: Sometimes, the reality of things could, and would, far exceed the faltering promise of either the former. Now my optimism was piqued; the rough and tumble of the dancing pair had set to spark the tentative tinder that held the corner of the room we were wedged into.

I knew there now seemed to be a completely different take on tonight's proceedings. Fully expecting something and not receiving anything was a long way from, at least, receiving the unexpected … most of the time. *Suppose an arrow in the back is a slightly better outcome than having an axe stuck in there* … unless, of course, they're encountered simultaneously. Then that would be nothing else, other than … just … shit.

My mind began to warm back up – thoughts now far away from the impending loss of Phil – for the entertainment to be offered tonight; though not quite to my taste, I did still enjoy everyone having a good time, myself included.

Jesse was still smirking at me, even as Carla made herself scarce quickly once Margus had offered his outrageous opinion – I'd hoped it was for her to hide a blush, but that would have been indiscernible to detect beyond the artificial hue of crimson, brushed generously across her petite, angled cheeks. He began to rub his chin and cheek, which he did constantly whenever he was about to speak, to offer an opinion.

'Getty, you seem … umm, quite enamoured by that pair over there,' he continued to rub his chin firmly, trying to hide the ever-increasing smirk. Luckily, he did, for I was sure it would extend from ear to ear. Sometimes I wished it did, for it was rare to see him even smirk, or smile, with some form of amusement. 'You do know,' he went on, 'and hopefully, you have worked it out by now, for if you haven't, we need much more to focus on your social interactional training, that the night be filled of extravagance, of flair, of more than just lust for some …'

I knew what he meant; my body was buzzing with what the shit just happened in the extravagant tavern moments earlier. Thus, all confirmed that many of the women I had eyed during the day, or at least the minority, would have been up there on the stage last night. Now, it seemed, the most charismatic of the town's population was occupied doing what they did best, flaunting their best and worst, a far cry from the proportional offerings from what I assumed. No less than my assumption, I was fully aware of everyone's potential preference for such proportioned lump, or lumps: or lack, there say … of. I let that sway me.

I took a moment to reflect on everything. That *moment* may have been more than fleeting, though less than it should have been. But … it was enough. My mind kept itself in the happy zone, just above that realistic line, tempting a brush of a higher optimism.

My expectation at the beginning of the day was high; now, it was even higher. It had to be, for I would not see the woman that caught my breath and all of my soul as she fell so deftly from the bar high up the night previous. It had to be something significantly more elaborate.

Unashamedly … it was.

We were hustled outside. Carla and her hands quickly herded all those contained within her father's tavern away as the large bell rang. A rhythmic ringing to signify that the *event* was about to take place.

It was apparent all knew the significance of the clanging, for all followed unconditionally, without cause for any disruption; it was all a little too … methodical for my liking. Then I thought of all the situations I had been privy to that resembled an inkling for my mind to touch upon. The thought amounted to not many, where it surpassed less than even one such memory.

Splitting the long, straight street again was the same setup we had passed the day before. Flanked on either side, a spillage of folk, seeping from all the doors on either side of the street, added to the already thronging mass – some flowed through more than others, mainly from the central tavern we made our way from and its twin directly opposite.

The long stage was barren of any life, though for how much longer I dared to wonder as I stared at the huge tent erected at the far end of the raised platform.

The crowd were also eagerly waiting for the spectacle to begin; I garnered such a notion from the way they smiled every which way, knowingly. A group of the young folk, leaning over the stage, began a simple chant picked up with cascading chorus as it rippled outward. It continued until the whole town was baying my unknown … with song.

After a few rounds, we joined in, once we could understand what was being chanted. Even my father, eyes closed, threw his fist to the sky with every shouted word of the chant, mimicking those we had tagged along with.

A final note from the bell rang across the air, holding a long note, bringing with it a hushing sound from most of those gathered. The silence was deafening, the anticipation excruciating. I don't think I had ever been on edge this much – I was hanging over that ledge, falling over and over, without actually hitting the ground.

A jumble of shouts erupted from within the tent, just noise initially, though I could hear the calls becoming more and more in time with every cry, until it was only a shout in unison … "Show us where you piss from!" over and over, drawing laughter from all that lined the streets. Louder so from the younger folk as they thrust their hips in the tent's direction, egged on by their mates, much to the disgust of the men and women who mingled in and around them.

The flaps moved ever so slightly. Even from the distance we were away, I could see a head pop, peeping, through the small gap before it closed just as quickly.

In time with the shouting, a drumbeat began, drawing up a higher anticipation.

I was expecting big things with such a build-up, even if it was just a bunch of burly men dressed to impress!

A spiralling flame shot forth from behind the tent. It spiralled upwards until it reached a height high above us, reaching its zenith directly above where we stood, before the flamework exploded in a massive shower of many colours. The colourful sparks spread themselves out to encompass the entire town.

Once the sparks of light had dimmed, leaving nothing but smoke trails, everything fell silent once more.

The first clue I had that something was about to happen was when those young folk who had been leaning onto the stage earlier suddenly looked down the other end of the stage and moved back sharply to make way for a small flare that erupted, running single file, on each edge of the stage, shooting away to make its way toward the large tent.

A crescendo of flame work shot forth from the front of the tent, leaving only a hovering smoke in their wake.

Then they appeared, strutting through the smoke left from the flamework, as though wading through shallow waters.

A well-choreographed dance was followed by all. Men of all sizes, dressed in all kinds – some not so much – stood hands on hips after the conclusion of their moves. Moving themselves to form an arrow shape now, they began to strut extravagantly down the street, high up on their stage, one owned … completely, by them, with an air of confidence that should have made even Jesse weep.

He was not. His eyes were still on the lookout for any trouble. Dark times were afoot. I knew that. I could feel and sense it with some unknown recognition of change. None of the others here looked as though they held the same cognition, the way they smiled, laughed, and went on with their nightly entertainment – I was sure now it was a nightly occurrence when they should have been fulfilling their role as one of the last bastions of defence before the periphery of the Haze of Sorrow would be broken – if indeed, it could ever be breached fully, and from what I saw, what I went through with my friends and family, confirmed that it could well be. Dark magic was at play that day, one that fed the wave of dread our way.

One thing that always caught me, every time I ever heard that word *magic*, observed it, or dreamt of it, was … how? How could the users do it? So deft of thought, so bereft of any strain. Surely it must have been hard to muster that kind of energy from nothing more than a flick of the wrist? *Wouldn't it?* That one time I set time to stand on the periphery of the Haze of Sorrow, *was it that easy?*

I thought no more of it. Otherwise, I would have joined Jesse in a bad mood, not that he was in a bad mood. It just looked that way. And I didn't want those around me thinking of me what I thought of Jesse.

Luckily, I did think no more. I must have been daydreaming of nothing for such a while that I only just dodged the big, puckered lips of Margus, who led the charging arrow of bodies.

They had gained half the street on me as I pondered something I knew nothing about … yet. I smiled goadingly at him, which was returned with a kiss through the air in my direction, amplified by the hand touching his lips to throw such an offering like a spear.

The connection between was broken as one of the younger lads shouting at the stage from before pulled at my coat, pointing at Phil. Though he did not speak, he only nodded to where a weight of curiosity lay. I knew what he was thinking. It never occurred for me to believe that the young would have been less exposed than most to such a being, let alone one covered in matted white fur – how he kept it so clean baffled me, for I never ever saw him washing in anything other than murky looking ponds, creeks or … at the very best, icy cold streams – which were seldom found.

There was no apparatus this evening for the men to clamber high, seductively, upon; only themselves acting as such. I watched on as Margus helped two of the other dancers up onto his shoulders, holding an arm of each as they set a firm foot to dig into his shoulder; they, in turn, did the same for two more. The last clambered up the back of Margus, thus completing the muscled diamond. Margus showed no strain; he only held a firm smile whilst he rotated a full circle, baiting the cheering crowd, drawing a louder roar as he winked copiously to many on the revolution. Not once, but thrice slow twists.

The biggest wink was reserved for me; he would throw it at me upon every revolution.

I was past any stage of uncomfortable. Instead, I had begun

to get in the groove, returning a wink or a fictitious blow of my lips – much to the delight of those around me, not least Jesse.

Then I saw her. The woman from the night before, the one who had taken my heart beyond its final beat if ever so briefly. A glance through the mix, and then she was gone again. I did not mistake her smile or how she dropped her eyes childishly.

Was I to follow? Maybe? Maybe not …

Definitely, this was the result after the minimal counteracting arguments were offered from somewhere inside my mind. I was happy with that outcome. I had to twitch my legs in any direction.

Follow where? She had disappeared suddenly. Had no inkling as to where she may have gone. But … I knew one thing for sure, she was on the other side of the elevated platform, and there was no way I would traverse the entire platform to walk when I could have just as quickly slid across the breadth of cheap timber between.

Soon as I placed a palm on the stage, Jesse slapped my chest with his gangly hand. Never before – and I knew he was quick – had I seen him move quicker. It was too late for my palm, but at least he had saved any other part of my body that was to touch the stage. I felt as if stung by the largest of Marsh Wasp, akin to the injection of its toxin. A repulsive barrier of some sort touched the surface of the stage, *it seems they do not just lay idle of mind,* I thought as I rubbed my hand on my thigh, trying to relieve the pain from the stage's sharp rebuke.

No relief came, only a sharper stare from Jesse. He threw his head down the street as if to offer the notion, "You'd better take the long road". The shake of his head, which he did quite often, finished his assessment of me and my foolheartedly action, "you lazy bastard", he said without moving his lips.

So, I did. I shuffled my way carefully along the periphery of the stage, leaving extra leeway to avoid touching the thing once more; I did not hesitate to think it may disable my hand further if I would accidentally touch it again, less my entire body.

A small train of folk straggled behind me, more so trailing Phil, as the string of young folk came, walked hand in hand behind him. He was not perturbed. He looked back and pretended to wrestle the one who tagged the fur creeping up out from his arse and over his leather trunks, seeing that one off with a soft cuff to the chin, to the back of the line, only for another to grab hold for a short while before they fell victim to the same playful gesture.

My father, Jesse, and all those who we had tagged along with throughout the day remained stum to where we had stood before. Seemingly enamoured by the show taking place only a short way from them. I left them to their own curiosities. I had my own, and I was sure to hark quickly upon it before any foul came into play like so often before.

Momentarily, I'd be thwarted in my pursuit of the woman I had craved for a little over a day's tick. None other than two older women who had made it their prerogative to have the best of evenings, the best they ever would have had, I assumed by the way they were crossing wistfully back and too, through my intended path. Dancing arm in arm. Drinking what seemed the *maltiest* of meads, judged by its overly condensed appearance, belonging to a body far bulkier than their own skeletal frame.

All I saw as I tried to make my way around them was that

they were loving every drop, trying their best to consume all within the glass. Once finished dancing, they sat in homemade chairs, wringing out their arms dramatically, the same way the men had burst out of the tent, not too far from where they had perched themselves. Not a drop would touch the ground: even the slightest overarch of a gulp was washed away with a swipe, a cardiganed forearm relieving the prominent chin of the tiny, wasted droplets.

They continued on soon as I approached, and I found myself on their merry roundabout one way, then the other, finishing more than a few revolutions locked in their arms before being able to continue on toward the midpoint, marked as the tent's central spire.

I heard a voice shout giddily behind me. That of my papa's, now broken from his gaze upon the stage, obviously following to keep tabs on my safety. I shuffled quicker, hoping to lose him, Jesse, and Phil too, before I could round the back of the large tent. Hoping to make my way back down toward the last place she left my eyes wandering to find her.

Lost them, I finally did; they seemed content to remain with my father as he was spun around, spun so fast his head lolled backwards, looking ready to pop off. That was until I locked eyes with Phil, who pointed and shouted something of a roar at me. He grabbed my father swiftly, pushed Jesse forward, and squeezed the two older women together to make an escape. I smiled as they all rushed on, but … I was too far ahead of them now, though.

Or, I thought …

Not looking where I was travelling, eyes on the trio in pursuit, a sudden jerk of both my arms upward shocked me like a bolt from above. If that wasn't shock enough, I found myself on the stage, surrounded by the dancers. They chanted something I could not fathom. The sound strangled as it tried to register coherence inside my frozen mind and soul.

The only sound I heard was the blood rushing through my body as I was hoisted high into the air, landing in their arms: not the once, a number unknown as I must have passed out around the fourth such lift in front of the ecstatic, baying crowd of hundreds if not thousands.

A light appeared, distorted at first, before it materialised into five faces adorned with a beautiful blend of colours. That seamless blend was broken by two black, bushy eyebrows on each – too black and perfectly shaped to be natural.

Then the sound began to form into something tangible; laughter, amused curses, and the familiar voiced shouts from the three who now looked on at me from where I was lifted.

I was lifted up, easily – ever so gently – by four big pairs of arms, turning the buoyant amusement to a raucous cheer. All five crouched to rest a knee on the stage, and all five offered me a hand, offering me their forever vows. A mix of shouts now came; obviously, all five of these people were known by their stage names, if not their real ones by now.

Then I saw her once more, and I knew I was done for, for she wore the widest grin. My heart sank for what that burning smile could have proposed. The pessimist in me assumed a wicked smile for me fainting on stage like a fallen leaf at the death of summer, and the optimist in me suggested … the same.

Though a wink before she disappeared around the edge of

the building made of dark-grey stone, that of one of the prominent taverns, gave me hope, if only a fleeting spark. It was enough of a crumb to follow. The problem, probably not the only one, but the closest at hand, was getting off that damn stage!

Boos rang around in a chorus – young and old – as I declined every proposal to push through a gap and instead jumped off the stage. The side I needed to be … and even further ahead of the pursuit.

Hampered as I pursued *her* by everyone wanting to show their disproval to barge a limb or shoulder into me as I made my way through them. I would eventually make it to that very corner where she disappeared.

A narrow gap left itself beside another similarly constructed building, leading the entire length along the structure until it was bereft of any light to reflect even the tiniest rodent's shining eyes.

I was about to follow down that long, narrow alleyway, but a tickle to my cheek was followed by a firm grip on my shoulders. *Phil! It could've been no other … what now? Not … now! How'd they get here so fucking quick, anyhow!*

My extended sigh was a common trait I had learned when all things seemed to go to shit.

Jesse added to my frustration. 'You're not thinking of going down there? In your state … Are you?'

I knew better than to say no, so a shrug of my shoulders was all he got. A quick slap to my head forced out a sharp, 'No!'

'Foolish boy. Have you suddenly gone mad?' he took a look down the alleyway. 'Just a dead end anyway, Getty … What were you after? A discreet beating, a fanciful interaction with some unknown fettle …?' My blush gave the answer away, but he spared me from further discomfort with my father watching on, shaking his head. 'Ah! Go on then, boy, I will stand watch. Just do it behind that crate there; seems to be some foliage requiring a new lease of life. A fresh watering will do them a world of good …'

'We might join you, Getty,' Phil smiled at me, but my father shook his head as if he feared the city watch would bang him up in chains if caught emptying his bladder out in public.

We had, by now, been left to our own doings. The show would go on, with the "Woos" and "Ahhhs" getting louder and louder.

After we had left our bladders to the respective plant pot, I took a look down the alleyway as I was now a little further in, and my eyes had slightly adjusted to take in more of the darkness. Jesse was correct. There was nothing but a stone wall at the end of the alleyway, with no sign of any escape into either building. The only way out of there, here, was upward, as nothing was possible to hide behind, save the crate where we desecrated someone's dying plants … Thinking of how she had navigated last night's acrobatics, I thought this would have been no mean feat to escape from. Jesse was right. Also, I was in no state to follow even my shadow!

The alleyway was suddenly filled with light, flamework exploding high above us, highlighting even the tiniest mosses stretched on the cobbles below or clustered to the walls. I cast my eyes up higher, to the top of the gable of each building, looking for any sign of where she had gone. The only movement, other than the trail of coloured lights, was a blackbird flying fast away, the boom obviously unsettling it from the temporary perch it had stooped.

As the noise drew to a quiet hush, the men on the stage offered their thanks to all and then promised the next show would be their most emphatic, bringing a raucous cheer from all in attendance. Margus finished an offering of the morrow's entertainment: a feast of epic proportions to be laid out on the stage following the bi-annual display from the children of the town's craft, by way of floats, the "Monster Swarm!" I heard an excited child shout.

*

Lucky we were where we were, for the masses began to meander their way from the central stage to either head home, if with an accompanying child or if frisk had set in with their partner, or head to the nearest door now flung open. Ours was a mere few steps to the entrance of the large tavern opposite our last.

A quick jig could be heard, inviting us in; a small band playing instruments with a smile rather than vocals. Heads and legs flicking from side to side in a merry fashion, no few who filtered in began to mimic the same, though slightly less merrily, as they rushed toward the brass-topped bar where a multitude of goblets were being filled from one of the many taps.

This tavern was an exact replica of the one across the street, except for the fact the pipework leading to each tap, bar one, was coated with ice. *So, a mage resides here; either that or some magical element has been applied.* Either option was fine with me as I licked my lips wantonly.

Jesse ushered us to one side, away from the throng of people pushing behind us. He seemed to know where he was going as he led us through a small doorway to one side of the bar.

A large room opened before us, decorated with paintings of many different things, too many to name. But one stuck out to me instantly, and I had to blink a few times before rubbing my eyes to look once more; high up, dauntingly above me, was a large painting of a woman holding a long spear, the very same from my dreams – the "Spear of Starlight" – of the manic woman who took that same item from the musical trio of Velosko, Amaria and Marcos after they were attacked by the strangest of ocean creature. It could have been the same woman, the "Slayer", but the face was smudged to a point beyond full recognition, whether by the age of the painting or for some other reason, I could not be sure. The brass plate, too, had been damaged and rubbed from countless touches, thus rendering any such marking impossible to identify.

Other such paintings, varying in age, scattered the walls and ceilings. I assumed most of those beasts, or mythical creatures some might call monsters, would be paraded through the town in the early evening tomorrow. If I was still around, I would be sure to take leave of my room and join in the festivities.

There were a few items I assumed also held some meaning; an old-looking wooden tankard, an axe made entirely of stone, and a large lantern with the glass blown out to droop from the ceiling.

The light in the room was produced by a mixture of the same looking lanterns, only much smaller, and a few burning candles held on a few shelves atop candelabras.

Only two small round tables offered any solace in this room other than the four cushion-backed chairs that completed each set; there was nothing more to fill the space of such an expansive and looming room.

Jesse made us sit on the chairs surrounding the table furthest away from the doorway. He always did that. It must have been a complex for him, one maybe to see who may attack us much sooner than they could – elementally less chance of surprise, I guess, and he was always sat to face that same entrance of that chance.

We sat, waited, and then some …

Was this Jesse's tactic to sober us lot up? If that was the case, it was too late coming, for I was now considering that climb up the end of the alleyway. Not because I was thinking warped and with gusto, but because now, I thought my reflexes were sound enough to achieve that task quite comfortably.

My legs became agitated by the lack of movement, so I began to stand, pushing myself up with two hands pressed on the table. Jesse slapped his hands to mine and cautioned me to *sit-the-fuck-down* with the hardest eyes he had ever taunted me with. As soon as I began to stand, the icy feeling in the middle of my back should have been prior warning that something was off with this room. The feeling dissipated as soon as my arse touched the green-cushioned chair again.

I looked to Jesse, who only held a stare of death. He held it for us all, until the ice was broken by the entrance of three others. They came over to introduce themselves; one the proprietor, the other his muscle and the last, or at least I thought, was a short fellow, the one to take our orders. That last appeared from behind us. I knew someone approached, for Jesse's eyes widened a mere fraction.

A hand touched my shoulder, and a cold touched my neck adjacent to the held shoulder. *Why is it? None ever offer introduction, always the shoulder ... or my hair!* Luck be blessed upon me, for I wore a few layers, the shoulders well padded, for I dared not think what such a cool touch would do to my bare skin, let alone through a flimsy woven shawl.

The mage ... I wondered where he was hidden before he introduced himself with the most cheerful of voices. 'Ah, young traveller, excuse my manners. But first, you should know your own. Did your father not raise you correctly? A seat offered in someone's house should be abided until the host grants you leave. That so ... Jesse?' My father dropped his eyes as if disowning me. I could have fallen through the floor ...

Jesse licked his lips, a little too much for my liking. Never had I seen the man so uncomfortable, scared even. 'Aye, that be right, High One ...' he wrung his hands together. At one point, I was sure he was to rise before he remembered himself too. *Who is this man, and why does he taint Jesse's behaviour so?*

The proprietor broke that layer of ice. 'Come now ...' he wore a brave face, outed only by the beads of sweat produced atop a balding fuzz.

'Come, where? Lawree ...' the mage asked, direct, matter of fact.

'To your senses!' Phil said, standing up to face the mage. I had yet to see the man. I was too scared to turn my head. But when my friend found himself in the slightest ink of potential ill, I would have faced the most evil, vilest of being. I stood to stand by my friend's side! Seeing Jesse only drop his head into his hands as I did meant nothing to me, no more than I thought of him within that minuscule amount of thought, him as just … a coward.

The mage held his arms out wide, holding up the drooping sleeves to match the overly large droopy hood he wore to cover his head. 'These boys have more balls than the lot of you!' Throwing back his hood, he revealed himself to be none other than …

'Dagda!' I shouted.

Though there was something about him that was slightly different, other than the short hair, he seemed much taller.

'No mind, Getty.' He patted my shoulder again. I could feel the ice-cold draught creep up my neck with each padded pat. 'I'm kin to Dagda. He is my younger brother.'

Oh, for fuck's sa— my mind began.

'—no, Getty! I'm not here to lecture or teach you anything. On the contrary, I'm only here as a *watcher*, one to report,' he looked to Jesse, 'ain't that right, old man …?' Jesse nodded. 'I thought to fill my time and use my talents, for … somewhat … to the betterment of all who reside in this sorry sack of a town. And that bludger there!' he pointed to the landlord, 'Be a better man for it! Ain't that right …!'

'Yes, of course, and we're most appreciative for it—'

'—come now, you sorry sack, we're all on the same side here …'

'My most sincere apologies, Nagda!'

I couldn't help myself. All fear had suddenly left my head, and I tried to hold it in. I failed!

I wasn't the only one to laugh at the extremity of such a name compared to the mighty Dagda. A sudden squeeze to my neck

214

reminded me of who we taunted.

Phil was angered and instantly flushed his fists, ready to fight with the mage, Dagda's supposed brother.

As the laughter dropped to absolute silence, Nagda let go of my neck, and he explained how the name would sound so similar in our language, but from where he hailed, such a slight difference in the sound would make a huge, distinct separation. 'The name cannot be pronounced in your primitive language. So we dumbed it down for you. On my home world, one I have not visited for a long while, it sounds much more complex. The slightest kink in pronunciation could well have your head on a spike … if you were that lucky.'

'How so?' my father asked, intrigued by the whole thing. He had lost the glazed look and seemed entirely with it now.

'May I?' Nagda asked Phil, as he held a palm to indicate attention to his now empty seat. Phil nodded, confused, full of testosterone or some misalignment of himself with that ancient spirit – or both. Nagda shuffled past, wedged between the stone table and Phil's hip, to take the empty chair. Adding much to Phil's confusion.

Jesse stood. My father began to do the same but was motioned silently to stay put. Jesse then nodded, in turn, to the proprietor, the muscle and the helper. The two empty chairs were then dragged unceremoniously across the stone-laden floor to the other table that sat alone, a fair way away in the vast room by the former. The latter gave options for selection of both food and drink before taking orders of all in the room bar the former, marking ink on a small slip of parchment.

My only question, before we took our seats, a short distance from Nagda and my father, aimed at the apparent order taker, was, 'Your strongest, please! Sir …?'

The man rolled his eyes before he answered, looking over to Nagda. 'Agda … sire.' The only one who laughed this time was Nagda, laughing so loud he almost caused the room to snow from his breath cast out with each outward belt. The frost that enveloped my father's face as he looked at me was almost comical. It would have been entirely if it was anyone else but him.

'Agda?!' I asked Jesse. Who only shook his head as if not to ask any further. A lesson I had learned a long time ago from the same: do not question the man, or woman, or creature, that would be the one bringing the produce. And! Most of all, do not question the produce or where it has come or potentially come from. For that would be the biggest mistake in all the lands and all the worlds. I was told; and never heard … thus learned the hard way.

'That'll be all, Sire …?' the other, obvious sibling of Dagda, asked.

'Yes, that will be just grand, my good man.' A smile gave me hopeful comfort he took me sincerely, no matter the slip to our initial introduction moments earlier. The nervous twitch with my smile hopefully went unnoticed. I gave myself some comfort that, hopefully, the strongest they had would put me out of a misery settling itself in the pit of my stomach. I was ready to put this day to bed.

Besides the odd show the town put on, the rest of the day had gone nothing like I had imagined. Far worse, actually. Now there were two otherworldly beings in this place – that I knew of. And not just any otherworldly beings, the same spawn of a demigod, of the Higher!

Agda left us, disappearing into the main bar, and the owner of the establishment offered us our seats. The whole room became a whole lot smaller as I sat down. All in my head for sure as the walls closed in. The Spear of Starlight – named as such, if in the right hands – loomed over me. The face of the "Slayer" now forged itself in that blur of paint, staring down, hard, at me. I said nothing for a moment, just focused on the ominous painting. The more I stared, the more hidden details would appear; symbols, text, even figures in the background behind the woman holding the spear.

Strange how they are not nearly as faded as the face or the brass plate.

That thought ran through my mind over and over as I turned to see my father and Nagda, deep in a primarily one-way conversation, my father nodding acknowledgement constantly.

A conversation of my own was about to take place with the man formerly known as the "Jester".

He knew it too, shushing me with a look and swish of a hand. Phil was keen to listen in too.

'Getty, you do know this is one of the last of that other world's defences,' he put two hands together, bouncing his fingers against each of its opposites. 'Do you really think *they* would leave that title to those who piss away all they're given? Hmm?'

'But why those two?' a nod to my father's table and one to the only opening in the room gave more than enough for him to guess who I was asking about.

'You still have much to learn, Getty ...' He looked to the

doorway too, knowingly, before the landlord entered, flanked by a pair of the servery team.

Even from this distance, and through the dull flickering light in between, I immediately knew which ale was my own. *Come to a place, taps filled with a magic to keep it almost ice, and I choose the warm mead! Typical* ...

I drowned the contents, something I would have been unable to do if it had been poured at the artificial temperature of every other tap. Then asked for another before my father even had his ale deposited on his table.

That was the way for the next hour or so. Jesse vaguely filled a few of my queries of the pair with even more to ponder, never actually telling me anything that would relieve that itch gnawing at my mind.

What was most revealing to me was that Agda was not quite the immediate kin of the mighty Dagda. Not quite, more a long distant cousin. He wouldn't go too much into the whole naming convention, only telling me I would one day find out for myself – if, indeed, I was the *one* that was to take such a path.

My father was a few more deep. Now much less bobbing his head and more animated with his arms and mouth as Nagda nodded agreement more than he.

The mead hit me harder than I expected, and ... was welcomed. Greatly. The dark room began to spin wildly whenever I closed my eyes for longer than a blink. Luckily, the chairs wrapped around to enable my arms to rest and keep my body from flopping to the floor in a stupor.

The room would eventually spin even when my eyes were

fully open. The talk and chatter was just an echo of noise and incoherence, but my thoughts remained sharp.

Until they did not …

Another Day

The last thing I remembered of the night was my father appearing over the top of me: which, at the time, I thought strange, as I was seated, so he must have floated somehow. But, no. I was lay flat on the stones, staring up at the painting. That was also my first memory as I shot upright in my bed across from Phil. He was yet to wake. Even the sunlight shining brightly in his eyes failed to stir him. The loud snorting and licking were the only signs he was still alive.

I wished I wasn't.

My head pounded thunderously. Bringing sweeping nausea for every strike to the anvil made of mush. From the angle the rays shone through the only window, angelifying Phil's face, I assumed it must have been about midday – at least.

Lying back down did not help. That only brought another wave of ill as blood rushed back into my head, adding to the volume already pumping through it.

My mother came by, knocking on the door, even though it was still ajar, with Phil's shondals acting as a wedge before she entered.

'Would you look at you two ...' A smile let me know it was in jest.

'You look radiant, Mama!' A croak crumbled off my arid tongue.

'You will too, later. Come on. Get your friend up. You're both coming with me for the afternoon.'

'Where? I was supposed to be leaving this town not far from

now, if even that time had already passed.'

'Same place I was being pampered the whole time you and your father were cavorting around that stinking town.' She pointed at Phil, 'Come on! Both of you! Hurry up!' Phil stirred a little, then rolled over, exposing his well-matted arse. A swift kick between the cheeks from my mother set him away from any further slumber.

'Jeez!' he stood, rubbing his arse while fully exposing his frontal bits.

My mother smirked. 'For such a big man ... you'd thin—'

'—Mother!'

Embarrassment now added to my ill health. I then pointed to Phil, to where his shorts should have been. 'Phil, 'sake, man!'

Excusing myself, I made my way to the small but well-appointed wet room. I emptied whatever was left in my stomach from the night down the porcelain-rimmed hole, much to the dissatisfaction, as offered by my mama's face. Then her head as she left, shaking it not so subtly.

Phil added to the mess at the bottom of the hole before we were dressed; our clothes had been dried and delivered to our room. I wore only a simple tunic that dropped down to my ankles, and Phil had pulled on his customary shorts: a pair of many the same he owned, his only outfit other than the belt he wore across his chest.

'Take your time ...' my mother said, peering in through the crack she left between the door and its frame, her tone full of sarcasm – which was not her usual way. I admitted to myself everything about her was radiant today; she bore a freshness I hadn't seen about her for a while – if ever – and seemed ready to take on the world.

We bustled our way outside unsteadily, the sun beaming hard in my eyes. It made the idea of a steaming bath all the more less appetising.

'Where's Papa?' I asked, already assuming the answer.

'Oh … he's already ready for a soak. Has been for hours since I dragged his sorry head and arse off the floor and out of our room.'

Poor bastard. If he feels even half as bad as me. I imagined him slumped in there, trying hard not to drop his head under the water, permanently, never to see the light again. Knowing that, too, at this point, I would find that a blessing with how my head felt.

*

We were led into a small changing room. One that sat between the main corridor and the entrance to the main bathing area beyond. Jesse was already there, robed, ready to go. A look of disdain on his face as he bid me a good *afternoon,* even though there was still a little left of the morning. I didn't question him, for I assumed he'd be packed and ready to go.

'And, you …' I responded sheepishly.

He was about to say more but thought better as my mother was still in the room. A grunting noise told me there would be more when she departed to the other changing room.

'Gretta ….' he nodded to her.

'Jesse …' she said as she flared her nostrils at him. A shrug of his shoulders was met with a slap across his face. Storming out, she shouted something that could have resembled a curse for his sake.

Jesse rubbed his jaw. 'Why's it always me?'

Phil answered the rhetorical question. 'You should know better, Jesse.'

'By what do you mean? It's not my fault that young man over there,' he pointed at me, 'can't control himself ...'

The confusion left on my face showed I had no idea what they were talking about.

'You've no idea, huh?'

I tried to cast my mind back to the previous night but could only remember bits, scrambled pieces. 'What? Falling backwards off my chair?'

They both laughed hard.

'Sakes, Getty ...' Phil laughed some more, harder. 'That was early in the night—'

'Very early,' Jesse finished.

'Oh ... well, that was the last *I* remember.'

'What in all sin caused you to change so suddenly?'

'I got tired, bored. Got a little pissed off with how the day had panned out. So ... I asked Agda to add a little spice to whatever shit I was drinking ...'

'Getty!' Jesse stood fast, 'You do know what spice could be around these parts? Please, *our saviour*! Tell me that you do!'

I answered sheepishly. 'Same as we add to food in less desirable places?'

I knew I had erred soon as they both doubled over with uncontained amusement. They laughed so hard their tears were almost audible as they spattered across the tiled floor.

'What happened!' I asked, hoping for an answer, none other

than "Oh, nothing". But I knew them both, and that answer would not be forthcoming.

'We will sit down later, you and I, and we will have a long chat. Dos and don'ts. Walls and floors ... blah, blah ...'

'Oh ...'

'Yes. Oh!' Phil jumped in.

The atmosphere around me immediately felt frosted. I robed up too. And waited.

A knock on the door was followed by someone peeking in through a small gap as they opened it slightly. 'You coming?'

'Yes, we're good. Give us a moment ...' Jesse responded. The door closed, and he looked at us both in turn. 'How're you boys feeling?'

'Honestly ...' I spoke on our behalf, Phil nodding with his consent, 'we've felt much better. Actually, never felt worse ...' Phil only nodded; it seemed he could not, or didn't want to, speak any more than he had to.

'Always good to be honest, Getty. Especially with oneself and its health.' He smiled again, a condescending smile that grated me every time. But I was too weak to complain or protest. 'Now ... you may think this afternoon may cause you some harm, but believe me, you will not regret it.' A wink directed at me told me there was more than my health at play here.

What does that bastard know? And why is he avoiding the fact that we were to be away and on our way by now?

The thick, humid draught of air from the other room hit me full-on. Even though the gap in the doorway had been minuscule, it seemed to enhance the flow of steaming air. I looked about for another pot to throw up into but saw none on offer, I had to swallow hard: more than a few times.

About to follow Jesse, then Phil, through the open dark, timber-clad door, I hesitated. The robe was my only clothing: was it to be removed before I bathed? Obviously, it was … Phil had no shame left in the face of my mama, but I … and then there was Jesse! Oh, I wished there *was* a hole in the ground to fall into, to follow my stomach.

Then my mother came in from the door we had entered. She was fully clothed, which meant she would not be bathing with us … yet!

Blessed be all the gods! Good and bad, and all in between!

'I will be venturing out with Malinga!' She gave me a cuddle, a tight embrace, 'I heard a rare event happening today …'

'Yes, there is!' I did, at least, remember that. 'When will you be off? Sure it would be a while before it begins, though.'

She smiled at me to give me a clue that she would be venturing out, much as I did yesterday.

'Do wait for me, Mama!'

'I will, child. Just rest up here first. You will be right as gold by the time you're done. Trust me …'

I nodded, taking her for her word, as I always did. 'Very well,' I kissed her cheek, which was now such a welcome luxury, one much returned for all the times her lips had blessed a cheek, or forehead, of my own. This time was no different, other than it was … potentially one of the last. My arms held her a little longer. A tighter squeeze returned, let me know she knew of my angst.

'Just don't ask for any spice! Or go into the big taverns or any tavern near the centre of town—'

'Getty, it's alright. Don't worry for me. I know all about it. Just come to me when you're refreshed.'

'Oh, you do?'

'Yes, my sweet Getty. Go! Go and relax.'

She left me with a smile and a wink. They both held something unsaid; the slight crinkle at the corner of her eyes told me she would be just fine. Though I dared not linger too long here, I was eager to see the parade and the other – fun – side of my mother if I could find her in time.

The door that had slowly closed was creaked open once more. Rather than a pretty eye, a stump of fur sniffed at the air. 'Getty, come on, you will not believe this place!'

I composed myself. There was no time like the present. 'Be right on my way, Phil …'

Phil wasn't exaggerating; it truly was a wonder. One that got me wondering if I could swiftly relieve myself of such to embark on a brisk walk beside my mama while she made her way downtown.

Between the wafting of air being pushed around via mechanical means, hand-held props that resembled giant palm fronds operated by the four bearers, there was a shimmering glimmer across a body of water even further ahead when the draughts between the steam permitted, the source of the shimmer came through a large, stained window; the biggest I had ever seen in my short years out and about.

It was annoying not being able to catch more than only a burst of a glimpse, *such a wondrous sight*. It would have been had the views not been so intermittent.

Even more so *wonderous* were those who drafted the palms. Be it from their sweating or the moisture that held rank in the cavernous room, their minimal, stretched clothing hung tight to their lithe bodies. I pulled my robe tighter around my waist as I walked by, following Phil, eyeing him rather than them, save me from crawling by, leaving any dignity I had left.

As we passed by each, they nodded a greeting. I hesitantly did the same, trying to keep only eye-level contact – no matter how hard that was. It wasn't until the fourth and last in the line that I lost all composure. She smiled at me, a smile I knew all too well by now, one that had replayed over in my mind for the past few days.

'It's you!'

A subtle shake of her head warned me to not speak further, and I was pulled away unceremoniously by Phil.

'Come on, you little horn bag, your father and Jesse are waiting …'

I shook my head, trying to wake myself fully before I looked back while Phil mangled me away, me sliding across the tiled surface, his shondals finding much more purchase than my bare feet. 'But—' Phil pulled me harder, causing me to twist and fall over. He saved me from hitting the floor as he pulled my arm up. I was now being led away, sliding on my arse, much to the amusement of not just *her* but by all who had now stopped wafting their palms to watch the unruly and horny boy being dragged away by some creature that would have been found in most children's beds – if a much-reduced scale, and even much so … less potential violence.

A smile touched my lips, too, at the thought of what they saw as they watched on. The steam in the room then took that image away for both parties, for the mist closed in all around us again.

I was dragged down a couple steps and then into another room before Phil picked me up and threw me in the air. The air disappeared all around me, and the shock of cold filled my entire body, taking its place, relieving any desire and lustful thoughts. Laughter ran hard in my ears as they resurfaced back into the steaming air.

Jesse and my father were lounging in the corner of the small ice bath, chuckling at my expense.

'That'll cool your balls off!' They all laughed some more at Jesse's jest.

'That girl, back there,' I managed to splutter out, my breath still caught, 'she was the one I had my eye on last night.'

I clambered through the ice as it sloshed about my body as I waded through, trying to find a step up out of the ice pool. Until instead, after a few laps of the ice pool, I ended up flopping over the edge back onto the warm tiles. I still bore my robe, which held the coolness of the water to my skin, even as my face and hands burned with the sudden shift of the temperature held in the humid air.

Jesse only watched me. He had something stuck on his tongue, looking sheepishly about as though scared to divulge any more than my father already had to my mother.

'It's all good, Jesse.' I looked at him with a wry look of my own. 'She has already departed. To have her own downtime in town. Said I'd catch up with her in a short while.'

He smiled knowingly at me. 'So … is that the woman you

were banging on about incoherently last night before you tried your hand at clambering up that alleyway wall …'

'Hmm … did I really?'

Phil offered his thought. 'Really! Not just the once; every time we dragged you away, you became so annoying at trying to get back there. Like a madman gone even more insane.'

'So, how'd I get back here?'

'Phil and your father held you down while I snuffed you with some of my own spice.'

'Oh … thought I felt a little wheezy this morning.'

'And I had to drag your arse all the way back here!' Phil chuckled as he pushed me back into the ice pool.

That time, I held in a breath before I hit the freezing slush. A breath held of my own volition, holding it longer still, I left my body under the surface for a while, letting the coolness seep through to my innards, to seep into where they were still hurting from the night before.

It felt good … really good.

Good enough for me to wake up spluttering on the side of the pool of ice from which I fell. Three faces were looking over me, full of anger, close to mine.

Much to my embarrassment, I had turned and coughed up what was in my lungs, almost hitting another face just outside of my vision as I let loose. A face now forever so familiar.

Further angst hit me as she tried to throw me back into the freezing water. The three angry faces turned to surprise as they pulled at my legs to stop such an action fulfilling its pertinent and ultimate potential.

Seeing no way of completing her task, she slapped me instead and spoke loudly, not quite a shout, but close, in some unknown tongue.

'She is angry at you ...' Jesse offered.

'No shit! What did she say?' I said, wiping my chin and cheek. He only shrugged his shoulders unapologetically for not knowing.

It was my father who surprised everyone. '*She* said she should hold your head under that frozen water there for a little while longer ...'

She pointed to my father, then to me before pointing to her mouth.

'How'd you know what—' Another slap to my face shut me up.

My father translated what she said next. 'She said she is sorry. She is sorry that you're a buff head, and she is sorry for hitting you. Even if you deserved it.'

I rubbed my cheek as she looked questioningly into my eyes, whispering something more.

'Is it really he?' my father translated once more.

Jesse nodded in affirmation. 'What tongue is that she speaks? I have never heard such of its like ...'

'It's the talk of the Deliverers,' the plump man who had greeted us to his home a couple nights earlier said as he conspicuously appeared through the thick, hanging moisture.

She bowed to each of us and moved swiftly to stand just behind his left shoulder.

'There are thirteen who reside in this town,' he said. 'Thirteen in Hereberry and sixteen who reside in the Capital. That is all. No more are allowed to leave the sacred citadel that sits atop the

Spike of Meldori, the highest point at the very far reach of the continent Ungola, far across the Simmering Shoals, to the east of this one.' He turned and offered a bow of his own. Deep respect shone heavily about his aura as he bowed even further than a man of his station would offer anyone other than their superior – and I assumed Maghari had not many! And none here ...

Jesse bowed, too, as did Phil. My father looked at me lying on my back and gave me a look that said I should do the same.

So, even though I was a kiss away from the forever embrace of death, I crept to my knees and bowed. Resting my forehead on the tiles. I closed my eyes, too – for extra effect, to enhance the respect offered.

Maghari spoke in the same language as she. I understood nothing but the last word spoken. Her name.

Lorel'eth ... he said, as he looked over his shoulder at her.

I whispered her name, if just to hear it slip away, off my own breath. I could never do such a word, nay mind a name, justice; it was a sound that felt too beautiful to speak of for if I should ever ruin even the pronunciation in the slightest.

Who was she! Why was she here? All manner of questions popped in, then out of my mind to make way for new ones. I had still not recovered from the earlier, momentary brush with the ultimate pariah of this or any world gone or forgotten – or one night to be forever so – so my body slumped forward, my cheeks sliding across the tiles, leaving my eyes to land close enough to Maghari's feet, for if I extended my lips from my teeth they would plant themselves upon his crusted, big toenail.

My saviour had since departed the room. And I prayed none

would call her back. Though I would not mind a kiss I could remember from a girl who had caused me so much heartache in such little time.

Did most boys my age act like this? or as stupidly! First Arigal, and now Lorel'eth! Not to mention a few others in some non-descript tavern, in an even more not-so village or small town! Never to follow through with the fluttering of eyelids, or was that my part in the jig of copulation?

I wondered further if Jesse had used his *spice* more than once to damper my potential advances. But then I thought better; the majority, if not all, were not of my own volition but the curse of the scene I found myself in. In such wonderful settings, dreams and readings of such times had all involved the tapping of liquid trade and folly of the mind bending through strong brewed offerings.

Two women I had not even the slightest knowledge of were the only ones I had ever craved: first, the Deliverer. She could be here to cart me off to some god-forsaken rock high up and even further away! Second, someone I had lusted over privately for the majority of my short life was once a destroyer of armies and gods only know what else!

Hmm … a Deliverer and a Destroyer. Both sound so similar, and I'm sure they may well be! Though Arigal had never laid a hand upon my face. Was that a good thing? Or a bad thing? I hesitated to think of what a slap would entail from Arigal – most likely my head flipping on forever through the cosmos, forever torn from a once messed-up body!

A slap was more than an honest contribution for such imprudent behaviour. Though I wish I remembered more of the night just gone to add justification to such. Not so much for

232

what I did wrong, but what I missed on one of the last nights I may have had with my father. He probably wouldn't remember too much, either. But, hopefully, he remembers all he discussed with Nagda: I was eager to learn more of why he was here and what he had been doing for who knows how long.

A word could only be judged on its merit, until that merit was revealed in the end by actions adverse. Much of those uttered were yet to be revealed. I imagined more than a few would be forthcoming soon ...

Too soon for my liking.

My eyes had closed for what only felt like a moment. When I opened them again, I was tucked up in an extravagantly large bed with even more extravagant coverings. Not in the room I was provisioned, but some other, much more ornate, much larger, and full of all kinds of exotics, including, I assumed, two of the Deliverers – confirmed when they spoke and waved hands around.

To my surprise, something I had momentarily forgotten during the day – if it was even the same day anymore, no less daytime – was *my* tome, resting beside my head on its own silk-covered pillow.

My vision suddenly was taken away to a large wooden door as it was opened quickly, revealing two familiar faces ...

'Getty!' the angelic-sounding Arigal spoke with an unfamiliar air about her voice, 'are you feeling any better?' She sounded worried for me. *For a show of empathy? Or was she being genuine?* Did I, or should I have cared which?

Dagda did not ... 'Foolish, child! Jesse told me all about—'

233

Pursing his lips, he pointed at me, and I prayed quickly his finger would not explode with anything to send me to another realm, or to asunder, or much worse.

He did none … other than slam the door shut as he stormed back out of the room. I exhaled a long breath. Then froze as Arigal came walking toward me. If ice could snap from being too cold, that was how I felt as she wrapped her soft, surprisingly warm hand around my wrist, checking to ensure it pulsed adequately.

A nod was a surprise for me when she confirmed she felt something throb in there. Her telling me to relax did nothing to draw the warmth back into my body. A smile offered with a little shake of her head told me she understood my rigidity; lucky for me, I was half-covered with a thick, fur blanket … for a pulsing underneath them was now raging away.

She was stunning, awe-bringing, heart-stopping, and delicate in appearance, even if she held a true warrior mentality! Not only that, she was, at the very least … many lifetimes my young age!

But, I had known her. Or I assumed I knew her from when she was merely a couple hundred years old, that I also assumed. She appeared to be even more immaculate every time I saw her. The blackness in her hair and eyes had given way too much softer tones. Though the streak was still visible, it wasn't as striking as how I knew her in my dreams; especially now as she stood before me, that streak of hair only a couple shades of pink from completely white.

'Be still, Getty.' I was sure she was joking, for I hadn't moved even my eyelids since Dagda had frozen me deep to the bone. 'A darkness approaches. One not of this world.' She spoke with a level of calmness that clearly belied the perceived drastic nature.

'What kind of darkness?' I managed to unfreeze my tongue enough to speak something legible, if strangled.

'One you know all too well, Getty.' She looked at the two Deliverers stood either side of the door; nodding, she offered one word to each, something I assumed was akin to "leave", only a little more polite.

As they opened the door to leave, I saw Dagda pacing swiftly beyond the threshold, turning on a heel to wear away at the carpet again. Maghari was also stood there, gesticulating with his arms; either trying to calm Dagda or, otherwise, I assumed he was angry at not being able to enter his own quarters. The two left, paying no mind to the two outside. Once the door was closed, Arigal walked over to lock it with an iron bar, whispering something inaudible as she waved a hand over the bar – an added measure of security, no doubt.

I wonder why Arigal would want me locked in a bedroom with her alone …? I knew for a surety that it wasn't what I hoped for. Then what? I erred, for we were not alone.

Both! Oh my, oh no …

Lorel'eth appeared from somewhere I hadn't looked and walked from where she must have stood – at the back of the large bed – over to Arigal. She took her long flowing coat from her gracefully. She folded it over her arm before retreating to the only door into this chamber.

'Arigal … what're you doing?' I asked, a little too sheepishly, shrinking as the words croaked sharply out.

'Be still, Getty …' Her smile was still no assurance she was not going to harm me. Lorel'eth shook her head donnishly as if Arigal should just slap me and give me a furious telling-off. 'I'm here to read to you. In a different kind of way.' She looked at the book resting near my head. 'I assume you have not read anything yet? Well ... anything that would make any sense?'

'I've tried, but symbols just float about, just appearing and disappearing. Sometimes reshaping themselves about the page.'

'Open it now. Read the first page. But do not tell me what you have read. Only if it makes sense, you are not to speak.' She stood with her hands clasped and dropped low.

So, I did. First of all, there was not much to the page, then suddenly script appeared, becoming more legible the longer I gazed. Before me was a page full of text. I cast an amazed glance at Arigal, who nodded, advising me to proceed to read it.

I took in each word as I read. Finishing the first page, I slammed the book shut and hid it under the fur blanket. One thing I failed to hide was the crimson blush I felt burning away the skin off my soft cheeks.

'That good, huh?' I was sure Arigal's softer cheeks held a slightly different blemish to moments earlier. 'Remember!' she held a finger up. 'What is written, thus recorded in that tome of yours, remains yours alone ... Understood?'

Nodding, I took her for her word once more. Mired in Maghari's bed, that was all I could do. I would surely not be moving out of it just yet, and reveal what lay beneath! Though I was doubly sure they both knew, garnered from my mortified reaction and widening of their lips clasped together.

'Blood and sand! How? Why?' I gasped at Arigal.

'I helped you!'

'What! You knew what was on the page!'

'No, no, Getty … I only helped you open your mind to something you felt deeply in this moment.' She looked to Lorel'eth as if the plant wasn't obvious enough. 'What you read upon that page, and any other in the future, was and will be *one truth* from your mind and body of what you wanted, something akin to an emotion dictated. What you saw was more than likely lustful, but that is your own desire. The next iteration of scribe may be one of pain, sorrow, a longing for something or someone, or something from the other half of the spectrum.'

I pulled it out again and scanned over the page that had been almost completely written upon. No sign of any floating symbols appeared in the spaces of the margins. Though when I flipped the page, a whole myriad of symbols appeared. I held a hand over the page, none making sense, and to my dismay, a revelation of such, the symbols floated across the back of my hand.

This told me two things. Two that I could immediately think of. One: the images portrayed were from my mind. And two, I was an absolute idiot!

'What happens now?' I asked, still holding a hand to the page, occasionally pulling it away and then quickly putting it back over the cream paper.

'Whatever you wish, Getty,' she again looked to Lorel'eth standing guard at the door, 'we have *a* Deliverer here … one of their few purposes is to *actually* deliver …' She looked at me as if I was, indeed, an idiot.

I must have been. For I had not a clue what she was expressing.

'They are of a race that has bred and continually breed, the

237

mightiest of warr—'

'Oh …'

'Yes. Oh, would be a welcome and unexpected surmise.' She twitched a hand to her side, and Lorel'eth came forward to stand at the end of the bed, still holding Arigal's coat.

Arigal returned the favour as she took the coat from her and put it to rest at the end of the bed. She unbuttoned the back of Lorel'eth's shirt, which she now wore instead of the tight-skinned robes that drenched her body with steaming moisture, though it wrapped her lithe body still the same.

'No! Arigal, stop!' I croaked long after when I should have. 'I'm not that way!'

'What, Getty?' She looked at me questioningly. Surprise on her mind by way of an upraised eyebrow. 'Would you prefer the personal company of another? We can arrange just as quick, but that wouldn't allow you to seed—'

'No! No, it's just …' I slumped. I knew of Arigal and her sordid ways upon Inarrel, a lustful way of sin like the Syltenerian way. Had seen many of her follies with a man, men, woman, and women. Some much younger than I too. Then I thought about what she was portraying and what that portrait of me in a few years could be. *My own child! I'm barely old enough to frequent a tavern – on my own!*

'Leave us, Lorel'eth …' Lorel'eth turned quickly, buttons still undone, revealing the smooth tanned skin beneath, more than a hint of a marking running up the entire length of her spine.

I could have crumbled, I wanted nothing more than to be smothered by a warm, loving embrace from her, more so than Arigal, who was now angrily shaking her head at me.

238

'I give you a girl, not just any girl! But one as steamy as you could ever imagine, willing to open herself up for you, to potentially bear us—you, a solid bloodline, and you wilt like warm, soaked spinach!' She looked ready to swipe me, so I sank deeper underneath the blanket. But she didn't let up.

'You're more than just you now! We are at war with a foe that transcends all of *us*. As you fucking know, all too well. We need to act as one for a cause greater than there has ever been and ever will be, for that will be the only option. We need fighters, Getty—' a slight noise from behind interrupted her rant.

I found it comical, *lucky she doesn't speak our tongue*, as Arigal turned to see Lorel'eth standing with arms outstretched close to the magically sealed door.

Arigal walked over to release the bar. Lorel'eth stood behind her, looking in my direction. A smile told me she understood the humour too. A quick flash of her breasts told me she was still game, fun, and maybe *slightly* interested in me.

She was bundled out into the hallway once Arigal dramatically flung both leaves open, snapping the iron bar as if an aged twig, much to the delight of Phil and Jesse, who now pottered around out there too; out of the way of the still pacing Dagda and a now reposed Maghari.

Arigal glared at me with a gaze full of scorn. She was going to say something but instead shouted to Dagda. 'You sort him out! I'm done!' Dagda grinned. A wide grin, which only set her to shout something more, a shout that echoed quieter the further she made her way away down the hall. Abruptly ending when a slammed door cut off all manner of obscenities.

Dagda sauntered in. 'What the fuck did you do, Getty?'

'You mean, what he didn't do …' Jesse winked at Phil and then at me. 'Come on, Getty. Get up. The light is beginning to wane outside. Were you not to be off to meet your sweet mother before the parade begins?'

'It's still today?!'

'Always has been, always will be if you ask that question, silly boy.'

'C'mon, Phil,' I shouted as I bounded out of the bed, just like so many times unbeknown to me. Forgetting I wore nothing but my bare skin, thus saving no one from the sight of my pale arse.

He shook his head sideways and looked about skittishly as he placed Arigal's coat around my free waist.

'What do you mean no?' I asked. It could have been our last night on the town. The last time I could potentially ever see him again before he became that ultimate warrior spirit or me being warped to another world in some distant time: the possibilities of no further interactions between us were endless! And he was saying no!

Phil hadn't the balls to answer, so Jesse intruded. 'He has someone he has promised to meet with this evening …'

'Oh …' I mouthed, almost too low for any to hear. The rebuke it told though, was very much audible.

'Getty …' He then proffered an unspoken apology. I knew he meant that truly. I thought I knew too with whom he was to rendezvous. I couldn't, for the sake of me remember her name, but definitely her face and how she had cuddled into him before everything got a little messy and a little crazier.

'Very well. Have a good night, Phil. I will head off soon as I can. Say, where're all my clothes from earlier?'

'Where you left them … you'd best go. Quick, then!' Jesse smiled.

I raced quickly out of the room, bumping slightly into Dagda unintentionally, which brought a large burly laugh from the man, all the while I held Arigal's soft coat about my groin, wading the straight corridors, no more mind of a heavy head – all that extinguished in every sense.

Keeping my eyes on the plush carpet, I failed to notice that Lorel'eth was barely halfway down the hallway. She must have been following after Arigal, keeping her distance to not evoke further wrath from the crazed woman, almost goddess. Luckily she heard my approach, even wearing nothing but natural soles, she sensed my approach and threw me over her shoulder with a defensive swing of me and her body.

As I sailed through the air, I caught sight of her face before I could hit the plush carpet with my arse, back, or whatever else – it was going to be painful. The look of horror on her face, the instant she realised who she had flung, filled my soul with much tenderness. A tenderness felt for real once my body clumped and trundled along what remained of the hallway. Only coming to rest as I crashed into the door that had been slammed not too long earlier by Arigal.

Luck would have it that they'd swing open in the direction my momentum took me, delivering me to the main antechamber, to at least give me bearing to follow back to the change room of the steam house. But nay, the anti-luck shone through as they emitted that opening from the opposite, so I slammed hard, noisily, into them.

I lay motionless for a moment before rolling over onto my

front. A petite hand was offered by my antagonist. She wore half a smile.

It was enough for me to want to grab it. Though I considered the strength that small thing held – the most recent event fresh in my mind. She pulled me up, me using minimal effort. *By the gods! She is strong!*

She looked into my eyes, looking for something more. Her first chance to really gaze deep into my soul.

If she found what she was looking for, I knew not. A sharp turn and a graceful brisk walk toward the opening to the steam rooms left me alone. I had to follow, not that my stomach was up to such a task. There had been so much going on that I had never thought of my father.

Where could that rogue be!

A question that would be answered shortly as he came from the route of the steam rooms. He carried the gear I'd left behind earlier, saving me some grace.

'Ah! Getty. You're up …' His genuine smile warmed me.

'I was just on my way to collect my things. Not sure it would go down well with Mama if I remained barefoot or baring myself to the entirety of this town, not that they'd mind much!' I gestured with my head down toward my waist.

'No, guess it wouldn't,' he chuckled, then continued. 'Tell a truth, I was going to go with you. But Jesse asked if I wouldn't mind accompanying him, said he was keen to visit a few of the taverns we didn't make it to yesterday.'

'Oh really…?' I asked, surprised at the suddenly independent father I thought I would never get to know.

'Aye, he seems to be on a mission to collect as much

information as possible on a few things. He said he picked up some more gossip later in the night. Just before you went on a drunken rampage. Insistent on following that mysterious lady – though now we know her not so – up a sheer-faced wall, or three when you could barely walk straight …'

'Oh …' I had been saying that quite some the past few days. It was much warranted and probably the best reaction I could muster in my current state of mind, even with limited bodily function – all of my own accord.

'I must run, Papa!' I grabbed my clothes and proceeded to dress in the middle of the large room, not thinking of who was watching. The scorn of my mother, if I missed the parade, would far outweigh the embarrassment of me being caught naked in the house's main room – all had probably seen everything I offered before, in any case.

'That you must, Getty.' He patted my shoulder before I lunged in and hugged him tightly.

'Be careful out there with Jesse; he always seems to attract some, *any* kind of trouble. Here … take this.' I picked up Arigal's coat and handed it to him. He returned a look as if what the shit was he to do with it. I only smiled. He paid that no mind, no burden for me, ever.

'You too, my boy.' He squeezed out, obviously an emotion playing its part, patting back. He'd seen it all before, though, so he wouldn't have cared. He'd tended my wounds, dressed, and undressed me for years, forever in my youth. A favour I could never repay but one I would try to emulate by sharing stories – something he loved to do so much with me. And, one day, I would tell my children stories akin to those he read to me.

Hopefully, I'd tell them stories of him, though any embellishment would do the man an injustice. He was already my hero, and I loved him deeply. Even more than I thought I ever could. His gentleness was his most remarkable trait. His second, close behind, was his patience: that one was one of many more I would never forget.

*

I made my way from the luxurious premises deep into the thronging town. The trail down the main street seemed much shorter than yesterday's. It was busy, and I hoped I wasn't too late already, as making my way through that throng — as I experienced last night — would be quite cumbersome.

I was saved from such as my mother greeted me from the outer rim of the bustling crowd. There was no stage this day. More of a barricade only set up on either side of where the stage would have been usually constructed. Those people closest to the barrier leant over the sturdy stone blocks, trying to look beyond those closest to them, down the street, toward where the tent from the night before remained: only the front flap had been removed, the opening enlarged. *How big are these kids' floats!*

I could see no such floats in the town and had no idea where they may have been hiding …

Nothing surprised me, not lately. On my way down from the premises, I had time alone to think of all that had happened, not only today or the past few weeks, but long beyond, about how my life had played out so far.

Still, I knew not who my birth mother or father were; that didn't matter to me too much. I thought more about how my life had been moulded, modelled, and twisted to suit a greater cause, much more colossal than I could have imagined.

In conclusion, I would never have found such a loving combination of a birth mother and father devoted indescribably to me!

That conclusion left me with more questions. Questions away from all that was happening outside my family's inner circle, best left alone for now – judged from the afternoon's weird interaction with Arigal.

Why would they take on such a task?

For surely it was nothing more than just that!

Why would they persevere with such a useless son!

For surely, that was ever more so apt.

The last ideology, though one of many unsaid, what held in the forefront of my mind, was … *why did they not bear their own?*

I wished they would have been able; they would have been so happy … though the jealousy I felt at that thought made me almost weep with shame. Their child would have been loved forever, enormously, even more so than I. I knew for sure. But, for now, I longed for nothing more than to rest again in that large comfortable bed, measuring how far the candle wax had dripped down away from each flickering flame during the night expired. The ingrained image of that flickering cast in my mind took me back, an assortment of tomes and scrolls flooded my mind, and I almost dropped to my knees in despair. The only thing that kept me upright was the sight of a few people watching me curiously as I made my way past the Blacksmith's Arms.

A quick shout brought me out of my forever reverie. 'Getty! Grace, you're still alive!' Polett laughed heartily.

'Oh, Polett, whatever should you mean?' I asked sheepishly, not wanting to hear her or any other's answer on the matter.

She laughed some more. 'Oh, you're a silly bugger! Heard you were ready for trying out your wings.' She laughed some more.

I shrugged my shoulders, not knowing the truth of anything as the wrinkle on either side of her eyes belied her young age.

'Phil came by later on in the night—'

'Did he now?' I eyed her suspiciously.

'Oh, nothing like that ... not yet anyway—' she laughed a little too loud. No *shame there, then.* 'Caught him carrying you over his shoulder, and I so happened to be sweeping someone's dinner off our porch when you all came by. So he dropped you and asked if I needed a hand ...'

'Did he now ...?' I eyed her, now a little more conspicuously.

'Yes. And he was such a gentleman about it. He helped me sweep up the inside of the tavern, too, while your father and Jesse carried you away.'

'Anything else happen while I was gone?' I barked, hoping the absolute envy was hidden, I had to backtrack, so I offered a little laugh, hoping she assumed I only jested.

'Well, my father and I – once we cleared the last of them out, which we don't do very often – we had a few drinks of our own, just Phil, my father and me. My father eventually went to his bed and then ... well ... me and Phil, just ... cuddled in ...'

My eyes would have given sarcasm an honourable name. 'Cuddle in ... really?'

'Aye!' She squeezed both fists into her hips, looking at me as if they would have liked to be planted into my face. 'You calling me a liar? Hey! Little lightweight!'

246

I knew she was telling the truth, enough truth to tell me they had not *been* together ... *yet*. But the way she was dressed, I was sure it wouldn't be long.

'A fact, Getty ... I'm due for a rendezvous soon with your cuddly, handsome friend.'

'And I hope you have a lovely evening ...' I offered wholeheartedly; I honestly did, if feeling a little jealous still.

'Huh! You men are all the same!'

She stormed off, away from where I was heading. I had to admit, she did look very enticing. Maybe I was less experienced in the way women were courted, but Phil was now a natural potential reborn killer! There was nothing soft about him other than his hair! Surely I was a better match!

The lucky bastard! I left a thought.

'Hey, Polett!' I retraced my steps the way I came, chasing after her. She turned as I caught up. A little pant broke any perceived sarcasm. 'Please do ... enjoy your ... evening. Phil is my ... best friend; he is a good man.' Resting my hands on my knees as I panted some more, I added. 'And, yes ... he would be the bearer ... of the finest cuddles! As I'd well know!'

I had but a moment to brace myself, to steady for all her weight to wrap around me.

'Thank you, Getty! You truly possess a beautiful soul.' Sliding down my body, she let loose a little the lower she slid. 'The majority of talk was about you. Your life, and what may be your life after here ...'

Oh, how morbid, I thought.

'But, honestly, and no ill toward you and your potential issues, all I was enthralled with ... was Phil. I suppose the more he upped your standing, the more I could only snuggle in, giving him comfort returned. If that makes any sense.'

'To tell my truth … I'm kind of jealous he would choose you over me.' A twisted smile shocked her until I softened it slightly. 'Let him know I won't be leaving until we have had one last hurrah!'

'I'll let him know, Getty.' She smiled back at me, a genuinely warm smile. 'Go! Enjoy the parade. It's close to starti—'

She was cut off by a loud, whooshing sound, abrupted by a silence with an even more deafening bang. I could see the sparkle of colour spreading about the sky behind me clearly in her gorgeously large brown eyes.

She hugged me tight once more and whispered in my ear, 'In another life, maybe …' before she pecked my cheek and skipped merrily away, skirt bouncing higher the more she skipped along, not looking back, not once.

Phil … you're such a lucky bastard!

*

I turned to see the last of the flamework dissipate into the ether. I made haste as a drumbeat began to rumble away. It eventually subsided to a low thrum as I searched for my mother.

Wandering about the periphery of the mass of people, I eventually found her. She seemed to be on the lookout for me too.

Soon as I joined her, I knew the why of the concerned look … Arigal eyed me from over her shoulder before turning swiftly back to the proceedings once we locked gazes. Whose was more sinister? I could only guess.

My mother needed no explanation; she had been told song and verse of the *almost* happenings earlier. 'It's okay, Getty.' She patted me down, heartedly, her way of saying she understood. Understood both sides but was taking mine. 'Come on.' She pulled me forward a little to leave me standing beside Arigal, who was clapping with a broad smile stuck across her face – genuine, or not?

I did the same as she put an arm around my shoulder, and then she whispered, 'Sorry …'

A slap in the face would have been welcome, but an apology … whoa!

'For what?' I asked cautiously.

'All of—for everything …' she shook her head slightly, but not her composure.

And that was that. No further talk for the remainder of the parade whilst an ample selection of known and unknown beasts, monsters of all shapes and sizes, trundled their way through town. Some I assumed to be of folklore, or made up by the children of the town, *much kudos for their creativity!*

I was sure not to mistake one of the creatures. It was unbeknown to roam this world, it must have been garnered from some mythical knowledge of the world of Inarrel – assumedly from the resident demigods acting as draught cooler and server … *I still had a few questions for my papa to answer on that revelation! Amongst other queries of his time with Nagda.* The mock of the bebockle was by far the tallest, hanging high above the others in the flotilla. I smiled as it passed us, the boys and girls that pushed and pulled, doing their best to mimic a sound they knew not, or what.

Arigal twitched an eye up as she looked toward me while my mind fully engaged in the spectacle. She was itching to say something more to me, maybe something fundamental ... could it not wait for a day, or even two, a few more hours at the very least?

She said no more. Not until the parade had concluded and everyone was milling off back to where they came from, some moving on to an established venue and setting, no doubt.

'What a pleasant showing, thoroughly well enjoyed.' She clasped her hands together, then hugged my mama, then me. Walking away, she waved a hand over her shoulder. 'I'll be seeing you before dawn, Getty. We have much to discuss ...'

At least I have more than a few hours til then ...

My mother took me to one side of the street, making way for the helpers that removed the barricades lining the street. One of those was very familiar, and he made himself known with a slap on my back, dropping the wind out of me.

He bowed to my mother, holding out a hand for her to grasp. 'Such a pretty lady, and how become with such a featherweight lad like our Getty here!' He nudged me with his elbow whilst winking a hidden eye at me. 'How may one prise such a delight away from such the effigy of foolhardy ...?' He finished, raising himself tall. He leaned down again and warmly kissed my mother's hand as she grasped his too.

A surprising giggle of embarrassment came from my mother's pouted lips. 'And who might my saviour from such a rotten little lad be!' She giggled once again, forever at my expense.

'My darling! You surely know the mighty Marg—'

'Mama, this is Margus. And I'm sure you're not his type ...'

'Well, well ...' Margus rubbed his rough, stubbled chin. 'Tell me?'

'Gretta,' my mother answered, a little too eagerly for my liking.

'Ah ... a flower could never do such a name justice. It befits the perfect, unique woman that shall forever be known in my heart as the beautiful Gretta!' He kissed her hand once more. After that, my mother watched my eyes roll about amid significant discomfort.

'Margus? Was it?' She let go of the big man's hand to instead link an elbow with his – hers at shoulder height to reach his. She led the way before asking. 'Take me and my *weed* here somewhere fun for the evening.' She looked over her shoulder at me – something else that seemed to happen far too often. 'I want my son to remember me as being fun before he departs us for shit knows how long tomorrow ...'

Margus glanced at me too, his head turning high above my mother's, his face out of view of hers, full of concern for my wellbeing. He mouthed something unheard, other than by sight. *We will talk later, you and I ...*

We surely will! I thought as they cavorted on ahead of me. I knew my mama meant nothing untoward to my father. I also knew Margus was playing only another charade, one of his many characters. He surely knew who she was as soon as he saw us. Seeing him without the makeup and crazily exuberant clothing made him no less pretty – a naked face that would be envied by the ponciest of monarchs. The nakedness only added another layer of masculinity that would shame the most battle-seasoned knight. He could, would, have any man or woman as desired. To top that summation off – if that wasn't enough – he could move … and sing all too well. And there he was, clinging to my dear mother as if she were his Summer Gala fancy.

'Hey, Margus!' I shouted.

'Yes, Getty …?' he replied as they walked ahead together.

'Did you end up back in the Hop and Shovel or the Prince's Cock?'

A churlish laugh told me all I needed. *The former, then … Maybe he would fill a few gaps from last night.* A *few* was probably a large underestimation. And I hesitated as Margus led my mama toward the large opening that graced the place where the *otherworldly* beings plied a trade – far beneath their station.

A walk of shame would greet me as we were led, this time, to a similar room to the one I found, then proceeded to lose myself in. Only slightly different. The portraits on the walls and ceilings were of a brighter, more pleasant tone, if still as ancient.

The room was on the opposite side of the bar from the entrance to the room last night. And the furniture laid out was lush, with ample lounging space compared to the dry, cold setting we had settled into when greeted with Dagda's kin – or so I assumed.

A woman was sat in the corner of one of the plush settings. Before we were introduced, I knew …

'Margus!' The woman jumped sharply and bounced off the soft surface she was sitting on. 'Who do you carry in tow?' She eyed up my mother with a hint of respect. Me … not so.

'This is the lovely Gretta. And her son, Getty!' A slap on my

252

back momentarily knocked the air out of me.

'Such similar names. Quite confusing. Welcome to you both. I am Ren'egda.' She then pointed behind us. 'And this is Agda, he will furnish you with whatever you may desire … anything …' She laughed at the last.

'Evening, ma'am.' He bowed and took her hand, just as Margus had. He then looked at me. 'Water? Will it be? Master Getty …' A switched look between the two of us by my mother set both our tongues to mud.

'I recommend the fermented juice of the *fleora*, Gretta.'

My mother asked Agda for the same, not knowing the drink's proper name.

'A good choice,' Agda concurred. 'One fiori!' He stocked a mental note. 'And you, sire?'

'The same, please.'

Margus eventually left my mother to embrace Ren'egda. Leaning in, they locked lips for more than just a peck; I assumed it was a deep, passionate joining of not just lips. They both wiped their mouths when parted.

'Ahh … it has been many nights since I have had the pleasure of such a greeting.'

'Oh. Has it really?' she nonchalantly chided him.

'For you? Sir?' Agda asked Margus.

'Whatever the shit this boy had a go of last night!' He came over and rubbed knuckles across my scalp quite haughtily. I still couldn't believe this was the same person from last night! He made Dagda seem less obtrusive, much less striking.

I looked up at him in awe, much more so than either Arigal or Dagda. His genuine, direct approach to all things left me shaken with wonderment. For he was much more an individual I had ever come across. I wished to be like him one day, just as brazen, just as becoming, striking, true.

I had no doubt he held no love interest for Ren'egda. I was pretty sure she was not his only, and further, he held the same approach to the opposite sex. Ren'egda herself was the equal of Dagda for every trait he held. To be described as beautiful, though she held darkish features, would have been an injustice. If any were the *true* kin of *he* in this town, then it was undoubtedly her.

Then I wouldn't want to be on the end of her bad side, for she would have more than a few of those.

What of one of the hells bells are they all doing here! How many more of them were scattered about eternity? I now believed they were not of all the same lineage – distant, perhaps – but not as immediate as their similar names relayed.

One day … I was sure to know their ways.

We were seated – more lounging on our sides on some plush chaises – when the first round of service arrived: savoury and sweet treats accompanied the drinks. Small nibbles of both kind, more described the like.

One thing I would do well to forget was the smell that came from the ceramic mug passed under my nose and over to Margus, a sure play at humour from Agda trying to make me heave.

Suppose the bastard has some humour, then, if only slightly.

My mama sipped at her drink, then tipped it back, gulping the whole thing down once she tested and enjoyed the flavour.

'Easy …' Margus laughed, 'easy, darling. Carry on like that, and you'll be trying to fly off the top of this establishment way before midnight.' A wink at me wasn't missed by my mother.

'Yes,' Ren'egda added softly, 'go easy, dear. There is much we must discuss.' Eyes trained on me told she knew full well who, or what I was from the very moment she laid her cold, hard – though stunning and consuming – eyes on me.

Margus, too, dropped the contents of his mug with only a few gulps. I hesitated for a moment before dropping the lot in one.

Ren'egda laughed and did the same, bringing much scorn and a furious shake of the head from Agda.

At one point during the early evening, Nagda poked his head around the frame of the opening that led back into the cavernous bar area. I caught his face as he drifted it back away slowly so as to not draw any attention, a pleasant smile plastered through the frosted frame of his hooded gown. Sure as the sun at dawn, my next drink was cooled to almost freezing.

Almost. I smiled at that. *A nice touch …*

The night went on, and I listened to more than a few insane stories that would have been cast as make-believe had I not known what I knew. No less than a few were whispered from my mother's lips, and some of those within earshot made me blush a shade far beyond that of an ultimate discomfort.

I had none of my own to share. Though I had a long life ahead of me. There was still time.

I hoped!

The night went on with much the same theme; a few bobs of

Nagda's head and plenty more sordid stories mixed in with the more surreal. I soaked in more of the room's artwork than I drank. My mother hadn't taken the advice of Margus nor Ren'egda, and they, in turn, took the challenge upon themselves. So, in the end, I was the only one with enough level-headedness to comprehend what was to follow afterwards as we ambled our way back toward the main gate of the home to our host.

It was Arigal who came to meet us first, approaching with a pace that belied her eventual words. 'We have run out of time.' A snort was the only response from my mother as she slumped over Margus's shoulder. 'Word came from Hereberry not long ago.'

'And?' I asked her.

'That darkness I spoke of earlier approaches quicker than we anticipated. Something is seeping through the air and consuming all to follow in its dark shadow, including even the tamest of creature.'

'How long, ancient one?' Margus asked as he shuffled my mother about to get himself more comfortable.

She grimaced before answering, and I knew it was not an answer I wanted to hear. 'Soon enough ...' she twisted her head to ask for a name.

At least soon enough is not as deadly.

'Margus.'

'Margus, a name I may not forget so soon, if ever.' She fluttered her eyes as she spoke.

Seriously, we were about to feel the wrath of some evil, and she was batting her eyelashes at the man.

'Bring her inside,' Dagda appeared at the gate, a smile toward my mother shrouding the serious frown I knew all too well.

'Very well,' Margus muttered as he walked past a still-smitten Arigal.

She turned to me. 'We need to get you out of here …'

'But what of my mama and papa? What of Phil and Jes—'

'You are my priority. Once you're away from this *thing* and all it brings with it, I will come back with Dagda and initiate the mechanism of defence the last town seemed to have failed to activate.'

'And that is?' I asked curiously.

'You would have surely met a few of those from Dagda's world by now. If not, you're an idiot. There would be some, however, that would have remained hidden, ready and waiting. Just as there should have been in Agnistol. I can only assume they are on their way ahead of the coming storm, for I would hate to think of the alternative—'

'And that is?' She looked incredulously at me as if I should know and had drowned my mind in drink.

'Fool boy, did you not hear me earlier …?'

'Oh!' It finally twigged. The darkness would then be supported by those akin to Arigal and Dagda. 'Shit!'

'Shit indeed …'

We walked swiftly, catching up with my mother and Margus. She had not yet advised the potential fate of my closest friends, nor my parents, not that I really wanted to hear, but I was not ready to up and leave them to whatever turn they could take if this mysterious darkness engulfed this town whilst they still resided. It seemed to flee wasn't an option for the *people* of this town; the defences had been set for a reason – to defend and repel, or optimistically it seemed … to defeat.

A rushing of guards flew past us, a line on either side consisting of maybe ten previously unseen, unknown combatants that must have been ready and able within the compound run by Maghari.

'They will relay the command,' Arigal whispered close to my ear. 'A command not ushered for centuries.' She turned to watch them leave the grounds. The last two of each column dropped back to close the gates and stood watch on our side. 'Each will have a specific person to seek out. The majority are not of this world, but one is a newcomer to this town, though she is far from such when the grander sense of things is considered.'

I tried to think past the now. It was quite a way from where I was mentally; I had no idea. Even the slight twitch of her face should give me the tiniest hint that I should know it was not enough to trigger her next.

'Jacara? *You would have met once* … ' she whispered even quieter than before. As if uttering the name upon her breath would set about a cataclysmic chain for which nothing could be returned.

'Guess it's no surprise fate allowed Phil to be here at this very moment …?' I asked pointedly.

'Not of mine, nor *our* doing,' she said as she looked at Dagda, who still wore a frown prescribed of concern. That was the most unsettled I had been for a while, ever since I had been almost skewered by Phil when he had attacked me when he was full of a manic state of mind.

'Is she dangerous?' Arigal looked sideways at me as if to go on. 'Do you know why she was imprisoned for more than a

258

millennium? And with such thought in their design to never let her loose?'

'I have no idea, Getty.' She shrugged her shoulders as if feeling a chill up through her spine. 'Why not just dispose of her?'

'Oh, I thought you would have known the reason. I thought the same, somewhere from when she was just a being in a bottle and when she scared the living shit out of me!'

'A bottle? Never mind, Getty.' She began to walk toward the main building down the long, wide pathway. 'I am surely grateful she leans on our side, not theirs!'

I was, too – truth be told. I had often wondered what had happened to Jacara – the spirit from the bottle – since we departed Elacluse. To know she was well was a comfort. To learn then she had made her way here; well, that kind of knowledge gave whatever small comfort to dissipate to dust from a stiff breeze. If even she was only that, for I had not seen nor heard of her since we arrived.

A connection I supposed brought Phil here.

From my constant prodding, he still had no idea why he ended up where he had; the only answer he believed was it was where he thought I would be or could be. The bails of circumstance were weighted heavily in one's favour – until they weren't. But what could I, or anyone, do about that …?

'We're but pawns of something much more than either of us could ever imagine, Getty. You will one day, if not already, come to learn that.' She led me away from where Margus was carrying my mother, over to where our carts had been stowed since we arrived.

'Wait!' I shouted, believing this to be the last time I would ever see my mother's face. 'I must—'

'Calm yourself … we are only seeking something important your parents brought with them.'

'That is …?' I asked curiously.

'Just some dusty old scrolls, some you may know of …'

I rolled my eyes at that. Knowing full well he had brought the entire collection of vellum. Lugging them a long way from where they should have remained. Then they set themselves upon a chest just the right size to contain all.

Why would she now be interested in that which was — by a long way — in my past?

One thing that crept deep into my mind was the lack, or non-existence, of a dream since that fateful meeting of both Arigal and Dagda. Since my readings had stopped. Even when Jesse had read to me of supposedly the same text, in book format, or any of those scrolls, it stirred nothing more than an irritation from not being my dear papa's spoken and true words.

An urgency about her demeanour set a little cone of flamework off inside my mind. But before I had the chance to ask about her own curiosity, I was overcome with a smothering. Unable to catch my breath, I assumed the worst. But as I fell to the ground, the worst thought became anew. It was not born from the evil I was recently led to believe, but from a swift swipe of Arigal's wrist to the base of my neck, just above my right shoulder, rendering me to a soft, becoming darkness of my own.

A smile followed something sweet she must have muttered to me, but the blood had far begone my ears to make any sense of what she may have said. And, for once, I was glad for the

260

unknown silence!

*

I was expecting to wake up far from where she had chopped me down, and it was ultimately a surprise I found myself back in my guest room. Panic set in as I reached quickly to my side, feeling for my book. Surprise caught me once more as I felt the leather cover and the more familiar groove of the prominent symbol etched into it.

'You're awake ...' a gruff voice said, one unfamiliar.

Sitting up a little, trying to move a stiff neck to see who spoke to me, I caught sight of ... *something* ... *Surely that thing is not of this realm, or anything close,* I thought as I gazed at a creature with dark red skin, its face covered with deep scars – a long, deep one split by a forever vacant eye.

'Getty, I'm sorry.'

Arigal!

'Why did you feel the need to subdue me?' I asked as I rubbed my neck.

'Practice. And a lesson for you to not ever let your guard down,' she giggled before being cut off by a grumble from the beast standing at the door.

I turned just enough to see who else was in the room. Finding no other soul, I let my head fall back into the small pillow, letting out a long sigh.

'We must be gone, way past now, Arigal!'

'Calm, Ock ...' She raised a hand slowly toward him.

'Be quick then, Arigal.' The man's – so I believed to be – voice grated. He slammed the door shut after he left the room.

And I could still hear him grumbling something from just outside, the rumbling sound transcending the timber.

'Pay no mind to Ock. Not yet anyway.' She sat at the end of my bed and placed a hand on the lower part of my leg. 'Now, tell me … did you perhaps dream of anything while you were out?'

I tried hard to think if I did but could remember nothing. 'I … don't think so. Why?'

'Useless child!'

'Oh …' I understood now her need to put me out. But not the reason. 'But, why?'

'A small chance you may have dreamt of something that approaches, and how it subdues.'

I blinked, and a flicker of an image, or memory, was caught in that blip of darkness. I kept the image to myself. But a slight hesitation to my breath brought Arigal closer to me, gazing into my eyes as if to read my thoughts, prodding for something. I lost myself in her eyes for a moment, and she sensed that, so she backed away a little and turned her head to look at the book resting next to me. To be honest, I thought she would have been happy to stare at the wall. Just lucky something pertinent was on hand.

She placed a hand on top of it, then softly placed the other to rest upon my chest, palm horizontal to where my heart should have beat.

It skipped a few – too many for my liking – before it began to pump once more, throwing a crimson shade to a significant portion of my vision's aperture.

'Easy, Getty …' she spoke easy. 'You should have no fear in

my company. And I'm sorry for forcing Lorel'eth onto you.'

'That was all a bit too much, Arigal.' Looking quizzically at her, I asked. 'Would she have done it?'

'Absolutely,' she answered with no hint of hesitation, 'no matter who was in that bed, she would have devoured every last drop.'

I shrank a bit more into myself at her use of that analogy.

She slid her hand down, further away from my chest. Looking into my eyes, she sought some indication of rejection. When she found none – whether it be from my body becoming completely rigid once again or from a long-time longing. She slowly moved it over my bare stomach and slipped it beneath my slacks.

'So … that isn't the problem,' she laughed softly, holding the most rigid part of me.

I tried to hold a groan within, though something crept out past clenched teeth. It was too much when she stroked softly. And an unintentional sigh of pleasure escaped.

What was I to do?

She shushed me, holding a finger on her other hand to her soft, wanting lips.

A bang on the door caught us. Frozen. 'Arigal! I'm done waiting. I'm off to see Dagda!'

'Oh! … Okay, Ock.' A trudge and a grumble cascaded to nothing, leaving us *all* alone.

A devilish smile gave me no cause to relax. Now with Ock gone, Arigal stood and waved a hand over the door. It banged into its frame even more than when Ock had slammed it shut, and then she gave it a good tug, testing its resolve.

'You should know, Getty,' she began as she swayed toward

me, 'I, too, have studied the ways of the *Deliverers* ... among many others alike I dare not allude.'

She yanked off the sheet I lay beneath, followed swiftly by my slacks, tugging them twice to combat the obstacle pitched between.

My world became something more from that moment on. The woman I had lusted for the majority of my life, the woman that had turned her back on the darkness, had pleasured me in ways I had never dreamed of; even knowing Arigal and her sordid ways from my dreams and my father's half-truth readings, I was in a state of pure bliss.

Her lips would never mouth words with the same weight they once had.

And I wanted more ...

Ock

I had many questions. Many would truly be an underestimation over time. For now, though I was content with only the few that proceeded through the whirlwind days in Dibrathella.

The first was for Arigal: *what in the world was that for?*

'Because you needed it! And so damn well did I …' Blunt. Direct even; Truth? Did I care? Would I dare assume she was without another in whatever realm she found herself? The truth was … I didn't care.

'Oh. Well, thank you then, Arig—'

'For what? I should be the one doing the thanking.' She smiled as I blushed. 'You should read your *journal* when you next get a chance.'

It was not the topic for conversation in the current situation we found ourselves in. I had told her about the image that appeared when I had blinked. It was not long after she lay beside me with a quickened breath, one I would do well to forget. I thought she would laugh at the visage and treat it as a figment of my imagination until I saw true horror flash across her eyes. She had dressed quickly and fumbled through the sheet she had thrown on the floor, looking for my slacks.

She threw them at me and ordered me to dress quickly. But then pointed to the shower nook. 'Meet me at the front entrance to the main hall. Be quick, Getty!' I had looked at her incredulously, expecting something sweeter following the first time I had ever … maybe a peck on the cheek. Again, I felt no hurt; I felt good, rapturous even. I felt obliged to obey.

That image in the darkness now approached. A whole horde of them. And not just resigned for the unfortunate people it had consumed. Even the smallest of animals was framed with a similar silhouette. One of horror. The darkness hid the true evil that had defiled all in its path. But I knew; my mind *filled* the blank, black canvasses that presented themselves as they emerged through the last line of timbers skirting the forest's edge.

Filled, though, would be further from what hung loose.

Closer they came, revealing skin and muscle ripped from all parts of the body that were not required to enable movement. A black substance coated and stuck to what remained of their bodies, seemingly to help them remain upright; even the animals that would usually roam on all fours stood on their hind legs. All were leaving a trail of oozing darkness to spread outward across the ground behind them to defile the landscape even further. The only thing that remained passably intact was the vacant faces of each as they sauntered slowly up the slope toward where we waited on our mounts.

It would have been comical, almost unbelievable, but I had seen my fair share of crazy in my short number of years. I took it all for what it was; shit was about to happen. And I was to be once again that shit stuck between either slice.

The first question I asked was to Dagda as he prepped me for tackling such a foe before we undertook our journey to rendezvous the darkness. He had requested that I travel the short way to where the two parties would meet at the edge of the Eflar Green – a large forest that split the two towns.

'Am I ready?'

'No. Not in the least,' he answered from behind me, yanking both hands down, tightening two straps of a small leather cuirass. 'But you must be … one day. Let's skip this mummying, babying and get you some real action. Eh?'

I tried to rub my ribs as the leather creaked into them to soothe a slight tingle on the once scars I could not scratch. 'I sure wish Phil was coming along …'

'What? And put one of the ancients in harm's way!'

Sure you're across all, Dagda? My mind cast back to all the shit Phil and I had been in – through – and pulled our way out of. No less the time evading the colossal rock being upon our first contact – and his first physical contact.

Ancient. I laughed at that. He was not much older than me, and he showed no signs of any transition, as proposed by the fascinating being that we helped escape from confinement after said interaction with the even more unbelievable.

Harm's way? I laughed even harder.

'Guess not.' I wasn't in the mood to disagree. I was still buzzing from my interaction with Arigal. A sharper downward pull of the straps told me he knew …

He came around to face me and placed a hand on each shoulder, adjusting the armour so it sat just beneath my chin. 'The neck is a prime target: don't forget that, Getty!' A tap to my head. 'The head can take multiple blows, even piercings, but the neck …' he swung a finger from side to side of his own, 'you need that so you can support them blows.'

I took it he knew what he was talking about, I nodded as best as possible, being restricted from dropping my chin.

Dagda advised me he was to remain in the town to help direct defences should whatever I was to do should fail. All in town must have been well versed, and the forever sounding of a siren had now reduced itself to an intermittent ringing of a large bell, signifying danger had not yet passed.

*

I turned my head, with difficulty, to look at Arigal. A wary frown creased her normally placid forehead. A look I had not seen for a while since she had ordered all out of my room back in Newton following another attack from the darkness, one I assumed was also responsible for the horde approaching from below.

The steep slope slowed them slightly: the people, that was. The animals came quicker as they reverted to their natural gait on all fours. I knew what I had been told to do. But I thought the task was mammoth, untested ... by anyone. At least I would have a few trial efforts at the lesser threats – for they moved the quickest. And hopefully, the swords of the guards behind me would finish off what I, or the barrage of arrows, could not.

I assumed Arigal would have some say in the proceedings too. Just what, and to what level was she to test me.

Even if all that failed, the being that had been in my room earlier, Ock, waited with a few of his own, waiting behind readymade defensive battlements. I thought they could at least wait up front and pick off all with their double-sided cleavers. And Dagda ... the more I thought about it, the more I thought it was a test. If I pulled through, there was more cause to believe I was this *Saviour of Worlds*. And if I didn't: "Oh well, another one, another failed pursuit".

I didn't believe Arigal would just stand by and let me be slaughtered, or worse, become another pawn of the Darkness; *surely she wouldn't.* I began to hesitate if she actually could.

No doubt, if I failed in my given task, the mass below would not make it past far beyond the top of this hill. And if it did, it wouldn't likely expand any further than the small houses or barns that skirted the perimeter of Dibrathella.

She nodded twice down the slope. A signal for me to approach. The slowness of her nod I took to move at a similar pace.

The fuck am I doing here … I had no trust in anything I was doing; the animals were racing toward me, the people consumed were still bulking past the tree line, who knew how many more would be to follow, and I was atop an already skittish filly.

I approached the nightmare with eyes half closed, expecting to be devoured by the foulness creeping outward at any moment. What happened next not only perplexed me but took my breath away completely. An arc of light spread from where the filly's hooves trod after she reared and then touched the ground, sizzling the blackness and subduing the animals before it dissipated not far beyond the ragged line.

If any fear was garnered from the impressive burst of magic, it was not shown on any of the faces that still approached at the sombre pace. One, seemingly more agile than the rest, made a break through the front line, charging – still slowly, but at a quicker rate than the rest – up the hill. The look of absolute terror as it gnawed at a scent of something was enough for my mount to spiral up and turn on its hind legs, leaving me planted with my back on the ground. A softness to the fall reasoned itself

269

as the stench of the filly's fear hit my nostrils.

'Enough of this!' I heard a gruff voice, full of impatience, as a shadow moved over me. A clue as to who expanded beyond the accent to the sharp slit of light reflected off a blade on either side of the shadow, *Ock!*

'No!' a cry from behind, obviously Arigal. *it seemed she was content for me to meet my end, even when stuck in a pile of horse shite!*

Thankfully, Ock was not. He held a hand for me to grab and pulled me up from my wrist as they clasped together. A look into my eyes questioned if I was ready to offer more, but a slight glint of my own fear must have flashed across my eyes as I watched them all approach. He pushed me back toward where I had come from, toward Arigal and the guard, as he and his slayers cut about their messy business.

Arigal smiled at me as she dismounted. 'Well done, Getty, you proved far more capable than I, or anyone, thought …'

I was about to offer my gratitude for the lack of confidence now extinguished, but she silenced any retort with the unsheathing of a blade – either coated or pure, it looked frighteningly menacing! She ran forward, whispering in some other language, concocting some weave of mystery to blast into magical force with her free hand – arm extended and palm facing the oncoming parade of death.

The guard remained where they were. And a few of Ock's companions walked back to where they had been stationed before the commotion ranked prevalent. I wondered why Ock had broken his allotted task to remain behind the lines as means of one of the last for defence. *It seems Ock does not care for protocol.*

Lucky for me, he preferred the more practical approach.

I assumed I had done more than enough to show any potential: with that little outburst of *something*. Even if I had no idea how that slight potential was released.

Was it me or the horse?

Surely it was me, for who would put so much faith in something that shits wherever and whenever it wants. But how? It just appeared from nowhere, without much of a thought …

Watching on as Ock and his team of scythes worked their way through the first lot, Arigal finishing them off as they crawled up the slope – even after they had been scythed into two, three, or more, pieces – I felt the urge to follow.

A hand on my shoulder stopped me as I began to effortlessly float back to where I'd lain in shit. A member of the guard it was. Someone I had not met prior. A big man with facial features not so far from Dagda. *Ah, not another one!* My feet stayed put, steady where they had trod thus far. 'Best you stay here, eh!' he said, and as he said it, I looked to the rest of the guard, pointedly beneath their helms to their faces, and sure enough, a slightly off replication of Dagda could be found in all beneath … Save one.

She came toward me from almost the end of the line of the guard that stood at the apex of the large hill. 'Would you come with me?' She pulled on my arm as if I had only one choice.

But something inside me burst out. 'Arigal!' I turned to see her running past Ock, then past those struggling to fight off the constant stream of death that poured forward.

She turned to me instantly, and in that moment, I may have almost sealed her fate.

Almost.

A hand clawed at her, eventually finding some purchase on

her shoulder. I saw just a glimmer of fear in her eyes before she stumbled, falling backwards.

'Arigal!' I cried once more. Panic and hopelessness combined to form something else.

My eyes then began to burn, so much so that all darkness turned to light, and the darkness fully converse: Arigal included.

As the brightness subsided, the whole visage of the landscape before me was a mess. The subtle degradation of blindness to my eyes left only one light spot. Stood tall beneath a toll of untold casualties of darkness. That void in the visage of reality walked toward me.

'So ...' she seductively said to me, 'you *do* have it in you!' She walked past me as if nothing had happened at all. As if even her being subdued was worth the risk of bringing an unknown, unseen substance out of me.

One striking takeback from that interaction was how the sky had cleared significantly, turning from absolute black to a haze of red. And how fast the bodies of those consumed by such darkness became nothing more than the most prime of substance, something unrecognisable other than identification type of creature: skeletons of all kinds resting on the greenery. No sign of that blackness that clung to and oozed from their bodies earlier.

*

Ock stood at the precipice of the slaughter, then walked slowly along it, prodding each skeleton with a blade, returning to the other side from where he had stood to do the same. I was about to go over to him, only to be stopped by his huge roar toward where they had come from. In the end, he made his way to me.

'There be no living thing back that way. Best we leave.'

'To where?' I assumed back to the town but ensured that was the case.

'You may say goodbye to your parents and friends. If you so choose.' He looked at me thoughtfully as if weighing something. 'Then we begin the true trials of your seemingly innate abilities.' A ruffling of my hair gave me no cause for optimism. People have rubbed me that way many times before and been utterly unbenign to my feelings or safety. But I felt genuine care within his words.

'Oh. It's that time, huh?'

A slow nod of his head, accompanied by another ruffle of my hair, gave me a glimmer of hope at least someone left in my life would be straight forth and offer me the obvious outlook. I felt Dagda held concern for me. He had shown that in the ways he had tried to steer me without actually telling me anything direct. I wondered if he would take my head or offer advice regarding the interaction with Arigal the next time we were alone.

The thought of her made my loins throb ... uncontrollably. Though my first time, I felt no shame to the notion I was only a tool to satisfy her need, to release herself through a passion; it was certainly akin to what I had dreamt ... if even more enjoyable than I could ever have imagined.

'You still with us there, Getty?' Ock chuckled while I dazed away at nothing. 'Come, let us leave those poor souls for others to offer a proper burial. Not much more we can do now.'

'Is that it?' I asked, still worried it wouldn't be.

'No, that is something we would call a "Bleak". There have

been many occurrences of them appearing. But so close to an assumed unknown haven … that brings genuine concern.'

'Who made them?'

'They're not made; they just are. They can be manipulated in many different ways. But … the bargain has to, eventually, be in its favour. That is where the real concern lies.'

'How?'

'A Bleak can take many forms. The fact it chose a succumbing plague, well … it means that whoever took it upon themselves would have to offer something fantastical in return.'

'Like what?' My interest piqued so much that Ock smiled.

'Plenty of time for that. Shouldn't you be far more concerned for your goodbyes?' He began to walk ahead and waved an arm in the same direction. 'Come, we have a little time to discuss things before we're back in town …'

Before I moved, I asked him a question, something that just blurted out from nowhere. 'Arigal?'

A wide smile and a shrug of his shoulders told me all I needed to know. All he said was, 'She will be one of your mentors. Remember that.' He thought some more on the subject. 'And so will I, so don't be getting any funny ideas …' A raised eyebrow flattened me again. 'Hear me?'

I laughed, then began to follow as he lifted the flap to show his arse cheeks.

Ah, Ock followed the same lines of my kind of humour! It was strange to see such a mammoth creature turn about a jest so soon after the massacre of darkness that had just taken place.

I suddenly felt shame creeping into my soul, for those that lay behind us had been, once, like me and anyone else. The only saving grace was that we had ended their suffering, and one day we would repay a debt for them in kind. To those that dared sway such a force into dark will. I would remember for all, even if I would never know their names.

Then I felt real optimism, a flutter of something meaningful. I felt pain, and I used that to form a decision almost instantly. I had to make it count for all I had been through; all I had experienced in this world and that upon Inarrel.

The horror of the scene I instead pictured with faces of joy, laughing as they held their babes, mothers, fathers, their kin. Gone. And for what?

I knew not the answer. Not that I really cared for one, or it. My point of view was emboldened even more; there was no fucking point to it! I didn't realise I was gritting my teeth, squeezing my hands tight, or shaking my head slightly until Ock placed an arm on my shoulder to calm me.

'It gets easier, Getty. Not the immediate aftermath of such, but why we do it.'

I understood completely. And relaxed every muscle. 'Does it?'

… Silence.

Guess there could be only one way to find out …

Farewell

Gazing forever deeply into a bare plastered wall for a while would set your mind off. Seeing things that weren't really there. They were there, in your mind, but not *really* there.

I had waited for a while whilst my mother bathed with my father in the residential baths I had nearly drowned myself in. No matter how much she twitched or fidgeted, I dared not look at her.

I could make out Lorel'eth standing to one side of the double door from the corner of my eye. One of the other *Deliverers* stood opposite – still as a rock, both of 'em.

A clang, then a screech of metal gave inclination the door was opening. Though it wasn't my mama or papa who would appear. 'Jesse …?'

He walked hesitantly toward me. A hint of sadness about his forever jovial face gave me no inclination of what he was about to say. 'They've left, gone, Getty …'

'Huh, what? Left, to go where?' I looked at him, but he kept my smile from forming.

'They have gone, my friend. Gone.'

I couldn't fathom a thought. I knew immediately that he had meant they had departed to go somewhere other than the higher place, but still, it couldn't register as anything more than a blatant lie.

'Come, now, Jesse! The old Jester is ba—'

'Listen, Getty. They're away. Gone.' He sat down next to me.

'It was your mother's notion. One fervently fought away by your father. She couldn't bear to see you leave. She was broken into pieces telling me this, so you needn't see.' He placed an arm around me and squeezed my shoulder as I let out a whimper of something, followed by a snort to stop anything projecting beyond my nostrils. 'Your mother is a funny one, she loves you that much she doesn't want to see you see her upset for if to make you the same. Funny that. I understand her thinking, though, even if I disagree.' He leaned in closer to me and whispered. 'My mother did the same to me. The last time I saw her was when we had finished our nightly supper. She had a smile as wide as the vastest of the ocean, and a peck on my forehead before she told me, "Off to bed, young man".

'I was seven winters. She was one of *them* …'

I looked up at him just as a slight trickle made its way over a pale cheek.

'I understood over time,' he continued, not bothering to wipe the trail away, 'that the last memory of her would be of her wide smile and the softness of her lips pressed to my forehead. Not the pained look of someone you love so much fulfilling a duty beyond your comprehension. The last you see of the woman you would ever love the most in your life telling you she has to go, never to be seen again.'

The anguish on show left me with the thought he had never told anyone else before. I was about to offer my customary condolences, but he continued on.

'Did I ever tell you, from where the moniker "The Jester" came?'

'No—'

It was me. My invention, my way of dealing with the heartbreak my mother left me with. With that, I replicated that smile in everything I ever did. People would ask me why I smiled so much, and I would show them; the fool and the jester becoming. First, silliness, then as I matured, so did the jokes, shows, games, and the tricks.

'Till one day, I had drawn such a crowd I became noticeable. By them!' He pointed a finger to the sky. 'I wouldn't doubt my mother had anything to do with it.'

I held no doubt the two Deliverers could hear every word being spoken, but they both now stood straight, rigid, and still as a great oak stuck in the doldrums. A gesture well received by myself, one I thought of as communion, not knowing their ways … *yet,* I recognised uniformity with what he was speaking.

'So, what did you do?' I asked solemnly, quietly.

'I did what they asked, for the chance of seeing my mother's smile once more …'

A whimper came from one of the girls standing at the door. It was quickly identified from which once she fled through the doorway holding a forearm to her eyes.

Not Lorel'eth. She stood firm. If it wasn't for the slight quiver of a lower lip and a quick glance toward me, I would have thought her for a marble statue.

As it were, I, too, dropped a few tears as I hugged Jesse in tight, patted his back and wrapped an arm around him.

'I understand, Jesse.' I did. I truly did. Though she may not remember it, and probably the reason she dragged my papa into those baths, the last memory I had of her was being slung over Margus's shoulder. Happy!

A goodbye would have done what? And, thinking further on of my father, the thought of him sitting, talking, and joking with one of Dagda's kin, then further still to him bouncing around the taverns of this well-acquainted town made my heart melt.

In light of all that. What my mama saved me from was me thinking of being a burden that one final time. And that was something I could live with. Though I was keen to hear what parting words she had left for me.

'What parting message for me did she leave with you, Jesse? Before she left?'

A long wipe of both cheeks was followed by a chuckle, one heartfelt.

'Oh,' the laugh continuing, 'she said nothi—'

'She said not a thing, Getty!' Lorel'eth said in my own language, fully intelligible, and carrying a similar accent to mine.

The shock of her speaking my tongue should have been far less hurtful than the words she had said. I should have known as soon as they stood to rigidity at the door! They understood every word spoken.

Before I could say anything, she, too, fled through the doorway before my pertinent question could be asked.

Jesse held two hands up. 'I didn't know! Honestly.'

'Hmm, why such prudishness?'

'Who knows … who knows anything these days!'

I felt that. Deep down, I felt it. I knew exactly what he meant. 'Did you know of Ock? Before today?' I asked.

'Ish …'

'And?'

'Yes. I had heard of him, though never met him before today.'

He looked at me questioningly. 'Why?'

'Oh, no reason; he just reminds me of you and Phil, truth be told. A combination of you both.'

'Is it his big head or his big love for humour ...' Jesse smiled and rubbed my head.

I knew then that Ock was a good person, throwing about the same traits as my best friends. I already knew Jesse held a moral, if confronting, soul. And Phil had eventually won me over once we escaped the depths of that stone-guarded cavernous space. Still, though, I knew not who I would be departing with, or even where to? But I did know when, and that couldn't come soon enough now that my mama and papa had left: probably taken far from here, back home, by one of those in town, or by Dagda himself ...

It was too late now to offer my parting words. The few I had conjured and memorised since hearing I was to be gone ... for good. Those words were now left, for the best, to forever remain in my head.

I did have just enough time to seek out Phil, though. Hopefully, he hadn't already given his goodbye kisses to Polett. I doubted it, so it was no surprise when I knocked on the door I had been directed to, along a long hallway on the second floor of the Blacksmith's Arms, that I was met with a clambering noise. A mixture of floorboards banging, and a slight ruffling followed by fully versed expletives.

The door wasn't opened for some time. When it was by the barest of openings, a couple of chains held the door tight to the frame. A petite face peered through just above the chain, Polett's cheeks and forehead dyed to plum from pumping blood, no doubt from an exertion I now knew all too well.

The image of Arigal's face, pluming a similar hue beneath me, would forever now be always too familiar.

'Ahh! Getty!' She slammed the door. A rankle of the chains was heard before she swung the door open and leapt up onto me, wrapping her legs entirely around, adding to a backward momentum that almost made me fall onto my arse.

I spied through, into the room, over her head to see a sheepish-looking Phil raise his arms as if nothing was untoward. The fact that his shawl was on back to front only added to the humour of the scene. A little bit of guilt crept into my mind for interrupting. That was immediately swept away when Phil held up two hands clasped together, thanking me with silent prayer.

Soon as she let off me, I asked how she was.

'I'm so glad you came here before you were to be off to wherever!' she replied, ignoring my question. 'When will you be leaving, though?' I didn't know how to take the question. Was she trying to shoo me away, or was she genuinely interested? Either way, I still knew not precisely when I was to leave or where I may be departing to.

'Soonish,' I mustered to quell either verity.

'Oh …' she looked downcast. I knew then that she was sincere in her questioning.

'At least … until I get back to the compound, I suppose.' I offered for my own recompense.

Phil finally realised he was hanging loose and shuffled his shawl around before putting his awful shorts on.

'Do we have enough time for a tipple downstairs? At least?'

she pleaded. 'And a bite to eat? You look … famished!'

I almost replied in kind to the last remark but held my tongue for both our sakes. She was right, though; I hadn't eaten since before my interaction with Arigal. 'Absolutely!' No sooner had I spoken my answer did Phil move his hands to pay homage to me once more!

'Great!' She squealed. 'Then meet us downstairs. We shall be right down!'

*

I didn't have to wait too long. Though I was already onto my second draught by the time I heard footsteps tap down the wooded treads – further enhanced, thus identified by the squeak Phil's shondals emitted when strained underneath his weight on the polished timber.

By luck would have it, a familiar voice also sounded as they appeared. 'Getty!'

'Margus!' I clambered out from the tight nook, walked briskly over to him, and clasped a wrist tight to his.

'How's your dear mother?' he asked, genuinely concerned for her wellbeing.

A pang of pain, shone by my dropped bottom lip, caused him to grimace dramatically. *A little too much, perhaps?*

'No … she's still with us!' I laughed, if a little overbearing. 'She has left, headed back home, I believe …'

'Oh! That's a shame. She's a wonderful woman! So full of life! Was hoping she would introduce me to your father.' He shook his head. 'from what she said about him, he sounds a remarkable man.'

'But you met him, Margus, the previous night.'

'Did I? Huh … How much drink did I take in!' He shook his head again. Before, he, too, was leapt upon by Polett.

An inaudible sigh from Phil told me she had a thing for wrapping on tight as he hopped from one leg to the other rather dramatically behind her.

It still perplexed me, the whole Phil thing. I could relate as I had been stuck in a tomb with him, discovering his true nature and calling. But for others to take to him unconditionally, on a first glance or interaction, well … it just did, and always will, stump me!

A man of such few words too.

All seemed calm in the town, with little apprehension about heading out. It appeared as it did both the other days, if only slightly quieter, which I attributed to the weekly day of rest; no showings in the town today. As if no drama had been caused by the almost incursion of some ravaging darkness: the Bleak. Did they know what had been on its way? I assumed so from the constant ringing of the bells on the hour above the large, central taverns. I hadn't heard it since not long after the scourge had been vanquished. Once word had been received by the bell ringers. One of whom had just entered and was still wrapped by the petite body of Polett.

He eventually set her down to sit on the edge of the bench where we were to all assemble for one final time … at least together. Or, more pertinently, with me.

'What brings you all here, then?' Phil looked to the ceiling; Polett looked to the floor. I looked to both in turn.

'Just a last hurrah before I'm off to save us all … to save

everything, ever was, and will be even.' My mind wandered far away.

Margus laughed, a full belly laugh. Before he caught on that no one else had joined in. 'Oh …' he sat down. And looked into my eyes for any hint of humour. He found none. 'When you off then? And more importantly, when are you coming back?'

'Soon.' I sat back, slumped even. 'Too soon … as for when I will be back, I haven't the faintest.'

'Well, I'll be glad not to be carrying your sorry arse around anymore!' Phil added, trying his best to lighten the mood.

I just laughed, acknowledging his option for humour over pain, even if they were coexistent. 'True. I would tend to agree with that surmise.' I batted his shoulder with a palm, as did Polett.

'Margus,' I began to ask. A raised eyebrow told me he knew a pointed question was coming from the tone. 'Why does this town flaunt such a wealth of festivities when, as I assume you know, this is the last defence to the hidden city not far away?'

'Ah …' His smile was a wide one. 'If you haven't guessed that by now, Getty. From everything you have seen, everyone you have met, surely it's obvious …'

Phil nodded; he knew. And Polett. *Why am I so slow at getting to the party!*

Then it hit me. Something from my readings came to me; the life and light of those that resided here was radiant. It was as if there was nothing ill about the place, no ill will from any of the residents I had met. I knew there would be a scuffle here and there when warranted, and sometimes outsiders would surely come to town and be rattled out if they were not of the right mind; that thought brought a forgotten answer to a pertinent question, one to what Jesse had been diligently garnering during our scourge around the town. I had to ask Margus plainly.

'Margus?'

He raised the other eyebrow comically. 'Yes, Getty?'

'What happened to those folk who came through here a short while back?'

'How far back you talking, Getty?' A hint of deception was detected as his last word raised in pitch, if ever so slightly.

'I think you know the answer to that, Margus …' Jesse appeared from nowhere. 'Thought I might catch you all here. Lucky you're together.' He nodded to Phil and me.

'Why is that?' I asked plainly. Too plainly.

'Oh, it's like that, is it?' Jesse was suddenly agitated, pained even; he hadn't sensed my try at sarcasm. I knew we were to part ways before long. He was to go on as before, as a healer, finder, and reporter, "The Jester" would return! Once more to his former self!

I stood up and embraced him tightly. I squeezed a little harder at the remembrance of the filth that spouted from his lips during one of our first times together. It was still hilarious, it was invigorating. So much so it had sparked a fire in me that had been laid to waste for so long, and I had loved it. Every curse, every taunt, every … flagrant … personal insult.

'Thank you!' I whispered as a tear slid down my cheek, followed by one on the other side. A sniffle in my ear gave me reasonable cause to believe Jesse, too, was a slight touch emotional.

I knew whose shoes I'd rather be in. It wasn't Phil's shondals or my leather tie-ups. But fate had a plan for me. As it did too for Jesse, and indeed Phil, even for all the duties he was cursed, and yet had failed or refused to acknowledge such a role for this planet's future. Fate had a role for countless others, I had no doubt. That was the role for Jesse now; to find those to carry their own tome – should I fail to be he, they!

Though the time spent was jovial, it was tinged with the inevitable sombreness goodbyes could, and would, always bring. This was one that may well be forever. So I clung on tighter still to the man who had brought me out of my void and into a reality, one now linked in so many ways to everything I had enjoyed, or so believed. I remembered a strength; that of my mother who sought him and convinced him, so resolutely, to take a chance on me. I remembered the brave and the stoic pair that raced up to the house as I lay prone in my bed while she accepted her own demise so that I may see out mine in time.

That was the thing that caught me then, the word *fate*. Was Arigal's fate set in stone?

Was it?

From what I could recall, she died a hundred times in my dreams. She had fallen once more for the man whose nuts, scrotum and all, would eventually be fed to the nightwolves. I certainly hoped that was not one set for me. But I had seen worse ways to be removed from any reality.

Phil came in next; he clung his big arms around Jesse and me. A wail of pain groaned out of his quivering lips. Bringing comical relief as we all laughed. Margus and Polett joined us in union, adding to the relief of a lingering sombreness.

No parting words were spoken by any as they left, one by

one. I was the last to take the stand and walk away from the nook that would be settled in my heart for a lifetime. Polett stood behind the bar, awaiting the first of the day's customers. She was casually wiping whatever she could to remain unengaged. Phil had been the last to leave, if running back upstairs could be classed as such.

Polett remained to serve me my last drink in the Blacksmith's Arms. I nodded to her to bid her farewell. The customary lunge into the air caught me by no surprise as I caught her expectantly this time.

'Go with him,' I blurted out, unexpectantly.

'I will, Getty,' she replied even more so. She smacked her lips to mine before she raced back up the stairs, leaving the downstairs of the tavern empty, save me.

The silence was deafening. The slight brush of stone with the sole of my shoe only heightened the quiet. The only other sound was one that rang around in my head, the answer from Margus as to the fate of the miniature outsiders. "We sent them back to the ether, ground up in our flamework. We knew them to be of shit, be we didn't know shit could burn so bright, or so well!".

That, and the grateful memories I would forever hold from my transition from being idle to being fully alive.

And within that moment, I knew I wanted even more!

Flourishment and Transition

I don't remember too much about the moments leading up to when my legs began their twitching, other than Jesse's face becoming increasingly animated. And, so too, his cursing.

'Getty!' He pointed at my right foot first. 'Look!' I didn't need to look; I knew full well what was transpiring as my foot began to wobble. 'Look at that pathetic little foot! The lazy shit hasn't moved for years! If ever at all!'

I struggled to contain my laughter. So, I didn't.

Then my calf began to wobble, followed by my knee and then my entire leg. Followed simultaneously by the other side.

'Calm now, Getty!' he shouted.

I couldn't. I let the momentum carry its way all through my body. Until a darkness crept over my eyes. My eyes shook, squeezed in the decreasing amount of light until I could not see anymore.

Waking, I found myself in a room eerily similar to that of my own. The only clue was that the window was now opposite where it should have punched the wall. Surprisingly, I remained calm and leapt off the bed as I had always done during similar inception. My legs slumped, and I scrambled with flopping arms to stop my face crashing into the floorboards. I failed in the attempt as it seemed I was not in that fervent dream I would occasionally find myself, but something else.

It began anew, over and over, waking in that room. Though this time, I was lying on my back with two concerned faces clambering over the top of mine, the bed to my right, the window where it should be.

'What happened,' a croak slipped out of my trembling lips.

The faces of Mama and Jesse looked at one another. My mother sought an answer too. Jesse, unable to offer one, left a silence hanging in the room. Until I offered more talk …

'I woke in some random room not dissimilar to my own. But things were off … I no longer had the mirage of that something at the end of my bed, and things felt slightly askew.' I pointed to the window. 'That was over there!' I pointed to the bookcase.

'What was on the other side? Where the window should have been?' Arigal asked, leaning on the only door frame in the room.

Twisting my head on the floor, I looked toward her. 'Nothing. Blank, save …'

'Save, what, Getty?' She moved over to the wall where the window stood.

'A fuzz … I think.'

She pulled Jesse up, straightening him with her hands. 'What happened, Jesse?'

'He just flopped …'

'So soon?'

It was my mother's turn to stand straight, her forehead almost touching Arigal's chin as she met her gaze. 'So soon? The meaning of that?'

I was still lying on the floor. Nothing twitched except my eyes and lips as I looked up at the trio. Something had happened that shouldn't have, not so soon anyway, and I guessed that I shouldn't be lying on the floor – not just jet.

'The boy should not have been able to move for months … at the very least. Yet he manages to move himself off the bed in only a matter of weeks?' She turned her gaze to Jesse, whether to remove herself from a burning scorn eating away at her chin I was unsure. 'How?' she asked him. Hints of amazement embellished the curiosity in her tone. She sounded excited at such a premature result. I must have excelled beyond wherever of whatever it was I was to fulfil, even as the blood trickling over my upper lip protested otherwise.

'His eyes went west. Then he stopped shaking for a moment. Just as you or I would, he switched to the side and hopped off the bed, eyes dead. So too, it seems, were his legs.' Jesse chuckled at his own joke.

He was left to nurse a whack to the jaw as my mother swung, connecting cleanly with it. Having only recently physically clawed herself away from the shadow beings, she was now full of a feisty confidence, which wholly suited her.

Arigal stepped between the pair, holding my Mama's wrists so she couldn't swing again at him – *or her,* I supposed. 'Stop this. We are all for the same cause,' she looked to them both, 'are we not?'

My mother's arms slackened enough for Arigal to let them loose. Leaving her to rub them both absently as she nodded – acknowledging the strength of Arigal's grip with a slight nod of her head.

I could only watch on as my mouth gave no alarm. I was still there, and the rest of me had since ceased shaking. It wasn't until Jesse fell backwards over my prone foot did attention return to me and the plight I found myself in.

It was pretty much the same from there, for a few months at

most. I would find myself opening my eyes, staring upward at a part of the room further away from the bed each time.

The last occurrence, from which I could remember, I actually made it to the door, and had managed to open it.

A world lay itself before me, one I knew all too well. And in that instant … I knew what that meant. For if I was to traverse the threshold, that would be the end of the boy. The end of everything I had experienced with my Mama and Papa in my waking world. The hesitation I suddenly felt was enough for me to back away.

Though the vista was beautiful, and no matter how free I would be of my body, my mind would not give in just yet. I gasped graciously at the beauty: it was surely Inarrel. That I knew for sure. Of the same planes I had known, it was Inarrel in a perfect stasis of calm and cohesion, not a tinge of sadness nor the darkness that had always hung in the air or on the lips of so many.

I could have stepped into that world. The figure behind that wall of fuzzing greyness, the one who greeted me before every dream walk of Vilenzia, would have wanted nothing more for me; I was also sure.

In the end, maybe the cause of Father's readings being nulled or the fact that I had tread beyond the realm of normality; something I didn't want to venture from.

Maybe that was the ultimate trigger, one to set my body alive, numbing my mind more than only slightly, redirecting focus: that's what Dagda had said, backed up by Arigal and eventually from Jesse as he had ventured questions of my sleeping mind – which was now only a void for any try at remembrance …

Every time I was hoisted back into the supposed comfort of my mattress, one that could have been constructed of stone, until one day, I began to accept its comfort, its softness, and then the caress of the sheet.

It was always Jesse, on his lonesome, that carried me with a strength that belied his wiry frame – like that an ant would possess, just not as pretty. He nursed me and tended to me. Soothed any inquiries I held. Absorbing my transition from being what my parents had loved, to, in the end, a cheeky little shit who knew too much for his own good, even more so than his mother and father.

The often tending of my wounds, those I knew not of how I procured, stopped almost suddenly and I was left with a void in my own heart since that day of rejection of a better life. One I assumed was left for me, a forever paradise to live out my days as something more than what I was to, or could, and should become …

I left that thought where it belonged.

A life of forever merry given was not sought without those that supplemented the required humour through whatever means necessary – be it drink or laughter … or both – those could not be sought on their own unless contained within one's mind, from within that of, usually, of a mad man.

My assumption to mould the latter led me to believe the raconteur, who undoubtedly led the whole sway and development of things, was much, and rightly so, I thought, apportioned to that ilk.

I didn't contemplate for too long whether the fact that my father had stopped reading to me had any effect on the expulsion of my ever sought after dreaming. But I didn't care as much anymore, as one of my main interests in that story had now elevated herself into my world, and that brought some parity with where I wanted to be.

I did envy the thought of what lay beyond where my father had always ended the readings. It was not far from the point where Arigal had let her one-time lover's blood splash onto stone as she departed. Whatever departures had occurred beforehand from the previous readings I remembered, that was always the same outcome for the poor bastard; an occurrence that was eventually set with a burning text into the vacillating surface of the respective vellum.

It was not until a few months had passed that I began to meander my way out to the hallway and then drop myself over every step that tested my resolve.

When I finally ventured outside, a growing residue had clung itself to something that was insentient. Left there purposely, for what I had eventually found out, left for a time, and point for my own thrust of something more than the physical, that mentally I would strike. An expectant flow that was far from what was expected or required. I had done what I was supposed to; scream some unknown – hopefully violent and acute – language at the black mess creeping up like a spreading vine across the stone that was the supporting structure of the bridge at the bottom of our valley. The shout I offered as I approached, from within a presumed audible distance where linguistical commerce could take fore, was met with only an increase in the blackness scouring more of the stone blocks surrounding the bridge, to a point where it eventually became a thing, something more than just a crusty stain.

Then there was the expected and eventual hurrah, a moment of elation I knew was coming once I had mastered the motion and further ingrained notion of walking. Then the sporadic option of opening my eyes during the crushing spark of the in-between dreaming.

In the end, I was left with the countenance to satisfy Jesse. No others were permitted to enter beyond the doorway without first acknowledging Jesse's wishes for me. And then that of my own. I left myself thinking. I couldn't care. And why should I?

Over the duration Jesse was in our home, he had lots to say about the world. I craved to hear more and more of his travels. The scrolls would be read to me offhandedly by Jesse, who never failed to embellish far beyond the pale, though I never found myself in that waking dream, walking upon the shore of Sinboran, or gazing over the Masked Arches in Jacob's Well.

In a kind of way, I was lost. Putting that aside, it was a relief when I could *actually* stand of my own volition in the real world. I had mastered the mechanics of it, and, in time, my eyes would remain stum, no more of the spasm then waking up on the floor. Jesse had proposed the idea that my mind was adjusting to a new way of thinking, a new order of things. That something in my head must have been ticking over ever so slowly, and the fuzz that once was, had now dissipated, letting in *real* dreams – if they could ever be called such.

It was pleasurable to move freely about my own home. I had even taken a few strolls with my parents down into town. I was not dissuaded by the stares that slyly made their way to me. Talk of the crippled boy had undoubtedly been small talk to some in the town, and as I walked – albeit with difficulty as my feet grasped at the cobbles before me – I nodded to each and all with only a smile, as did my mother and father. The oddity about the side of the town we lived – a town split by a nonsensical, meandering river – was that there were no taverns, not that I was yet at an age to be allowed admittance. But several small cafes lined the limits of the cobbles, overlooking the slow-moving, winding water, tinged with a brownness most likely effluent from the many farms that touched its banks most of the way upstream.

When I first ventured into the town with Jesse, we crossed over the arched bridge that split the town. It was made of large stone blocks, cut to perfection on every visible face, and it was the only bridge that crossed the vast expanse of water. It was the first time a black, sour liquid had passed my lips. To spit out a drink would be rude enough on its own, nay mind across the chest of a young bargirl and her frilled, pearly white shirt, thus rendering a first slap ever across my innocent cheek.

By the end of that night, I had consumed enough to *actually* walk straight, all the way home, even if shouldering the mumbling and stumbling Jesse.

It seemed we hadn't taken my mother's word for "stay out as late as you like" literally enough, for when we arrived at the door to my home, sounds were heard from within that would have caused me to blush even if I was a crow. So, we sat … for a while. The whole time Jesse making gestures with his hands to accompany any of my mother's unbecoming, passionate moaning.

The time came when I was to venture to those distant lands, the ones that Jesse had spoken of with much verve and character. It was probably the hardest thing I had ever had to do, certainly the most emotional. Judging from how my mother reacted to me leaving was much in line with how she left me in Dibrathella. No goodbye, no kiss to caress my forehead. Nothing.

It was only a temporary venture until they would join us and judging my father's reaction as I looked at him, only a shrug to his shoulder and told me she meant well and that she doesn't do emotions too well. I remembered all the times I knew she was holding back a breath, the sound of silent tears falling as she sat with her back resting on my door, night after night until it all became too much for her.

The sounds within the house when Jesse and I made our way back told me there was a longing for my mama that had been hindered since I was housed there.

As before, it was probably better this way. The clinking of pots couldn't throw me; I knew she was just in the kitchen banging them in the sink to tell me she was okay when, in reality, she was most likely sobbing uncontrollably. So, I nodded to my dear papa, bid him farewell and hugged him tight.

'Take care of her.' A nod and the customary frown told me all I needed.

'We won't be too long away. Hear?' he whispered. As we broke away from the embrace, he pressed his palm to mine, transacting a small medallion, one I still wear to this day. One, as I lived and breathed, would remain steadfast to my chest. Even when I'd be gone, skin and muscle to dust, I hoped my pallbearers deemed it a part of me.

For that is who I am.

Who I was.

Who I always would, will be.

In this life and the next.

And whatever may lay beyond *even* that.

A Supposed ... Afterword

Now that we're a little more acquainted, I'll let you know that I hoped I would not be rereading this in haste, reflecting upon my life thus far, for not much of that may even remain. For I did not dictate, nor scribe the added text, it was a reread from something I was motioned to conduct when revelling through my greatest hour or during darkest peril.

So, I dictate to you, whoever or whatever you may be, the first half of *my* tome, a half I hope will be continued on. For that is all that be scribed for now. The remainder should be full of much more laughter. Though my heart knows better. A day will come when I will be released from the shackles I now find myself in, able to test the resolve of the petty iron that moulds my prison.

Pain and death would await. Much more than I dared to contemplate. Why read or write of pain when others will do that anyway? The deepest pain of mine, a pain felt two-fold, will surely be written by others, for if I would, or could, ever describe the pain of my mother and father's demise ... then I probably wouldn't have found myself here, alone, in a cage constructed of wrought iron, wrapped with some charged, barbed metallic string, with only myself and this tome ... half complete. I take that as a sign, one of hope that I may yet get to convey to whoever may be game enough to listen.

There may be more to my life than thus far.

Much more than that I have disclosed. Though ... the scribe may not next be I.

Well … not completely.

THE NEXT CHAPTER TO
"THE SCROLLS OF VILENZIA"

Vellum II
A Quest of Many

COMING IN 2025

NOW THE BETRAYAL BEGINS!

AND, OF COURSE, DECEIT!

WITH A LITTLE SLAYING ... NO ...!
LOTS OF THAT!